THE SLEEP OF BIRDS

Also by Sara MacDonald

Listening to Voices

THE SLEEP
OF BIRDS

Sara MacDonald

HEADLINE

First published in 1999
by HEADLINE BOOK PUBLISHING

10 9 8 7 6 5 4 3 2 1

Extracts from *To The Lighthouse* and 'The Moment: On Being, III'
from *Collected Essays Vol. IV* by Virginia Woolf are reprinted by
kind permission of The Society of Authors as the literary
representative of the Estate of Virginia Woolf.

'The Sleep of Birds' from Elizabeth Jennings'
Collected Poems is reprinted by kind permission of
David Higham Associates.

All characters in this publication are fictitious
and any resemblance to real persons, living or dead,
is purely coincidental.

British Library Cataloguing in Publication Data

MacDonald, Sara
  The sleep of birds
  1.Detective and mystery stories
  I.Title
  823.9 '14[F]

ISBN 0 7472 2219 3

Typeset by
Letterpart Limited, Reigate, Surrey

Printed and bound in Great Britain by
Clays Ltd, St Ives plc

HEADLINE BOOK PUBLISHING
A division of Hodder Headline PLC
338 Euston Road
London NW1 3BH

Dedicated to
Sue
Nigel, Stella, Fleur, Tom, Lulu,
and Jack.
With love.

ACKNOWLEDGMENTS

I am grateful to The Society of Authors as the literary representative of the Estate of Virginia Woolf for permission to quote from *Collected Essays Vol IV* and from *To The Lighthouse*.

I am also indebted to David Higham Associates for permission to use Elizabeth Jennings' lovely poem 'The Sleep Of Birds'.

My thanks to Kathryn Major for taking the time to lay out clearly the legal aspects of domestic violence. To the kind Hollingsburgs who sorted out a wonderful new computer in a grave moment of crisis. To Rosemary North for her eagle eye and friendship. Last, but not least, to Tim, for use of fax machine, e-mail, photocopier and for endless support.

The Sleep of Birds

We cannot hear the birds sleeping
Under the trees, under the flowers, under the eyes of our
   watching
And the rustling over of sheets of our unsleeping
Or our final whispers of loving.
How enviable this solemn silence of theirs
Like the quiet of monks tired with their singing hours
And dreaming about the next.
Birds are remote as stars by being silent
And will flash out like stars at their punctual dawn
As the stars are snuffed by the sun.

Does this quiet sleep of birds hide dreams, hide nightmares?
Does the lash of the wind and the failing wing and the falling
Out of the air enter their sleep? Let us listen,
Open the window and listen
For a cry of a nightmare to underline the night.
There is no cry, there is only
The one feathered life who's not awake and does not sing
But hoots and holds his own, his own now being
A lordly and humorous comment upon the darkness,
A quiet joke at the changing demands of the moon.

Elizabeth Jennings

Chapter 1

Silence for a moment, just the sound of heavy breathing, his and mine. Then the phone screeches out into the room, making us both jump. Jake turns and stares at it as if coming from a long way away. His left hand uncurls from my bunched sweater and he flexes the fingers of his right hand where he has bruised them, and abruptly lets me go.

I slump to the ground, automatically turning and painfully pulling myself into a foetal position, protecting my stomach and head for when he returns.

He picks up the phone 'Hello?' he says. His voice is gentle and relaxed. 'Beth, how nice! How are you? . . . Good, good, that's really good news . . .'

I close my eyes. My head is ringing and I cannot tell whether the darkness is evening or I am losing consciousness. I can taste blood in my mouth and I cannot lick my split lip.

Beth. So near to me, yet impossibly far. A pain far worse than bruising starts up in my chest.

'Well, actually, Beth, she's in the bath. Can I get her to ring you back? I'm sure she'd love to come for that. . . . OK then, take care. Bye for now.'

Oh, his voice is soft, low as honeybees. He hums softly as he comes back towards me. My body tenses; I begin to shake, try to curl up tighter, but I cannot because of the pain under my ribs.

I always worry about my teeth. I dread losing any of my teeth.

Jake bends slowly to me. 'That was your friend Beth. She wants you to go down for the weekend. Various academics are descending on St Ives for Virginia Woolf lectures and she thought you would love it.'

His voice is conversational, smooth as oiled wool. I flinch as he places a forefinger gently on my cheek. 'Open your eyes, my darling. Look at me when I am talking to you.'

I manage to open my eyes.

'There we are. Good girl. Don't whimper, Si. I'm not going to hurt you.'

He moves away and gets a cushion and lifts my head, moves my plait out of the way, smoothes it over my shoulder as if he is stroking a snake.

He kneels beside me. The knuckles of his right hand are bleeding and he licks them. His eyes are bloodshot, his blond stubble stands out on his chin like cut corn. He shakes his head slowly as he watches me. 'What a silly little thing you are, Si. Now, we are not going to have any more talk of leaving are we? *Are we?*' His voice rises just a fraction.

'No,' I whisper quickly.

'Of course you will have to tell Beth you can't possibly go. You see, I can't trust you any more, can I, Si?'

I try to stop the tears rising in my throat but I can't. They trickle out of my eyes and I can't stop them. I hurt and I am afraid.

'Oh, Sigrid, Sigrid, I never want to hurt you, you know that . . .' He tries to pick me up off the floor but I scream out in pain. He goes away again, fetches a rug and puts it over me to stop the trembling, tucks it in lovingly around me.

'Right, here's what we'll do. I'm going to run a warm bath full of your herbs. Then I'll lift you carefully upstairs, bath you and pop you into bed with a hot-water bottle. How's that, darling? How's that, Si?' Again his voice rises just a fraction.

I mumble something. He goes away.

I can feel the flagstones under the rug, as icy as death. I can smell the earthy, doggy smell of the rug in my nostrils. Breathing is difficult, darkness and dizziness swing towards me. I wonder if I am going to die this time.

I hear the bath running a long, long way away and then he is back, lifting me slowly and gently, shushing my whimpers of pain. The water is good, warms me, stops the shaking. I can hardly see out at all now as my eyes swell up.

Chapter 2

I wake in the night. The pain is excruciating and I am afraid of what it means. It hurts to breathe, and although I feel cold, my body is covered in an icy sweat. I feel the warmth of Jake's body beside me and his deep, even, untroubled sleep isolates me in the dark.

I try not to move, try to lie quite still on my back, so that the huge, sore ache that I am will still or fade for a while. I do not want to die. I do not want to die here on Dartmoor where the silence and darkness and space swallow me up. Where the vast rolling spaces seem to echo my loneliness like a hollow laugh.

Into this endless night I lie and feverishly, for comfort, think of my friends who have slipped and faded away, confused by my conflicting signals and Jake's charming distancing. I think of Beth, and then I stop because I will cry. There is only Beth left now. Beth, John and the twins.

The breathing beside me does not change and I wonder at it. Wonder how I have come to this. To accept as normal, to make right what is so wrong. Perhaps I have had just too much practice.

I think about Jake's gentle, dignified father and his dark, cool, sophisticated mother, living their lives in peaceful retirement in Cyprus. What, in Jake's safe, middle-class, Hong Kong and Dartmoor childhood, could possibly have made him violent?

Then, just for a second, I let myself think of Ginna and Gramps and Norway. But the loss rushes in like a tidal wave and swamps me, a far greater pain than my bruising at Jake's hands.

Why couldn't they forgive my mother?

Why couldn't I forgive them?

Behind my closed eyelids, into the endless humming of this

7

black, trapped night, I see the log burner packed with sweet-smelling wood. I heard the soft crackle, like scrunched silver paper, of firelight catching bark and flaring gently to warm and fill the shadows behind which were the soft and safe movements of people who loved me.

In the morning I open my eyes, muzzy-headed, to a mist drifting in strands through the crack in the window. The silence is eerie, muffled and heavy.

I know it is early, but I hear movements below me. Stiffly, I move my arm across the bed to find Jake's side already cold.

It hurts to turn over so I lie watching the four squares of window lighten slowly and begin to reveal, behind the mist, a clear blue sky. A blackbird flies low across the window, squawking and I suddenly recognize this heavy silence. It is snow.

I hear him coming up the stairs. He puts a mug of tea on the bedside table. He does not put the lamp on for then he will have to see my face.

'Si? Are you awake?'

I move slightly to show that I am.

'It's very early, but I'll have to leave now because of the snow. I can't afford to get snowed in. Clifford is hanging my paintings this morning and I want to be there.'

He pauses, looks down at me. My face must be emerging into early morning. A face that is not mine. A face that is becoming mine. A face that Jake has given me. A face that is swollen and bruised and bloody.

'Oh, Si.' There is a break in his voice. There always is, after-wards. 'Did you sleep all right?'

I nod. It is what he wants to know.

'I'll be back as soon as I can. I'll probably have to leave the car on the road, but I'll be back by late afternoon, I promise.'

He pauses, won't go. I am watching him but I cannot make my voice come and he does not like this.

'You will rest today? Stay in bed as long as you can. I've banked up the fire so it's warm downstairs, OK?'

I nod again. Go. Go.

He bends and kisses me. 'See you later.'

I must deflect him from unplugging the phone and taking it. I say through swollen lips, 'Drive carefully.' It comes out in a croak.

'What?' He bends to hear me.

'Drive carefully.'

He smiles at me, his beautiful face lighting up. 'I will, my darling. I'll see you tonight.'

He turns and moves quickly out of the room, his thoughts now concentrated on the journey ahead, as I hoped. He runs down the stairs and there is a moment's rustling as he pulls on his coat and gloves, a brief pause when I know he's checking his reflection in the mirror. Then the front door slams. The BMW glides silently away.

I imagine the pattern of the wheels on virgin snow, a quiet crunching noise in an early morning of low-flying, excited birds, unable to find their food. The back seat will be full of canvases and Jake will be humming as he drives, forgetting quickly how much he has hurt me.

Painfully, I get my legs over the side of the bed. A wave of sickness swamps me. After three tries I manage to get upright and walk to the bathroom. The pain in my chest makes me gasp.

I look in the mirror. This person bears no resemblance to me. But it is not my face that worries me, it is my ribs, which I know are broken. The pain is so excruciating that I have this image of a rib piercing my lung.

Sweat breaks out on my forehead and I think I might faint. I clutch the basin, sip some water, then hobble back to bed. I lie still and the sickness subsides.

I turn to look at the phone and that blessed little waiting message. One message. Message one. Beth is on the end of that phone. I only have to dial. But no one must see me like this. Where to go? How to go? I must not fall asleep again. I can't think. I'll just rest a moment.

I reach out and cautiously press 'Play'. If Jake hadn't been late and in such a hurry he would have noticed the answerphone. There have been so many times when he has unplugged the phone and took it with him. I'll just listen to a voice, any voice. It is Beth. Her voice fills the room.

'Si, you didn't ring back. Just feel I haven't spoken to you for ages. Jake always answers. You always seem out or in the bath. No offence, Jake, if you are listening to this. I am just ticking off my best friend because she's so bad at getting back to people. Si, I really think you would enjoy this weekend. Do try and come. Give me a ring tomorrow, please. Love you lots.'

I play it three times and this cold sullen little house of Jake's listens as I weep and does not like what it hears.

I must not be here this afternoon when Jake returns.

Chapter 3

I wake and know I must have slept for hours. The sky is blanket grey and I see it is snowing again, feathers of snow swirling across the windowpanes. I turn on my side and painfully, stiffly, get myself upright again. I manage to get out of bed, pull my dressing gown around my shoulders and go to the window.

All is covered and muffled and descending. I am going to be trapped here. I fight panic and know what I have to do now. I pick up the phone and ring the doctor's surgery.

'Hello? This is Sigrid Watson. I'm really sorry to bother you . . .'

My voice comes out cracked and unintelligible, even to me, and the receptionist says, 'I'm sorry, you'll have to speak up.'

I start again. 'This is Sigrid Watson, out at Trelarva Farm Cottage.'

'Oh, Sigrid, it's you! This is Jill. What on earth has happened? You sound awful.'

Relief wants to make me cry. Jill is the practice nurse and I sometimes walk with her and her dog. She is married to a prison officer and she is kind.

'Last night I tripped and fell badly, landed on the flagstones. I thought I'd be all right in the morning but the pain in my chest is getting worse.'

'My dear girl, you haven't fallen again!'

My heart lurches. I had forgotten she had been on duty last time.

'Jill, it's snowing hard. I'm going to be trapped here soon – you know what it's like.' She must hear the panic in my voice.

'Jake isn't there to bring you to the surgery?'

'No, he's in Plymouth.'

'Hang on, Sigrid. I'll just go and speak to one of the doctors.'

She puts the phone down and I watch the snow. If I could be trapped here on my own, if I knew Jake could not get back to me, then I could bear it. But he will get back to me, he will. He knows Dartmoor like the back of his hand; he grew up here. He has snowshoes and langlauf skis. He always carries everything he needs in the boot of that car.

Jill comes back to the phone. 'Sigrid? Look, two of the doctors have started their rounds early because of the weather, but we have a locum attached to the surgery. He has two more patients, then he will be with you. Can you hang on for about an hour?'

I am close to tears. 'Yes,' I whisper. 'But please don't be long. Will he be able to find me?'

'Sigrid, I'm off duty in an hour so if necessary I will come with him. OK?'

'Thank you, Jill.'

'Just one thing, are you upstairs in bed? Can we get in?'

'I can get out of bed. I could probably get downstairs, but I don't think the door is locked.'

'Good. Now just take it easy until we get there.'

I put the phone down and shuffle to the wardrobe for my small packed rucksack, which Jake found last night, but I can't bend to pull it out. I go to the bathroom and wash my face, try to do my teeth, clean myself up, brush my hair. Outside the window the grey sky descends to meet the ground, covering the quarry and softening the distant tor.

When I am walking up by the quarry, the ghostly sadness of the place will rise up from the black water like a palpable cloud of misery, touching me with an icy hand. I see clearly the shaven heads, the vulnerable exposed necks, the tired arms raising pickaxes high, to shred the hard grey stone. I hear the sharp repetitive clunk as sparks fly from the rocks and the melancholy clink of chains dragging those wretched prisoners' ankles. The sound seems etched into the rising cliffs of black rain-soaked stone.

The despair and desolation lives on in the quarries, wafting with the mists, hovering over the looming prison and the clutch of prison officers' houses in Princetown, and reaching this cottage.

I shiver now and turn to the mirror. There is not much I can do about my face and already I am concocting a story that must sound remotely plausible. I raise my arm with difficulty to unplait my knotted hair.

Now I must dress. But I can't. The pain in my chest almost stops me breathing. Sickness rises in my throat and I fight not to pass out. I stumble back to the bed and darkness swallows me again.

I am woken by the sound of a car slowing down outside. There are voices, a knock on the door, then quick footsteps up the stairs. I struggle upright, try to get my feet on the floor, to wake from this strange, deep sleep.

'Sigrid?' Jill is beside me. I hear her sudden intake of breath. I can't understand why my eyes won't open.

'Lie her down,' a man says quietly. I hear Jill walk away, I hear the running of the tap, then she is bathing my eyes gently and they open again.

'Sigrid, this is Greg Tremain, the doctor.'

He is tall and fair and very young, and he is going to ask me questions.

'Let's take a look at you, Sigrid. You've certainly been in the wars.'

I want to smile; it is something my grandmother used to say.

'Where is the pain in your chest?'

I touch the worst place and he examines my ribcage and I wince. He gets out his stethoscope, listens to my breathing and runs his fingers over my stomach and side. He is not smiling any longer. He sits on the edge of the bed, looking at me.

'How exactly did this happen?'

'I fell badly. My foot got caught in the lamp flex and I fell on the flagstones and caught my face on the side of the metal fender.' I begin to shake with the effort of lying.

'OK. Take it easy, you're going to be all right.' He turns my head, touches my cheekbone and forehead. 'Very nasty.'

He gets up and moves away, opens his bag and gets my notes out. Outside the snow is still falling.

'What time is it? What time is it now?' I ask anxiously.

'It's about one thirty,' Jill says, coming to the end of the bed.

Jake could be on his way back. Having left early this morning, he could have started for home by now because of the snow.

'You won't leave me here?'

The doctor comes back and sits on my bed again. 'Absolutely not. Sigrid, I think you might have punctured a lung. You need stitches in your head and you have extensive bruising. You will have to go to hospital, but I think you know that already.'

I nod.

'I just need to take a few quick notes, then we'll take you in to hospital. We can't rely on an ambulance in this snow. All right?'

'Thank you.'

Jill says, 'Sigrid, tell me where your things are and I'll pack a bag for you.'

'My bag is packed,' I tell her. 'I just need my toothbrush and things . . . It's in the wardrobe . . . I was going away, you see.'

The doctor and Jill exchange a quick glance.

'How old are you, Sigrid?' Greg the doctor asks.

'Twenty-four.'

'I see from your notes you broke your arm badly a year ago, had a fall from a horse six months ago, and a garden rake came up and hit you a month ago. Those are a lot of accidents for a young girl to have.'

There is silence in the room. They both watch me. They do not mention Jake. They do not say, 'Where is your husband? Can we contact him?' Thank God they do not say this.

'OK, Sigrid, let's get you into hospital. I'm afraid it's not going to be a comfortable ride for you. I'll leave you with Jill while I ring to say you're coming.'

He goes downstairs and Jill finds me some socks, helps me put my dressing gown on properly and gets blankets from the airing cupboard.

I ache to leave. I sit on my returning panic and need to whimper. I know – I just feel it in my very bones – Jake is on his way home. He will have remembered the phone. He will be afraid I might have rung someone.

Jill helps me downstairs. Upright, I feel very wobbly. The doctor has brought the car right up to the door. It is a Range Rover, I see

14

with relief, with a light on the top. But it is too high for me to manage. I wince with pain. I can't do it.

'Just a minute.' Greg the doctor lifts me on to the back seat and Jill puts pillows underneath my head. For a second I meet his eyes. He is probably not much older than I am, and good-looking in a bland way. He knows perfectly well what my injuries are due to and he is angry. He is too young to know that it is my fault for not being what Jake wants me to be.

At that moment I hear the car, Jake's car, purring quickly down the lane towards us through the falling snow, and the whimper escapes from me. I have clutched the young doctor's arm before I can stop myself.

I feel blind and utter panic. Jake will use his velvet voice, he will persuade them he will look after me, he will persuade them he can take me in to hospital if necessary. I know he will . . . he will—

'Sigrid, Sigrid, calm down. It's all right. It's all right. We're leaving now, this minute, together. I'm going to shut the car door on you before you freeze.'

I close my eyes tight shut against the sound of the familiar footsteps crunching over the snow towards the car. I wait for that lovely voice.

'Mr Watson?'

'Yes. My wife . . . What's happened?'

'Your wife says she had a fall last night. She's in a bad way. She should have been taken straight to hospital when it happened.'

'Oh, my poor darling. That is entirely my fault. I just wanted to get her into a warm bed. She assured me she felt all right, and this morning she was fast asleep when I left. I feel terrible. I had an important meeting, you see, but I was anxious, which is why I came home early. Shall I take over now? You must be so busy in weather like this . . .'

The car door opens and Jill gets in and puts hot-water bottles under the blankets. I am shaking and my teeth chatter. I am so cold. I am so very cold.

I hear her call out, 'Greg, Sigrid is going into shock. We should get going.'

The voice does not stop. 'Oh my poor Si. She really is such an accident-prone little thing. I'm beginning to feel quite concerned . . .' His voice floats about, getting everywhere, into all the cracks.

Greg the doctor's voice is cold. 'Sigrid is my patient and I shall see her safely into hospital.'

'Of course, of course. Quite right. Thank you both so much. I'll follow you in my car.'

Greg gets into the car, holds my wrist, says something inaudible to Jill, then I feel a needle in my arm and slowly the voices recede and the car starts up and we begin to crunch slowly away from the little house I have come to hate so much. Jake's house.

Jake will follow like a shadow. He will raise his arms and the huge shadow of him will engulf me. Then he will turn with me and run back to that cottage and love me better. He will woo me with his dark chocolate voice full of love. The voice he uses only for me.

He will cover me with the strength of his pain, a huge encompassing black blanket of twisted emotion for me, just a girl with a long blonde plait he spotted at a university disco . . . persuaded into his lectures.

His single-minded intensity will play me like a violin. He will touch my body and make it sing. He will know deep, deep inside him what excites me most, what makes my body tingle and sear with transient joy.

He knows that the silky voice makes me ache with longing. He will whisper, 'See how you love me, Si? Only me. Only me. My silly little girl. My silly little Si.'

And I will be happy. I will be grateful that anyone can love me, want me, be at all interested in me. Grateful that he is being nice to me, gentle and kind. That we can seem for a time like other people.

For a short while I will not have to dread the tic starting in his cheek, his lips compressing into that sudden tight line. My stomach need not heave with anxiety. I will not have to rehearse in my head over and over a sentence before I dare say it. Try it like a taste on my tongue to test the shape of it in case I provoke a sudden burst of temper.

Out of the car window the sky darkens, full of relentless snow, which cuts Dartmoor off from the rest of the world. There are no voices in the car now, only the chug of the diesel engine.

I feel the salty taste of something in my mouth and realize hazily it must be blood. I float suddenly and feel unconcerned, and the feeling is not unpleasant for the pain has subsided to something I can manage.

Jill, sitting beside me in the back, leans over and looks at my face, takes my pulse again, smiles at me.

'Not too long now, Sigrid.'

Then she leans forward and says something to Greg the doctor. He reaches up and switches on his light. I see it reflected dreamily in the window as it revolves and the car increases speed.

We must be on the long winding Ashburton road now. Up, down, up, down, over the bleak moor, across little bridges, past small clumps of cold Dartmoor ponies with their shaggy, bear-like coats . . .

I smile. I do not really mind if I die. I can feel the dark dusky afternoon begin to engulf me. As dark and vespertine as Jake's voice. I cannot fight either and there is such a joy in giving up, sinking down, down through the soft white snow, into the sudden peace of it.

From a long, long way away I hear a siren start. It must be an ambulance somewhere out on the Plymouth road.

And the dark shadow follows. Follows.

Chapter 4

Waking in a city feels different. You know immediately, despite the birds singing, that you're surrounded by buildings.

Before I open my eyes I can hear the heavy shush and roar of traffic gathering momentum. Before I open my eyes, before I remember where I am, I feel relief, because I know I am not on Dartmoor.

When I do open them, I can remember nothing about how I got here into this bed. I remember Jill and the young doctor coming to the cottage and I remember I was in his doctor wagon, but I don't remember anything else at all. It's like a strange, floating amnesia.

I ache with a dull consistent ache, especially my head. The light is diffused, grey and yellow from streetlights, so it must be early. Far away I hear voices and the clink of teacups. I turn my head carefully and see I am in a small room on my own.

Why can't I remember anything? Why can't I remember faces and being put into this bed? Familiar anxiety surfaces and I will those voices and jingling teacups my way.

Silence. No one comes. I look down on the covers to see if there's a bell. My left hand is covered in bruises and I have a needle inserted into the back of my hand, and I'm on a drip. I can't seem to move my right arm.

Then, I hear rubbery-soled footsteps coming my way and I watch the door. It swings open and a nurse comes in and beams at me when she sees I am awake.

'Hello there! Welcome back to the world, Sigrid. How are you feeling?' She fiddles with my drip, checks something I cannot see below the bed, then she smiles down at me and checks my pulse with her fob watch. I murmur a reply to her obviously rhetorical question before she pops a thermometer into my mouth.

She remains standing, looking down at me kindly, and talks loudly and slowly as if I am a retarded child.

'I don't know how much you remember, Sigrid. You were brought in yesterday afternoon by your doctor, because of the snow. You lost consciousness on the way here.'

She whips the thermometer out of my mouth, looks at it, shakes it down and replaces it above my head. I try to say something but the croak is back.

'You're all right. There's nothing to worry about. In a moment we'll come and give you a wash and make you more comfortable.'

'. . . very thirsty,' I manage.

She turns and gets a stick thing out of a packet and moistens my lips. 'I can't give you a drink just yet, love. We need to check you don't have to go down to theatre.'

'Why?' I manage another croak. 'What's the matter with me?'

She leans down on the bed rail so that her face is nearer. 'You have had some internal bleeding. We have to make sure it has stopped. You were too poorly to do an exploratory last night, but all the signs this morning are that the bleeding has stopped. We have given you a strong painkiller, so you shouldn't be in too much pain.'

'No, I just ache.'

'Good girl. I'll be back in a moment. I just want to get another nurse to help me lift you.'

She squeaks to the door on her rubbery shoes. As the door swings shut behind her, I remember Jake. I try to close the thought out. I must not think. I must not think. What time is it? Will he have gone home?

I look at the door. What if I hear those expensive leather footsteps coming slowly down the corridor towards this room? A shadow will cover the glass, the shadow that follows me everywhere. He will walk in. He will kiss me. He will bend over me and lull me with that soft voice. Pretend it never happened. Just something in my head.

What will I do? He has never hurt me this badly before. Will he be sorry this time? Will he be angry or frightened? Will he tell them a story that is different to mine? What are they going to ask me?

Will they leave me alone? Will they simply accept what I say?

Oh God, I'm so tired. I close my eyes and feel such a deep, exposed pain begin, inside and out. I feel tears of self-pity behind my eyelids and breathing is so difficult. I hear the fast, loud rasping of my breath in the empty room.

Suddenly there are arms lifting me deftly and quickly upright against the coming darkness. 'Sigrid . . . Sigrid . . . Come on now . . .'

Something is clamped over my mouth and I gulp it and float, and the pain subsides.

Hands push my hot hair from my face and pat my shoulder gently. 'Calm down now, that's it, that's it. Calm down, slow your breathing. Good girl, that's better. You're all right. You're all right.'

I want to smile. It is as if they are calming a horse. I feel a needle slip into the back of my hand and a strange taste comes up in my mouth and I smile as warm, sickly darkness comes.

I can smell toast. It is comforting.

When I wake I am turned slightly on my side. I can see a black pair of shoes, black tights and a skirt. Small white hands are folded neatly on crossed knees. Black jacket and a wide checked tie. I meet her eyes with a jolt.

It is a young policewoman.

Chapter 5

'Sigrid, I'm Police Constable Alison Munro, from the Domestic Violence Unit, based here in Plymouth. One of the nurses asked me to visit you as I was already in the hospital. The staff are concerned about you, Sigrid. They consider your injuries non-accidental and I'm here, unofficially, because of that concern.'

She pauses and leans forward. 'I believe you told your doctor that your injuries had been sustained in a fall at home.'

I nod.

'Sigrid, your own doctor and the doctors here in the hospital consider that your severe injuries are not due to a fall, but the result of a serious assault.'

I look at her shoes because I have nothing to say.

'Sigrid?' Her voice is gentle. 'Did your husband do this to you?'

Behind her the sun is hidden by the buildings so it must be afternoon. The sky is blue so the snow must have stopped.

'Are you afraid to tell me the truth? There is no need to be afraid, I assure you . . .'

Little does she know.

'When you were admitted last night, your husband gave the hospital a statement of what he says happened to you the night before last. I would like to hear what you have to say, Sigrid.'

'Is he here? Is he in the hospital now?' My heart starts to race.

'Yes. He's waiting until you are well enough to see him. Do you feel well enough?'

I meet her eyes. I am unable to hide what I know is in my eyes. Fear. I can't breathe . . . I can't breathe.

She jumps up from her chair. 'Sigrid, relax . . . relax. Don't get upset. It's all right . . . I'll get a nurse. I'll leave you to sleep now and come back later. I just want to say this to you. I've done this many times. The fear of speaking out is the worst fear. Once you've got over that, we can help you, we really can. Please think about it.'

The nurse of this morning comes in. She takes my wrist protectively.

'The consultant is on his way to have a look at you.'

'I'm just going,' the policewoman says. 'Goodbye, Sigrid. I'll come back later, when you're feeling better.'

The consultant is tall with silver hair and tired eyes, and an expensive suit. 'Sigrid,' he says, 'I'm Mr Whiticker . . . He looks down at me in an avuncular way, 'Well, we've patched you up. You'll be as good as new in time.' I wonder if they have to learn clichés in medical school.

He jingles some change in his pocket and I wait. He sits suddenly on the very edge of my bed, gingerly, watching me.

'Having said that, your injuries are nasty, Sigrid. I will list them because you may be surprised at how severe they were for a fall at home. You have a fractured skull and a broken collarbone. You have severe lacerations and bruising to the right side of your face. You narrowly missed losing the sight of your left eye where the eyelid was split.' He stares down at me. 'You have four broken ribs and severe bruising to your arms and body. Your left lung was pierced and your abdomen was so bruised it caused internal bleeding. You narrowly missed having a ruptured spleen.'

He reaches out, turns my hand over and fingers the purple marks on it. 'How old are you, Sigrid?'

'Twenty-four.'

'My daughter is the same age so it is hard to be objective. Another assault like this and you could lose your life. Old bruises show it's not the first time this has happened. Please do the right thing, my dear, the brave thing, because whoever did this to you needs a great deal of help.'

He pats my hand distractedly, his face sad, as if he's seeing his own daughter here, not me.

He smiles suddenly in an effort to charm me. 'Don't worry, there

24

will be no lasting damage to your face. I suspect under all that atrocious bruising there is a very lovely young lady. Right, sister, I shall examine my patient.'

He checks me over with gentle cold hands, and just before he goes out of the door, he says to the sister, loudly, so I can hear, 'Sigrid is not well enough to see her husband yet. I suggest he goes home and gets some sleep. Will you please tell him that?'

He turns and waves at me. 'You are doing fine. Dr Marshall will see you tomorrow. By the way, does your husband always wear gloves?'

I look at him, startled, and he and the nurse exchange glances as they swing out of the door.

I see Jake now, out there in one of the waiting rooms, drinking coffee and charming the nurses. He will have come in out of the cold in his expensive camelhair coat and he will have found soft leather gloves the colour of pale tree bark to cover his bruised knuckles.

He will keep asking how I am. Can he see me yet? Poor, poor Si. Will they list for him my injuries? I am amazed I can have such injuries and be lying here thinking at all.

A small fat nurse comes in and brings me a cup of tea that tastes of nectar. She chats to me as she changes my drip. 'Is there anyone we can ring for you, to come and see you? Your mum, dad, brothers or sisters, Sigrid?'

'No . . . thank you. Everyone lives too far away; it would just worry them. I'm all right.'

'It would be nice for you to have someone here. A friend?'

I hesitate. Beth? I dare not even imagine the joy if Beth were here.

'You think about it. I'm going to settle you on your back for a while. That policewoman wants to have another word with you. I should speak to her if you can, because she isn't going to go away easily, dear.'

She swings out of the door and PC Alison swings back in. I just want to sleep. I just want to be left alone.

'Sigrid?' She sits down again. 'Have you thought any more about what I said?'

I don't answer, but I watch her face.

'Your husband has written you a note. One of the doctors told him you are still too ill to see anyone.' She hands a piece of paper to me, but my eyes are too swollen to read it and she knows this. 'Shall I read it to you, then I'll leave you to sleep?' Her voice is gentle but firm. The nurse is right; she is not going to go away easily.

I don't want to hear anything Jake has to say at this moment, but I nod.

She opens the piece of paper and reads.

'Si, darling, I have been trying to explain to everyone what happened to you the night before last. They seem to be blaming me for not bringing you straight to hospital. I just did not realize you were so badly hurt. Please forgive me, and for disappearing the next morning without checking you out properly. You can imagine how dreadful I feel. It is just you were sleepy and warm, darling, and I wanted to leave you that way. The doctor tells me you are still too weak to see me. I do hope you will feel well enough before I leave tonight. If not, sleep well, my love.

Jake.'

PC Alison Munro is watching me. 'Your husband is not very happy with us or the hospital. He believes we are interfering unnecessarily and unfairly in your private life. He has implied he is trying to protect *you*.' She pauses.

I look at her wearily. What now? Do I sense a very slight shift in her attitude to me? I am used to this happening when people see that handsome face, listen to that soft, persuasive voice.

She folds the letter primly, puts it on the bedside table and opens a large sheet of lined paper. 'I made it clear to your husband that no complaint has been made by you against him. He said he understood the hospital's concern over your injuries and he would be more than happy to talk to me voluntarily and clear up any misconceptions. I'm going to tell you what he said, Sigrid.'

I turn to the window. What time of day is it? White clouds blow swiftly across a sky of hazy blue. I close my eyes. I have had enough of today.

'Your husband says that on the night you were hurt, Wednesday, the twenty-fifth of February, he was working in his studio attached to the house, preparing for a coming exhibition of his work in Plymouth. He says he heard crashing and things falling inside the house. He suspected what it was because it had happened before and he rushed back inside the house.

'He says he found you throwing yourself around, getting up, hurling yourself at the furniture. He tried to grab you but you tripped and fell heavily against the metal fender, which cut your face and forehead.

'Even then, he says, you did not give up, and he had to forcibly restrain you to stop you going on hurting yourself. He says he grabbed you and held on to you with difficulty because you were in such a terrible state. He admits to hitting you once to try to calm you down. He told me he was frightened and angry with you because these sudden fits of yours are becoming more and more frequent and he hadn't been able to stop you hurting yourself before.

'He says the phone rang, startling you both, but it stopped you throwing yourself about, and he went to answer it. He spoke briefly to a friend of yours. Then he carried you upstairs, bathed your injuries and put you to bed. He says he kept an eye on you all night, but he now sees he misjudged the seriousness of the damage and was quite wrong not to get you to hospital straight away.

'He assures me, Sigrid, that his motives were not sinister but protective. He says he has realized for some time that you are very unhappy and probably need help for your deep depressions. He says he loves you very much indeed and that when he first knew you, you were recovering from a nervous breakdown and rather unstable, but he really believed the peace of Dartmoor would help you recover, help you to paint again. He has come to the conclusion the opposite is true; that you've grown to hate it, find it forbidding and lonely, and have become increasingly isolated. He says he should have got medical help for you as soon as you started to injure yourself, but he was so afraid you would be admitted to some psychiatric unit, which he didn't want to happen.

'He says what he told you in his letter – that with hindsight it was quite unforgivable to leave you alone the next morning, but he thought you were sleeping and comfortable, and he would be back before you knew he was gone. It is, he says, something he has to live with, something he deeply regrets.'

I bet.

Alison sits back, watching me. She does not say anything for a minute. Then she asks, 'Is that an accurate statement of what happened?'

I am so very, very tired. 'What do you think?'

'I'm asking you, Sigrid.'

Suddenly, so suddenly it is frightening, the suffocating pain in my chest explodes. Tears gush down my face, stinging my eyes. I know I am making horrible noises but I can't help it. I raise my hand up to an awful hopeless despair. Jake has wished me, willed me dependent and mad for so long now. Soon, soon, I will believe his words too.

Police Constable Alison jumps up. A nurse comes rushing in, then another and another, all around my bed like sparrows, murmuring, hovering distractedly, avoiding my wires and drip, trying to comfort me, patting me, placing tissues in my hand. They all seem deeply upset.

Someone whispers, 'Come on, Sigrid, shop the creep. You're safe now, you're safe with us. Make sure he can never touch you again.'

I cannot stop weeping, the weeping won't stop. 'I hurt. I hurt.'

'We know you do, lovey, we know you do. In a second we'll give you another injection and the pain will go again.'

'Just tell us. Say it quickly, Sigrid. Did your husband do this to you?'

'It's my fault,' I wail. 'Don't you see, it was my fault? I made him angry. I couldn't be what he wanted. I was sad because someone I loved died. But I wasn't mad. I wasn't . . . like he made me out to be . . . I never had a nervous breakdown . . . I tried . . . I tried . . . to be . . . but I kept getting it wrong. I provoked him.'

'No! No! It was not your fault, Sigrid. Men like your husband want you to believe that. There is nothing wrong with you, nothing at all.'

As I calm down I look round my bed. All these busy nurses fussing and caring about me. I have been so devoid of female company I have forgotten what it feels like. It feels warm and loving and . . . safe.

I lean back on my pillows, shaking with exhaustion. The pain in my chest makes me feel sick. PC Alison says quietly, 'Sigrid, on the night of February the twenty-fifth, did your husband assault you in your own home?'

'Yes.'

'And are the serious injuries you sustained due to that assault?'

'Yes.'

'Thank you.'

'Well done.'

'Brave girl.'

I am a child again. They are treating me like a small child and I don't mind. I don't mind at all. I close my eyes and relief floods through me as the nurses smile and filter slowly out to attend other patients.

Alison touches my arm. 'Sigrid, the police try to stay objective, but we are human and we sometimes find it difficult. Yours was a particularly nasty and sustained assault and I do understand what it cost you to tell us. It was very brave of you. We can charge your husband now and the law can protect you.'

She gets up and smiles at me. 'I am going to enjoy the next bit of my job, wiping that charming smile off that handsome face. Here's the night staff. Sleep well, have a good night, I'll see you in the morning.'

Two nurses come with a bowl of water and gently wash my face and hands, brush my teeth so carefully through my swollen mouth that I want to cry with gratitude. They make me comfortable for the night, give me more painkillers, then ask me again if there is anyone they can ring for me.

I smile as I begin to float and the pain recedes. 'Beth,' I say, and tell them her number in St Ives.

I wake suddenly in the dark, my heart thumping. The door of my room is propped open by a chair and I can see two nurses on night duty at the small desk. One is facing me, the other is crouched on the end of the desk. They are chattering. Is this what woke me?

There is the familiar beating of fear in my head, like bats flying. Then I remember my terrible dream, still vivid.

I am bending, looking down into a deep pool and I am admiring the colours of the weeds below the water, a speckled green and brown, when someone calls out to me, warns me to be careful because I am not looking at weeds but at the brown moving skin of a large snake crouched in the bottom of the pool.

I back away in terror and the huge brown snake rears suddenly up out of the water and I turn and run, sure that it will get me, but when I turn I am on the seashore and the snake has got someone else, someone small in a red dress with long hair, who is floating face down in the water.

I cry out because I think it is a child and I run at the snake, which rears up at me again, its mouth huge, with long curved teeth. Suddenly it disappears and I go to lift the small body in the red dress floating downwards and I murmur to her, but when I turn her over it is my face and I am dead and my long hair floats out around my head, as browny, yellow, rubbery seaweed.

I cry out now to the nurses in the corridor as I relive it, but a bell goes off loudly somewhere and they both hurry away and the corridor is empty and silent.

I feel a shadow descending, creeping my way, and the whirring of wings in my head that accompanies fainting fear becomes louder and louder. I close my eyes.

When I open them he is there. He is. Shutting out the light from the corridor behind him. I cannot make out his face, only hear that soft voice making my skin crawl.

'Oh, Si . . . Si, I am so disappointed in you. You should not tell lies, my darling. That was very wrong of you. You know and I know what happened. I won't tell them about the insanity in your family, and in the morning you will tell them the truth, what you did to yourself. There's a good girl.'

If I keep my eyes tight shut it might be another nightmare.

'I am going now. I wasn't allowed to see you, my own wife, I am not supposed to be here, Si. But you know better than anyone, don't you, how good I am at persuading people? You know better than anyone, my own little Si, that I am always and forever going to be one step behind you. Always and always, for ever and ever. Amen.'

Gently, he hums. Gently he pulls the needles out of my hand and I scream. I scream loud and long and he is gone. I open my eyes to see the door swinging and the chair falls with a crash.

Two nurses come running, but they do not believe me. 'Sigrid, he cannot get into the hospital. There is a security guard and the doors are locked.'

I shriek at them hysterically. They can't protect me, they can't. I point at the door and the fallen chair and my hand. 'Sigrid, Sigrid, the chair is light and can easily fall; needles do sometimes come loose in sleep. Come on now, come on, be sensible, no on can walk through locked doors.'

They give me an injection and a nurse sits on a chair beside me and eventually, as the sky lightens, I fall asleep.

When I wake I see there is a policeman sitting outside my door. So it was not a dream. They did believe me.

When I wake again Beth is here and she holds me and holds me and holds me as if she will never let me go.

Chapter 6

'Why?' Beth asks gently. 'Why didn't you ring us to come and get you the very first time this happened? We're two hours away from you, Si, only two hours . . . I can't bear the thought of you going through this for so long.' She brushes my arm tentatively with light fingers, as if I am fragile glass. 'I can't believe I am sitting here, seeing you like this, so bruised and thin and . . . defeated. The most wretched, the worst thing, is . . . I knew something was wrong when it was so hard to get you on the phone or to entice you down to Cornwall, but I put it down to either Jake being possessive or you being terribly involved in a new life and marriage.' She sighs and smiles ruefully at me. 'If only human beings obeyed blind instinct and not intellect, and worried less about what people might think.'

Beth does not expect me to answer. I am sleepy with drugs and I have a temperature. I curl my fingers round her slim wrist and close my eyes. Beth goes on talking quietly. 'John is talking to the consultant. We would like to take you home as soon as possible. It's one of the times, darling, when I'm so glad I'm married to a doctor.'

In the distance I can hear the supper trolley, although it is probably only about five thirty. Curtains are beginning to be drawn in the windows of the wards opposite. My view is made up of moving people in lighted windows, of floating pink and grey sunset clouds above the flat roofs. I think how quickly and how easy it would be to become institutionalised: the wonderful safeness of routine and knowing the exact time because of mundane things; of being childlike, because I'm being spoilt like a child, without responsibility or the need to think or make any decisions.

As if Beth knows what I am thinking she says, 'It will be so

33

lovely to have you with us again. We won't crowd you, Si, or probe or . . .'

I turn and look at her lovely and worried face. 'I know you won't, Beth. It's just you have John, the twins, Huer's Cottage and Talland House to look after. You have enough to do, as it is . . . I should stand on my own feet.'

She stares at me, horrified. 'You wouldn't go back to Jake, for God's sake, surely?'

My body grows hot. 'Of course I wouldn't! Of course I wouldn't, Beth.'

John swings cheerfully through the door. 'All organized. Another few days, Siggi. You have to get rid of that temperature before we can whisk you away to your bossy friend here.'

He puts his arm on Beth's shoulder in a gesture I know so well. 'Don't be upset, darling. Siggi's going to be fine.'

She looks up at him. 'Si thinks she ought to stand on her own feet.'

'You both have enough to do without having me, John.'

John sits on the edge of the bed. 'Bollocks! We happen to love you. We have known you since you were a shy, awkward, beautiful and hopeful eighteen-year-old, clattering up and down our stairs with Dan. It seems such a long time since you and Beth spent time together. Don't deprive us of the joy of having you with us for a while.'

'I want to come,' I whisper. 'I so want to come . . .'

Beth gets up and kisses me. 'It's going to be all right, you'll see, The past few years with Jake have just been a blip between Dan and lots of good things to come. I am dying to share Talland House with you . . . show you all the things we've done to Huer's Cottage. The twins are clearing their playroom for you as we speak.'

Her voice dips and rises as I close my eyes against a huge orange and black sunset filtered with long thin black clouds like cigars.

'We'll leave you to sleep, Si . . .'

I shared John and Beth's large terraced house in my first year in Bristol. They were struggling to pay their mortgage and I had an elegant room on the first floor that looked out on to a circle of grass and large and beautiful trees near Clifton village.

Older and wiser than me, Beth mothered me, disapproved mildly about Dan and me being so caught up in each other. 'You might regret it later on, Si. Wish you would spread your wings a bit. The world is made up of so many interesting people, why limit yourself to coupling so early . . .?'

'Beth, mind your own business. What the hell do you think we did?' John would say, laughing his head off.

After I had lived with them for a year John was suddenly offered a chance of a year in Zimbabwe, in the hospital at Harare, and so off they flew, and Dan and I shared a flat together after that. Beth and I never stopped writing. Beth finished her Ph.D. in Africa, had the twins and then completed her dissertation on Victorian women writers.

When they returned to England, John joined a practice in St Ives and Beth discovered Talland House. She fell instantly in love with it on being shown round and was persuaded by the amused owner to help him rekindle the Virginia Woolf connection and bring the house back to the attention of the literary set. For Beth it was like a dream come true.

Before I fall asleep a little flame of excitement flares at the thought of seeing all Beth has done, at the thought of leaving hospital, leaving Dartmoor and Jake behind me. I shiver. Beth is right. She's got to be right. I can, I can leave it all behind me. I can start again.

Chapter 7

I watch the sun rise up over the sea, tingeing the harbour a flushed orange, setting the sea on fire in great dancing sparks, turning the dawn from a sepia photograph to a gentle colour-washed day.

Fishing boats nudge and chug out of the harbour and across the bay, right through my field of vision. They are etched against the sky, silhouetted, little one-man boats, with lone fishermen standing at the tillers in woolly hats or yellow sou'westers.

They circle to find the right spot before throwing their lobster pots, attached to a marker, overboard. Then they turn home for breakfast. In early evening, when the tide is right, they chug out of the harbour again to pull in the full pots, their wake cutting a frothy line back to the harbour in a deep purple sea.

Here at Talland House I'll make tea in this small empty flat that is waiting for summer visitors, then I'll curl back on to the sofa bed, wrapped in an eiderdown, and watch the day lighten through the French windows, which lead to a small black wrought-iron balcony. I watch the sun climb over the Island and harbour, across the sweep of the bay and up the sky, lightening Godrevy lighthouse. Virginia Woolf's lighthouse.

I do this most mornings. I cannot believe how long I sit here watching, listening to the waves breaking on the beach below me, before the early traffic starts and blurs the sound.

The movement of the sea is hypnotic. I float and dip, float and dip, across and under, across and under the sea. Sometimes the small black head of a seal will appear, or a rare flying of dolphins across the sky. And I marvel, marvel and ache with release because I am here and no longer in the muted beige colours of Dartmoor.

I am here in St Ives with Beth and John. They both drove up to bring me here from hospital, afraid I might change my mind. The snow had disappeared from Dartmoor except for a sprinkling like spilt sugar in the highest places.

We did not go back to the cottage.

Beth and I are the same size and she said we would share clothes. She went to Marks and Spencer and bought me underclothes and warm childlike pyjamas because she said that both houses can be cold.

She told me she went away and wept when she first saw my face. She wept for herself too, because she had liked Jake, had found him attractive and charming, and she could not bear to have been so wrong about someone. John is just plain angry, but he never cared for Jake; they have nothing in common. John is a very unvain, dedicated GP.

They bore me lovingly back to their family, to Huer's Cottage, which lies below Talland House, perched strangely on the cliffs above railway line and sea. It has wonderful great views across the harbour, and looking down on the sprawling white-washed town, rising up pink-washed from the curve of the sea. The view from the cottage takes in the sweep of Victorian houses, cottages, flats and hotels, which spread out, hugging the cliffs, higgledy-piggledy, back to back, side to side in an eccentric Cornish mixture of steps and gardens leading to the coastal path.

John has doubts about whether a huer ever really lived in the cottage, but it is nice to think so. Along the coastal path, a few hundred yards from the cottage, a granite huer's hut, the Balking House, stands facing firmly out to sea amongst the new balconied villas built like Spanish haciendas, with a perfect bird's-eye view of the ocean.

Here, in the old days, the huer would stand on the cliffs, and when a shoal of pilchards was sighted, making shadows under the suddenly disturbed water, his loud cry of 'Hevva!' would go up to alert the seine fishermen below. Then the huer would direct from the cliff top – with whistles and cries, and hand signals with branches or horn – where the fishermen were to cast their long seine nets to capture the incoming shoal and draw it into the shore.

The fishermen would beat the water with their oars to keep the fish in the nets as they drew them to the beaches. Pilchards! Huge shoals of pilchards ... shiny green, slippery silver ...

Men, women and children would run down to the sea. But even in Virginia Woolf's day, fishing was in a decline and it was rare for the pilchards to swim into the bay. The boats, dragged by horses down to the beach every September, mostly lay idle on the beach below Huer's Cottage, waiting sadly, their coiled nets ready for the huer's cry.

When I arrived, Hanna and Amy, the five-year-old twins, hugged me painfully, rushing to get their new school uniforms to show me because they had just started school, and proudly clinging on to Mutton, their black, almost-Labrador so he could not knock me down.

Beth had given me the twins' playroom on the top floor. My room was full of flowers and books, new clothes and light flowery curtains beautifully made by Beth, blowing inwards from the square granite window full of blue sky and constantly changing sea, of station and beach and cafés, and people moving like Lowry figures along the path that links the beaches to the town.

I wanted to cry with gratitude, and everybody bustled about pretending they didn't notice. It was all too much. I sat on my bed, and when John came up with my rucksack and sat beside me I tried to explain about the isolation of the cottage in Dartmoor, where the dark swooped suddenly down in a creeping mist at the end of a day, trapping me into the damp claustrophobia of it. This warm, happy, noisy, ever-moving household felt like coming back from the dead.

Beth moves, beautiful and serene, between the present – her life in Huer's Cottage with John and the girls and Mutton – and the past – Talland House and its ghosts, sitting elegant and strangely beautiful above the town, with its fading grandeur and breathtaking views.

Leslie Stephen, Virginia Woolf's father, came across Talland House in 1881 while on a walking holiday, and rented it for the family from the Great Western Railway. The railway line had just been extended to St Ives, and every year Virginia and her family came to spend the summer in Cornwall. It is a strange and wonderful Victorian house that stands above St Ives, with its shutters and beautiful wrought-iron balconies outside the windows, which in Virginia's day went all round the building.

Once it stood in large beautiful gardens sloping to the sea, separated like rooms, and surrounded by escallonia hedges. The garden is still lovely and has that tranquil and timeless quality, but land has been sold over the years for building and a car park.

Inside, the staircase has gone, and the top of the house had been turned into flats long before the current owner bought the house. The house has not been loved and cherished over the years, and Beth has had a free hand helping to refurbish the rooms exquisitely and expertly, with their stunning views of the bay. The present owner, currently abroad lecturing for a year, is trying to recapture the feel and sense of the house in which Virginia Woolf spent much of her childhood.

Downstairs, the drawing room, where the Stephen family sat and read and talked with many famous literary figures, has wonderful high ceilings and decorated cornices, a stone fireplace and long window capturing every glitter and colour of the sea. Beth has her office and entertains Virginia Woolf devotees downstairs. Here she will sometimes light the fire and we will sit together when the twins are at school.

As soon as I arrived, Beth gave me a set of keys for Talland House.

'You must have your own keys, Si, so that when the twins jump on you, when you need to be alone to paint, or just to be alone, you won't have to ask, you can just disappear.'

Beth is the most generous person I know. She loves to share what is precious to her. She knew I would be enraptured the moment I crossed the threshold of Talland House.

At Huer's Cottage I go to bed early each night and lie listening to the sounds of television and footsteps on the stairs, and children arguing and John getting cross with Mutton, and Beth shouting, 'Bed, you two!' I lie sleepless, catatonic and make myself relax, uncurl my body, breathe deeply, sink into the noises and feel of this old creaking cottage full of warmth and family life.

I listen to the soft sound of the sea breaking below me, watch the myriad harbour lights with relief after the suffocating darkness of Dartmoor.

But fear has become a habit I can't let go of yet.

I get up as the sky lightens, a pink flush on the horizon. I tiptoe down the creaking stairs and let myself out of the front door of Huer's Cottage, and the vast sound of the ocean, glimmering in the dark, rushes at me. I make my way under the railway bridge, up the steep path to the road, enter the drive to Talland House and stare for a moment up at the windows of the still house.

I go up the back steps, puffing because I am still weak and unfit. I let myself into the empty flat and collapse, breathing heavily, on to the bed. Out of the french windows, beyond the wrought-iron balcony, the sea, from this height, is still, like black glass. I wrap the eiderdown round me and wait for the sun to rise and for the small fishing boats to edge out of the harbour.

I love being quite alone here. It is where I face myself each day. It is where I sleep and dream and read Virginia Woolf. I have started to keep a diary too. Beth has left coffee and tea, and there is a small fridge with things to tempt me to eat.

For a while Virginia Woolf's nursery is my own, my secret place. I know this is where I will start to paint again. I love to begin and end the day here, where the sky is full of fiery colours and a fading purple sea.

One afternoon I fall asleep to the sound of rain. I wake in the dark, the house is quite still, the air heavy with a strange hovering expectation. Beyond the window the sea is breaking with small smacks like someone shaking out a cardboard bag.

Lights in the distance, beyond the phosphorescent sea, twinkle as if all life is over there. It is cloudless, and stars sprinkle the dark sky. As always my dream woke me and Jake's voice is in my ear, as soft as those waves out there and as powerful.

'Are you painting, Si? What have you done with your day? So sad, you showed so much promise, my darling.'

'I'm sketching . . . it's coming . . .' I reply, stung.

'Darling! Wonderful. Show me.'

'I'd rather not, not just yet.'

41

'Come on, come on, this is exciting, the first work you have done since . . . Dan.'

'Jake, please, please, let me be. Let me do things in my own time.'

But he has found my sketch book pushed quickly under something as he came in the door. He is opening it and turning the pages and I have to swallow the scream of rage. I am allowed no privacy. This is *my* work, *my* private jottings, not for anyone to see, especially not Jake.

He stares down at my little pencil sketches and purses his lips, closes the book with a little smack. Smiles me that smile. 'Don't give up the day job, my darling!'

The atmosphere in the room seems to change suddenly from expectation to anger. Is it my own long-suspended anger that fills the room?

In the dark there is a rustle of a dress and when I look towards the window, a figure in white is leaning over the black balcony staring out to sea. Her hair is dark and pulled back, knotted. Her profile is beautiful. Long and sad.

I lie very still, wondering if I am dreaming and if I am not dreaming whether I should feel frightened but I do not feel frightened. I do not even feel surprised. Of course Virginia Woolf is here. I am inhabiting her old room.

Pictures of her are all around the house. Like her books and her life, they dominate and are as much a part of the fabric of the house as the lives of Beth, John and the twins, who spend so much time here lovingly decorating, painting, researching and discovering past lives lived and visited here.

As soon as I entered the wide hall of Talland House, through the heavy arched door, and stood where there had once been a curved staircase, I felt the stillness of ghosts. I have seen Beth half-turn and speak to someone behind her when the room is empty. I have watched John glance at a shadow and the twins look up suddenly from their play and smile.

I curl into the warmth of the eiderdown. When I look up again Virginia has gone from the balcony. My thoughts fill the cracks of this still evening, whispers rustle like dry leaves through the room.

An echo of conversation hovers on the lips of someone I cannot see. Words form like a familiar ache behind my tongue, a quick breath upon my cheek. Meaning is a shape in the dark. Words, like the slow breaking of a wave, carry hope to some distant shore.

I open my eyes. Virginia Woolf stands looking down at me. She is very beautiful. Frail, intangible as a faded painting. There . . . but insubstantial . . . like dappled leaves fluttered by the wind, making moving, shadowy patterns over a lawn.

She seems so real. My skin prickles in fear and wonder. Perhaps Jake is right and I am unbalanced. Impatience fills the air like the humming of insects on a summer night. As if I am being told to trust and cling to what I know to be true, an ageless wisdom of instinct and spirit. Virginia moves. She fades, becomes an illusion.

She is gone. I smile at myself. I desperately want Virginia Woolf to haunt me, as if a communion with spirits is a continuity in itself and death nothing more than a vanishing trick.

If I am mad there is a wonderful liberation in my madness.

From far, far away, like a distant echo, I hear Beth and the twins calling my name, wondering where I am. I return with a jolt to the present. I get up and shut the door of the flat and call down to them that I am coming. I am coming . . .

Chapter 8

Beth is sitting in an old chintzy armchair stitching. Her feet are tucked under her, her head is bent, her hair flicked behind her ears, out of the way as she concentrates.

She is wearing a long white sweater and blue jeans, and she is pregnant again and looks radiant curled up with her embroidery. I watch her with love and admiration. She is a beautiful person who is happy. She is happy not because her life is easy but because she has that rare faculty for happiness.

She will find joy in tiny moments, in even the most difficult circumstances, and she will imbue them with an enthusiasm that captures all around her, like blowing on a wilting fire until suddenly it bursts into flames.

I am sitting curled on the large sofa, wrapped up in the old faded pink eiderdown and we are both listening to a tape of *To the Lighthouse* – again. Eileen Atkins reads it so beautifully we both fell asleep last time.

Virginia Woolf's words ebb and flow, ebb and flow through this large corniced drawing room at Talland House. We are waiting for visiting Woolfies from Japan. There is a faint smell of furniture polish and pungent narcissus.

The door out to the hall is open so we will hear them come, and I am aware of the fridge humming faintly in the kitchen. The Aga, which keeps the house warm and dry, plops gently every so often like fish rising.

Outside, beyond the window, birds fly, carrying twigs, calling out one to another in the cold blue air. Buds are unfolding, the palest green emerging on sticks of shrubs and climbers – delicate, tiny

45

knobs of spring preparing to burst open. In the garden of Talland House, bright red and pink camellias are in flower, and thousands of white and yellow daffodils sit in clumps under the trees.

The snowdrops are over, gone as quickly as they came, great carpets of them mixed with white and blue wood anemones. Spring is coming. What shall I do in this spring?

Inside the room the soft voice on the tape describes Mrs Ramsay standing on the quay, looking out towards the lighthouse across the wide sweep of the bay.

I stood on the harbour wall yesterday looking across to Godrevy lighthouse and the great and wonderful sea rolling in to the acres of yellow sand. Now, behind my closed eyelids, I see the same view as Virginia saw, and time blurs and hovers in this peaceful room, where the only movements are Beth's fingers moving quickly in and out of her tapestry, and the only sounds the faint hum of machines inside the house and the swoop of chattering birds outside.

I see, long ago, the green baize door swinging to and fro between the kitchen and the rest of the house, and the sound of a ball bouncing down a curved staircase, and childish banter rising and falling to my breathing.

That moment of half-sleep, that moment when the spirit soars with a sudden elusive essence of being – of being here in this place at this moment – floods through my body in an aching joy, a pumping of blood, a life force that is mysterious, continuous and inexplicable.

It is like being a small child lying at the top of a large old house, sick and feverish, and suddenly hearing someone you love climbing slowly up a million stairs towards you with tea, a boiled egg, toast.

The thought of the buttery toast and the yellow yolk dripping down the egg cup is already a taste in your mouth. A tray will be placed on your knees, someone will sit beside you and you will be safe and comforted. A wild moment of weepy happiness floods through your veins. It is the end of a long, lonely day in your sick bed.

This is how I feel with Beth; the same sad joy of an ageless connection with things; the end of something long and unending. But I am poised, timeless, until the next part of my life begins.

Beth turns now and grins at me. 'I think you are turning into more of a Woolfy than my earnest Americans.'

I grin back. 'Not learned enough!'

A coachload of literary American academics have just left, having moved excitedly through the house exclaiming, 'Here, Myrtle, Woolf would have stood here, just here at the front door, looking out at the garden . . .' 'She walked . . . from here to here . . . Virginia walked into this beautiful drawing room to debate with Thoby about life, about Shakespeare . . . Sat over in that corner and wrote . . .' 'She stood, must have stood at this window for hours watching the bay. Oh boy . . . look at that view.'

Beth and I were so relieved the twins were still at school. They tend to cavort precociously about, doing handstands, declaring: 'Virgin Wolf did handstands 'ere, 'xactly on this spot . . . 'xactly on this spot where Mutton did the most *humendous* wee . . .' Then they collapse in giggles, utterly ruining any atmosphere of academia.

The phone rings suddenly and Beth uncurls, switches off the tape and answers it. 'Beth Elliot.'

Her face changes; she glances quickly at me. 'Yes, she's here.' She puts her hand over the phone. 'It's your policewoman . . .'

I get up and take the phone. 'Hello?'

Alison Munro says, 'I'm sorry to bother you, Sigrid. How are you?'

'Much better, thank you,' I reply warily.

'Just two things. As you know, Sigrid, after we charged your husband, your solicitor made an application for a civil injunction to the County Court. Your husband did not contest that injunction and agreed with the solicitor acting on your behalf not to make any contact with you.'

'Yes.'

'Did your solicitor explain exactly what this means and the next step to be taken? I did talk to you about this while you were in hospital, but I do appreciate you were very unwell.'

I am silent. Beth has gone into the kitchen to make tea. I want Alison the policewoman to go away.

'We are preparing criminal proceedings against your husband,'

47

she continues. 'If the Crown Prosecution Service decides there is enough evidence to prosecute, you are required to attend as a witness, Sigrid—'

'No!'

'Sigrid, please . . . I would like you to think very carefully about this.'

I am shaking and I sit down. 'My solicitor told me that I would have to be cross-examined twice, once by the barrister for the Crown and again by Jake's barrister. I didn't know this when I made a statement to you. I won't go to court—'

'Sigrid, if you refuse to give evidence the case will collapse. Surely after all you have been through you don't want this to happen?'

'My solicitor says that the Crown Prosecution Service has to make a decision whether or not to prosecute first. It may not come to court.'

'But if it does, and I hope it does, surely you won't be reluctant to give evidence?'

'I'm sorry, I'm really sorry, I know you've worked hard, but I won't go to court and be cross-examined. I have the injunction now. He can't come near me or contact me.'

'Why not, Sigrid? Do you know where he is? Because we have no idea. We haven't got the manpower to ensure that he doesn't molest you again.'

'I don't want to go to court. I don't want to see him. I just want it to be over.'

'But it isn't over, Sigrid. The sheer truth of the matter is, despite any civil injunction, he is free to turn up on your doorstep any time he feels like it at the moment, which is why the police want to take criminal proceedings.'

'Don't say that!' I cry. 'Why are you trying to frighten me?'

'I'm not. I'm trying to protect you. I want you to protect yourself, Sigrid. We can only do so much. I'm sorry if I've upset you. I'll speak to you in a week or so. All I'm asking is that you think very seriously about what I've said to you, maybe talk to your friends. Meanwhile, take care of yourself.' She puts the phone down. She is annoyed.

Beth brings me a mug of tea. The afternoon is spoilt. I am safe, surely I am safe here? He won't come here. I look at my hands. My stupid cowardly hands are shaking and I spill the tea. Beth takes it from me and hugs me.

'He'd better not come here,' she says fiercely. 'I don't believe he would dare, darling. I don't believe you have got anything to worry about at all.'

We hug, rock together for a moment, framed in the large tiny-paned window full of sunlit sea, before the sun slides behind the houses. The Japanese Woolfies have obviously got lost.

We lock up Talland House and walk downhill, back to Huer's Cottage. As we arrive the school bus turns at the top of the road and the twins stream and clatter in, arguing like magpies, and I hug them roughly to me.

Beth is wrong, of course. I know what PC Alison Munro says is right. It can't be over. Jake won't let it be over.

Chapter 9

Suddenly the weather changes. Spring is gone and winter is back. I wake to a great blanket of sea engulfed in a swirling grey mist. St Ives has disappeared. It is like being back on Dartmoor.

Huer's Cottage is freezing and draughty, and I sit up in bed, hugging the bedclothes to me. I look at my hands, my arms. I touch my body, curl my arms around myself. I do not know who I am suddenly, or what I am doing here.

I sit shivering in early morning, fighting familiar despair, as if the mist has triggered the isolation of Dartmoor and wherever I turn I cannot escape the claustrophobic endlessness of it. I do not even want to get out of bed and go to Talland House.

I look out at the vanished sea. That great moving mass of water, full of power and strength, subtle and hidden, rising and heaving like the belly of a great, ever-moving mammal – somehow threatening with its relentless grey swell and rhythm.

I move out of myself up to the ceiling. I look down on myself. I have been here before and I am afraid of fragmenting into a thousand pieces. One telephone call, one conversation, and I am enveloped by blind fear. And guilt. I should not have talked to the police.

The first time I experienced this feeling of wanting to fly away from myself was when I was a child. I used to travel many miles. Away, away in my head to favourite and safe places. Then, suddenly, the ability to do it left me. It came back when Dan was killed, as if all my new-found strength and happiness died with him.

Jake descended, like some golden god. He swept me away and decided to save me from my 'strangeness'. Perhaps he is right after

51

all and I have inherited my mother's imbalance, which made her feel this sudden overpowering and terrible melancholy.

There is a knock at the door and John brings me tea. 'I hope you are not going out in this? It's cold and it's early. I would rather you stayed put today. Talland House will be even colder than it is here.' He places the tea on my bedside table and looks down at me. 'What is it?' But he knows. 'Siggi, just put the court case out of your mind for now. Let's talk about it nearer the time. You know Beth and I will support you. It's going to be months and months before anything happens and in that time you're going to feel stronger and stronger.'

I nod, and he peers at my fading bruises before he departs for his busy practice. 'Your face is healing beautifully.' At the door he turns. 'You are going to feel depressed and wobbly for quite a while, you know. You've taken a hell of an emotional and physical battering. And whatever Jake managed to make you believe, you are perfectly normal.' He grins at me. 'I would be more worried about you if you didn't have the odd wobble. Trust me, I'm a doctor!'

I smile at him as he shuts the door. I drink my tea to the sound of the twins and Mutton thundering up and down the stairs. I get up and go to the window. The mist is clearing a little, but the landscape is almost empty out there. A woman walks a dog, and a man, a distance away stands on the edge of the beach in a long white mackintosh.

I stare at him, but he does not move; stands quite still just staring out to sea. My heart jumps painfully. *Jake has a long white mac. I have always hated it.*

The twins burst into the room, closely followed by Mutton. 'Mornin'. Mornin', Si. Mum says, would you like breakfast in bed?'

I turn from the window as Beth puffs up the stairs after them. 'Bathroom, you two, this minute. I told you to knock. I told you only to put your heads round the door first.' She looks at me. 'What's the matter, darling?'

I take her to the window and point to the man in the long mackintosh. 'I think . . . Oh, Beth, I think that might be Jake.'

Beth peers out and then laughs. 'Sigrid, that is *not* Jake, that's Mr Trevorrow. He always wears that long dirty white mac. He comes every morning and walks his Jack Russell on the beach. It's only because you usually shoot up to Talland House so early that you haven't seen him before. See, there they go . . .'

I make a face. 'Sorry.'

I go downstairs with her and when we have waved the twins off on the school bus we sit and have coffee together. The kitchen is warm because it has a Rayburn. 'I think I might walk into St Ives and buy some paints and new brushes later on,' I say.

'Good idea. I'll pick up some bread and cheese and we can have lunch together at Talland House. I had a phone call earlier. The Japanese Woolfies have finally found us!'

'Let me do something. I'll get the lunch.'

'No, Si, I don't want you climbing up the hill carrying things. I've got the car. What would be a help is if you could stay at Talland House this afternoon. I've got an antenatal appointment.'

I smile. 'I'll take my paints up there, just in case the weather clears up.'

When Beth has left for her doctor's appointment after lunch, I wash the plates, make myself more coffee and curl up on the sofa in the drawing room at Talland House. The Japanese have been and gone, and no one else is coming to visit as far as we know. The weather has not lifted. The afternoon is dark, as if evening is already approaching. I switch on some music.

I feel as if I am waiting for something. Half asleep, dozing to the music, I sit up with a start. I suddenly realize what it is I feel. *I am waiting for Jake.* It doesn't matter what the police, my solicitor, Beth or John tell me, it is what I know. It is not possible to protect me from Jake. *'I am always and forever going to be one step behind you. Always and always, for ever and ever . . .'*

Jake is behind me, beside me, inside me. I will never be free.

Beth has lit a fire in the granite fireplace and the flames flicker on the pale green walls and high decorated ceilings. I catch a tiny movement of displaced air, a blur, and Virginia Woolf is there sitting in the little nursing chair with a book in her hand, her finger marking a page. She is young today, her hair loose. She looks at me quizzically, as if she is thinking: You think you are the only person in the world to feel despair?

The light changes slowly to a bruised purple, full of rain. I stare at Virginia Woolf's lovely face. It is hard to see that unlined, clever face, full of excitement and anticipation, and imagine what was in her heart and mind when she walked out of her house in middle age to find a heavy stone. Left her walking stick in the mud like a marker, and waded into that fast-flowing river.

It makes me weep to think of her bending to find the exact right stone to fit her pocket. Had she seen that smooth, certain-shaped stone lying on a path one day, and planned her end ahead?

Or did she, suddenly emerging from her house in this terrible melancholy haze of despair, spot it like a distorted signal, as lying there with a purpose, her mind slipping away from her, to a distance from which she didn't know if she could retrieve it?

Virginia Woolf marks the page of her book with long thin fingers. I like the feeling of her here. I like to believe she is here, tangible, listening. It makes my own thoughts form and take shape.

I think about Dan. When happiness ended so suddenly. Loss swings in and makes me draw breath with pain. I have survived without him. How can this be? We met on the train from Edinburgh to Bristol. We were both going to Bristol University. It was friendship at first sight. Or lust. Or love. Whatever it was we were best friends from that moment. I was on a high. I was safe. I was away from home. I was out of reach.

Friends used to joke, nastily sometimes, because Dan and I did nearly everything together and because we did not need anybody else and that is unnerving. We would sit together screaming with laughter, content and insular, and it would make people feel excluded. But it wasn't intended. It was just how it was.

We could have been brother and sister, we were so alike physically, and our lives were similar. Dan was very fair too. We both had Scandinavian mothers who tended to be gloomy. My mother was Norwegian, Dan's had been Icelandic. Both our mothers had died when we were in our teens. His in a car crash.

I was an only child who had longed for siblings, Dan had a much older brother. We had both been lonely, with parents who were cool and detached with each other, who found it difficult to express feelings or show love openly. All this bound us together like a spider's web. It was truly like finding the other half of oneself and feeling total exhilaration to have done so.

Outside the mist lifts an inch from the sea. Fragments of it blow away, carrying faint wisps of the colour of the sun buried within it. Virginia Woolf get up from her chair and wanders about the room, restless, as if she too is remembering something. Her book remains on the chair.

In our last year, Dan and I spent a lot of time planning our year out. We were going to do a stint teaching in a school in Zimbabwe and visiting Beth and John; then, when we had saved enough, travel round Africa. We couldn't believe our luck. We were so excited about the trip.

Sometimes it seems like yesterday, not five years ago. Neither Dan nor I took hard drugs. We smoked cannabis, sometimes, very rarely, at parties. That was all.

One evening Dan went off to this party on his own because I had flu. I never saw him again. They said he took something. I refused to believe it. We had exams coming up and Dan was so anti hard drugs because of what they had done to a school friend.

He took something which made him think he could fly.

I close my eyes tight shut against my thoughts. I clutch the eiderdown to me so I am covered in warmth, but my body trickles with icy sweat, as it did that night.

He jumped. He jumped from the Clifton Suspension Bridge.

It was Jake who came to tell me. Jake who knew before me. Jake who looked after everything. Who looked after me. He was one of the best lecturers at Bristol. Everybody, even the men, were fascinated by Jake. He was tall and golden and beautiful. He lectured on fine art and his lectures overflowed with women students who fell in love with him. But Jake appeared to be fascinated by me.

Virginia is standing framed in the window, her back to the sea, watching me.

I think he was only fascinated with me because I was in love with Dan and I was not interested in him. After Dan died, he was gentle and kind, very practical and caring. I was struggling . . . I got behind in my work. He gave me time. He was a brilliant painter and I learnt so much from him. All the same, I couldn't finish my course.

I felt guilty. I was surviving without Dan.

Did you have a choice? Virginia Woolf's voice is a draught moving the curtains gently outward like a parachute. Soft as a breath. She is wearing a long black skirt with a white blouse caught in at the waist. She is girlish and thin.

I stare at her, so fragile, so insubstantial. So real. A ghost who has never left, who lives on in every creak and flicker and shadow.

I am amazingly ignorant, I tell her. But I am learning from Beth. This house is full of the essence of you and I want to feel you for myself. I want the house to give me my own version of you. I want to listen to the walls give up the voices and laughter of your childhood. I want to sense you here, even when I cannot see you. I want to believe you are here with me, even if you are only in my head. I want to read your words as if they are a clue.

Virginia Woolf smiles slowly, a young girl silhouetted in the window against the misty sea. Her full lips twitch with amusement. She raises a hand to tuck a stray strand of hair behind her ear. Then she is gone.

There is no book on the chair. Only my memories of Dan filling the late afternoon.

Chapter 10

The next morning I wake late and a thin yellow sun tinges the edges of the clouds and reaches into the window with long thin arms to the end of my bed.

The mists have disappeared and the sky is blue, but out at sea, by the lighthouse and beyond, small white waves ride high, and the doors and windows of the house rattle like a low growl.

'There is going to be a huge storm,' Beth says, sitting on my bed. She has brought me up a cup of coffee, fresh and strong and delicious. I sit up in bed and clutch the hot mug and think how aware everyone is of the weather here, when you can see it rolling in from a distance.

Beth places a yellow envelope in front of me, looking at me anxiously. 'Jake?' she asks.

'Yes.'

I turn the bright distinctive envelope with the familiar handwriting to me and my stomach gives a sick little lurch. It is obviously a card and I think I know what it will say.

Beth is still watching me. As I start to open it she reaches out and touches my hand. 'Si, promise me you would never go back, whatever he says.' How well Beth knows me. 'You've made the break now. It's over. However seductive or pathetic his words, it's over.'

I tear the flap and pull out his home-made card. It is one of his small abstracts. It is lovely. I stare at it with a surge of grief for what might have been. Inside he has written:

Dearest Si, Just a note to remind you my feeling for you will never change, but I am forced to accept that yours for me must have. I plan to take a trip abroad, joining my family in Cyprus and then travelling on to the Far East to prepare for my next exhibition in Hong Kong.

I have informed your solicitor of my intentions. Perhaps you will be good enough to confirm them to him. Take care, Si. If you need anything write c/o my bank, I have put some money into your bank account to tide you over until you get some kind of job. I hope you will be able to cope. I tried so hard to protect you from yourself . . . And I loved you very much. Jake.

Beth still has not taken her eyes off me. I keep my face quite impassive. He is not begging me to go back. He is not begging at all. I pass the card for her to read. I look out to sea. I won't think . . . won't think . . . How typical of Jake to combine his prodigious talent with cool, detached words.

Beth reads quickly and pushes the card away from her, her face as closed as mine. 'Clever,' she says quietly. 'Dismissive in the guise of loving. ". . . until you get *some* kind of job . . . I tried to *protect* you from *yourself* . . ."' Bloody Nora, Si, he makes you out to be some sort of certifiable neurotic.'

She gets up off the bed and paces about angrily. 'Honestly! No mention of what he did to you, beat you to within an inch of your life. No "Sorry, Si, I lost it. Here is some money until you start painting again." Tried to protect you! Balls! Who is he kidding, himself?'

I smile, she sounds like John.

'Is it true, what he says in the letter? Do you really think he will go away and leave you alone?'

'It sounds true. His father is a retired Hong Kong judge. If he knows Jake is in any sort of trouble with the law he will vouch for him, I'm sure of that. Maybe he has advised Jake to go away, to travel, to show he means to leave me alone.'

'I sincerely hope so. I suppose Jake also thinks it is far less likely you will go ahead if it comes to a court case . . . Sorry, I'm banging on, not asking you what you feel. Are you upset, sad, angry or what?'

'I just don't know, Beth. I just don't know what I feel.'

But am I telling the truth? Would I really have liked Jake to beg me to go back? Begged to be forgiven, begged for another chance? Would I have been happier to have him profess eternal love? Jake would never beg for anything, I know that. So I suppose I am hanging on, as always, for a Jake who only lives in my head, but which I have trained myself to believe really exists.

Beth says quietly, 'You have very confused feelings about Jake, don't you? Don't look defensive, Si; he could be utterly charming. He was clever and fascinating and great fun, I know that, I saw that for myself. How could you not have regrets? He's your husband, for God's sake!' She leans forward and holds my arm as if she wants to make sure I hear her words. 'But he's dangerous, Si, and you know it. Every time you remember the good bits, remember the fear, remind yourself what he did to you. Only yesterday you were terrified poor Mr Trevorrow was Jake standing out there.'

'I know, I know, Beth. I don't have to be reminded of the fear, believe me. It's with me everyday . . . I see Jake everywhere, or I see his car, or someone like him turning a corner. I feel as if I am waiting for him to come, as if his power over my fear stretches great distances.'

'Rubbish!' Beth says firmly. 'He is a flawed human being who needed to possess you and break your spirit. You will probably never understand what made him treat you like he did, and you must leave it like that. Let him go, Si. It was not your fault. Please accept that and move on. Don't become obsessed with Jake or he will have won.'

I cannot say anything because I am near tears. There is so much I wish I could tell Beth, but I can't. The silence has stretched too many years. The silence has grown and become a part of me, like a small drip of acid eating away at the fabric of what I am or what I have become.

We hug, Beth and I, rocking gently on the bed that is filling with sunlight in the quiet house empty of twins. 'It's all right, it's going to be all right,' she whispers over and over. I must repeat it to myself like a mantra, until I believe it.

Mutton comes and pushes his cold nose between us worriedly, and whines. Beth laughs. 'Mutton cannot bear anyone to be unhappy. I'm going downstairs to heat us a croissant. Then, shall we walk him? Because this sun isn't going to last.'

'Yes . . .' I bend and kiss Mutton's large velvety head. 'OK, Mutts, I'll get dressed . . . Beth . . . thanks.'

'Don't thank me for anything,' she growls. At the door she asks, 'Were you talking to yourself or talking in your sleep early this morning?'

'No, I was reading *To the Lighthouse* to Mutton. He couldn't sleep either.'

'Of course you were. Silly me.' She clatters down the stairs humming.

Down on the beach the sea is turning grey and choppy. The wind whips sand into our faces, and empty crisp packets and chocolate wrappers blow across the sand and catch at our legs as if they are propelled by machine.

It is unpleasant, and even Mutton is ready to turn for home, his eyes and mouth filled with sand. Bent double, unable to talk against the breathtaking force of the wind, we turn our backs to the sea and drop Mutton back at Huer's Cottage, then toil on up the hill to Talland House.

At the top of the drive we stop, out of breath, by the small wall and look down over the bay at the angry white-flecked sea and at the tankers beginning to emerge on the skyline, seeking shelter near the harbour.

'Here was the Lookout place where Virginia Woolf used to stand and watch the shipping in the bay. In those days there were cargo vessels and small steamers making for Hayle harbour. Before the Porthminster Hotel was built below us, the family used to stand here and look down at the station and watch for the signal to go down. Then it was time to go and meet visitors from the train.'

Beth turns and, with her back to the sea, waves an arm across the tarmac drive and deserted car park, towards the house. 'Imagine a vast Victorian greenhouse, up against that white-painted boundary wall, full of peaches. Wonderful ripe, furry peaches. The hot exotic, fruity smell drifting out of the door and across the garden, making the children's mouths water as they played.'

Beth takes my arm and we walk up the drive towards the back

door. 'Imagine two or three acres of garden rising up all around and behind Talland House, running downhill in front, towards the sea. Lots of separate little gardens divided by hedges. Passion flowers with great blossoms like bees, climbing up the house, urns full of tumbling flowers. Primroses . . . red hot pokers. Oh, and there was the Love corner under the greenhouse, and the coffee garden and the Fountain. The kitchen garden, there, where the car park is, had strawberry beds . . . There was a pond where they sailed paper boats.'

Beth sighs. 'Si, this house was a little island, a blissful green oasis looking down, down on the bay. Perfect. Utterly perfect.'

How Beth loves this house. How she loves the discovery of lives lived here and fading photos brought up by the locals. And where fact is blurred and awful sixties changes made, there is always imagination and the movement of ghosts.

Beth will stand last thing at night, when the flats are full of visitors in summer, on the lawn with Mutton, breathing in the scent of roses and night-scented stock. She will look up at the lighted windows and listen to the faint sound of music and bath water running and small footsteps running over wooden floorboards, and she will wonder about lives she knows nothing of, played out up there, in all those rooms of Talland House.

We both stand with our backs to the wind and the sea, and stare at the strange flat-roofed house with its long windows, its black wrought-iron balconies and the faded, white façade, the face of Talland House, which is about to be painted.

'Bliss!' Beth says. 'John and I have all the fun of fascinating people coming from all over the place and none of the awesome responsibility of actually owning the house.'

I look and imagine that I see small shadows pass within the house. Virginia, Vanessa, Thoby and Adrian, looking out as children, down on to a magic garden, shimmering through a sea mist, waiting for the sun to burn the cloud away, before bursting suddenly, the sky a flash of blue, into a blazing, endless summer day.

I see small footprints in early morning grass, the toes a clear outline where they tiptoed, holding their dresses up out of the dew. I hear a garden gate click in a lazy afternoon full of bees' hum and heavy closing eyelids, and a small fist clutching a handful of grass and lifting a lawn-crumpled cheek to listen. Such afternoons evoking for ever, on and on into adulthood, the memory of a vivid glittering haze of sea and sky and the echoing sound of seagulls screaming and wheeling over the rooftops. Bringing back the smell of the sea, blown inland, of salt and pungent metallic seaweed. Of childhood holidays recreated over and over, even into old age, in a seamless bid to recapture in the same smells and sounds and glimpses of luminescent blue sea and sky, a searing perfection that fades with childhood.

Beth is looking at the roof. 'I hope to God we don't lose too many tiles,' she yells over the wind. 'Come on, let's go inside. It's freezing.'

A huge wind bends the trees double in the garden, and the vast macrocarpa firs in the gardens of the hotel above the house sway alarmingly.

Once inside, Beth and I watch from the drawing room window the dramatic bruised storm clouds roll in from the horizon, massing together, bleeding into sea and sky until they are one. Darkening the day suddenly like the middle of an epic film where God's wrath explodes across the sky.

I stand enthralled, but Beth shivers. 'Come on, Si . . .' She raises her voice over the rattling of the windows, checking the catches on each one. 'Let's get home before the storm breaks. Mutton will get neurotic and my conservatory door is open.'

We blow back down the hill to Huer's Cottage. St Ives is disappearing, vaporizing away into cloud as the weather closes in. I turn. Behind us Talland House is already invisible. Soon Beth and I, shut into her little cottage, will become sea mist and cloud cover. We will disappear into the weather. I smile. It is a strange, safe feeling.

Chapter 11

That evening after supper, as we sit around the table lazily finishing a second bottle of wine and listening to objects hurling around outside in the gale, the maroon for the lifeboat suddenly goes off. Against the noise of the rising wind and the rattling of the house, Hanna and Amy come rushing back into the kitchen.

'Dad . . . Dad . . . can we go and watch it launched? Can we . . . can we . . . please, please?'

John sighs and drains his glass. 'Go on then, hurry up and get yourselves wrapped up. It's bitter out there.'

Beth sees my face and grins. 'Go on, you too, and I better come in case I miss anything!'

'Heaven forbid,' John grumbles, smacking her bottom lightly.

We blow down the hill and along the path by the beach into the town, clutching each other and the children, and trot, at a pace dictated by the wind behind us, to the lifeboat station.

I feel as if we are a part of the fabric of a fishing village anywhere. Down the ages, men, women and children, hurrying to a fixed position. Scurrying towards the harbour, towards an angry, unpredictable sea that is throwing violent waves over the sea wall, making the twins squeak with excitement as the wind tosses us like playthings, making us acutely aware of the impotence of man against this immense destructive force.

The lifeboat has already shot into the uneasy sea and is plunging like a frisky horse out of the harbour mouth, leaving a wide wake behind it. There is a flurry of activity on board, sou'westers are still being pulled on, ropes gathered, orders given, then quickly the boat turns and heads out into the waves.

We watch it dip and plough out of the harbour into heavy seas, disappearing into the darkness. People lean on the railings, clamber about the harbour wall and mutter and gossip about a tanker listing ... a fishing smack trying to get back into Newlyn ... someone taking a small yacht out after being warned about the weather.

Overhead in the clouds, we can hear the rescue helicopter, and see the lights flickering up in the sky and a sudden uneasy silence falls. Everyone is thinking of the terrified people somewhere out in that horrific sea, fighting for their lives.

We walk round the harbour, trying to keep warm for fifteen minutes, the twins calling out to school friends, climbing about on the low wall, getting overexcited and silly. People drift about, stand outside the pub drinking beer, gazing out in the direction the lifeboat took.

Eventually Beth insists on taking the twins home to bed, ignoring their howls of protest. 'The lifeboat could be hours out there, as you both well know. Now, come on, be fair, you have to be up for school in the morning and I have enough trouble getting you up as it is.'

She grins at me. 'Do me a favour, Si. Stay and have a beer with John, his tongue is hanging out.'

'Are you all right coping with those monsters up the hill in this wind?' John asks hopefully.

'Yes ... yes, of course I am,' Beth laughs, and winks at me. 'See you both later.'

John and I battle our way to the bar and as we edge back outside, clutching our drinks, someone calls to him. He turns. 'Hi, there, Matt!' We push through the crush, out into the cold night and John introduces me. 'Si, this is Matthew Tregonning. He paints wonderfully. Matt, this is Sigrid Watson. She's staying with us for a while, and she also paints beautifully!'

John takes a gulp of beer, terribly pleased with himself. Both Matt and I burst out laughing, mutually amused by him. 'And John plays a mean game of golf for a sedentary doctor!' Matt says to me.

He is a tall man with dark curly hair and laughing blue eyes. He holds out his hand and meets my eyes with an easy warmth. 'Hi, Sigrid, glad to meet you.'

I take an immediate and instinctive liking to him.

Just then a cry goes up. 'She's coming back. She's coming back.' We move back to the harbour wall and watch the lifeboat plunge and lift nearer and nearer, until we can see the dark, frightened and cold faces of foreign seamen. 'Off the tanker . . . must be in bad trouble . . . Korean crew . . .'

'Poor bastards,' John says. 'I expect they are paid a pittance to crew unseaworthy rusty old tankers.'

We turn away, not wanting to watch the sailors struggle sodden and shivering off the lifeboat. It seems like voyeurism suddenly. An ambulance is blaring down the hill, then another and another. I hope no one has died; I hope they were all saved and are just pathetic and cold and frightened.

'One for the road?' Matt asks.

'Oh, if you insist!' John takes my arm. 'Just a quick one, Si?'

I am suddenly tired. I have walked more than I have since I arrived and I ache and I am very cold. John notices suddenly and while Matt gets the drinks he says, 'Sorry, that was thoughtless. We'll get a taxi up the hill, Si.'

Matt coming back with our drinks, overhears. 'I've got the car outside, I'll give you a lift.'

'Matt has a wonderful little gallery overlooking the sea, Sigrid. You must go, it has some lovely things.'

'Yes, please come. I'll give you coffee.'

I can see he and John are good friends; they chat easily to one another without excluding me.

Matt has a battered VW, which makes a lot of noise, and he drops us at the top of the hill. 'See you soon, I hope, Sigrid.' He grins at me with crooked teeth. Oh, how I like imperfection.

As we walk up the small road to Huer's Cottage, John links arms with me suddenly. 'Siggi, you're humming to yourself again, just like you used to. How lovely to hear it.'

I laugh. So I am. I never know I'm doing it.

In my bedroom, I go to close the curtains while I undress. Lights flicker on the tankers out at sea and on the horizon. I feel the nearest to happiness I have felt for a long time.

Huer's Cottage, like so many in Cornwall, has its front garden across the road. Steps lead down into it from a small wall edged with overgrown buddleia, small wind-bent firs, and Cornish palms, which rattle in the wind. Beth and John prefer the back garden, which is more private and slopes upwards to the cliffs from a dilapidated conservatory.

As I stand at my bedroom window, I catch a small movement behind the palms. I see the glow of a cigarette. Then, somebody moves out of the shelter of the wall and further down the garden, where there is another gate on to the lower path to the beach. The streetlight catches and elongates his shadow for a moment. The blowing branches of the trees distort the image of long coat and broad-brimmed hat.

My happiness vanishes as swiftly as it came. It could be Mr Trevorrow again – it could be anyone. I know that. Teenagers cut through the small gardens, use them as a short cut at night. I know this, because it makes John cross.

Maybe Beth is right, I am becoming obsessed. But for the first time since I came to Huer's Cottage, despite being at the top of the house, I keep the curtains drawn against the night.

Chapter 12

Matt's gallery is tiny, like a small doorway into hobbit land. It is full of small exquisite pieces, and strong diverse paintings cover every wall. It is not a gallery for tourists wanting cheap knick-knacks to take home; the summer hordes do not pour in. Each piece is very expensive: beautiful sculptures, elegant wood carvings, mirrors made out of different bleached woods, tableaux of gulls and rooks in varying mediums. Pottery and glass in inventive shapes and brave colours.

Just being inside the doorway stimulates, ignites my dormant sense of excitement at the possibility of exploring other people's work and creating my own. Each time I come, there is something else to admire.

Matt sits inside, painting. His work too is varied and startling, much more imaginative than I had supposed. I had expected competent coastal scenes which sold, not his intricate abstracts. I realise suddenly there is much more to Matt than his niceness.

He is framed, as he paints, in a vast back window full of stretching blue sea, so that the sea dominates the gallery and his flat above. I have not been here in a rough sea, but Matt says it is very exciting and quite terrifying.

I have started to come often and I am meeting his friends, who pop in and out like I do, discussing their work, how it is selling, drinking coffee. It is good, so good, to feel young and single again and to talk about things that really interest me, to have the courage to say something suddenly, without testing it on my lips first.

Since the storm my depression has slowly lifted, the huge black cloud has drifted to the horizon, and it is Matt who helps keep it at bay. I have started to paint again – small watercolours of Talland House as Beth and I imagined it once to be, set amid those gardens of camellias and azaleas.

I put a pale face at the window, a hint of a girl in a white dress in the garden, lifting the gate latch.

Matt loves them. He propped the first small unframed canvases against a bright jug, near gleaming silver hand-made earrings, and they went, sold, just as they were, almost wet – and I smiled and hugged myself in the dark nights because maybe Jake was wrong about my work – it wasn't a fluke, they sold. Wrong when he said I could not paint my way out of a paper bag.

Today the morning is like summer although it is not yet April. We are sitting up in Matt's flat with the window thrown open, drinking white wine and listening to the thud of waves breaking on the rocks below us, listening to the sound of seagulls screaming and weaving over the harbour and the noises of traffic and voices of St Ives filtering in to us.

The wind blows my hair from my face and Matt fingers the disappearing bruise on my forehead gently without saying anything. I don't know what or how much John has said to him and I don't want to talk about Jake because the black cloud comes nearer.

'I know Jake Watson's work. I don't like everything he does, but he is certainly incredibly talented. A friend of mine went to his last exhibition in Plymouth and thought he had lost his way, though,' Matt says now, watching me as if he knows I am thinking of Jake.

'I don't know,' I say. 'He was certainly temperamental before his last exhibition.'

There is a silence I don't fill, and Matt pours me more wine and smiles. 'OK, let's change the subject. This is the time of the year I love best, you know, before St Ives gets flooded with people and we can't move. The season used to start later, but since the Tate Gallery opened people come almost all year round.'

'It must have helped you and all the little galleries, though?'

'Definitely.'

'Matt . . .' I say slowly. 'It isn't that I want to be secretive about Jake or why I am here with Beth and John, it's simply I hate talking about it.'

Matt leans forward and kisses my forehead. 'You don't have to explain to me. We are friends, remember? It's just, I've burdened you with my love life, so I was feeling guilty.'

'Well, don't,' I laugh. He is getting over Lindsey, an American student of stunning beauty, who came last summer to work in the gallery but found St Ives too insular and claustrophobic and went back to London. Matt tries to hide the fact that he was quite cut up about it.

He spends his life running his gallery, organising exhibitions, but his obsession is surfing. He takes off at every opportunity with his friend Rob, and often a whole group of them travel round the coast in search of surf.

At this moment in my life Matt is the ideal friend, for there are no complications. He is a lovely, unambiguous person.

We finish our wine, gather up Mutton and Matt's mongrel, Alice, and walk through St Ives, up to the coastal path. Matt wants some cigarette papers and while he goes inside the newsagent's, I stand and wait for him outside, holding the two dogs.

I'm daydreaming, miles away, thinking of how wonderful it is to be doing normal, trivial things again, without accounting for every move I make.

But when I look up my heart leaps with shock. Jake is standing over by the harbour wall away in the distance, wearing the grey flecked fisherman's sweater he paints in.

Matt comes out of the shop and I throw the leads at him and run down the road, past the lighthouse station, down towards the harbour. I am furious, blood-red with rage. I won't let him play games with me. I won't let him play cat and mouse, taunting me with just keeping his distance.

I run awkwardly, still unfit, panting after the figure, who is now slowly, contemptuously walking away.

I catch up with him and grab his arm. I am shouting, incoherent with rage. My voice is loud and dizzying, like running blood in my ears.

He turns. It is not Jake. It is someone quite unlike him. He looks at me, shocked, and I let go of him quickly, apologize, as shaken as this strange man by my reaction.

Matt has run after me and I stand breathless, fighting tears. Matt takes my arm, embarrassed, and repeats to the man, 'Sorry . . . sorry . . . she thought you were someone else . . . So sorry.'

Matt leads me to the harbour wall and hugs me. 'Hey, come on, it's all right . . .'

I hold on to him, shaking. 'Matt, I think I'm going mad. I'm beginning to think Jake was right, I really am losing it . . . I keep seeing him everywhere . . . In a white mac he used to wear, in that fisherman's sweater . . .'

Matt smiles. 'Oh, Mr Trevorrow and his long charity shop mackintosh. Sigrid, everyone wears fisherman's sweaters. Look, I don't need to be a detective to realize that that bastard knocked you about. Of course you're still frightened. Of course you're still seeing him everywhere – that's what fear does. Come on, let's walk. I'm a brilliant listener you know. I'm known round here as Mattie Rayner!'

I laugh. Oh, Matt. Thank God for Matt.

We turn and take the coastal path, walking hand in hand, and I tell him a little about Jake and Dan and the cottage on Dartmoor where I was not allowed to make friends with anyone, where anyone I did make friends with Jake did not like.

I tell him how, day by day, my confidence in myself and in my work dwindled and my ability to think for myself diminished. I tell him about Jake's anger, which I could provoke in a second without meaning to, and the fear that began to grow day by day.

Matt stops walking for a minute and turns me to him, again fingering the fading sallow bruise on my face. 'I just can't imagine hitting a woman. I can't get my head round it.'

I reach up and place my cold cheek against him. The wind has suddenly got up and is as cold as a damp breath. I smile. 'Of course you can't.'

Behind him the wind has whipped the waves into flying spray below us. The cliff circles us, making the proportion of land and sky feel unbalanced, as if I might tip over the cliff. As if I am an insect crawling along the edge of a table and might at any moment drop like a stone on to the far distant sands.

Matt is wistful. 'Surf is up . . .' he says.

Laughing, we turn back and collect his wet suit and surfboard from his flat, and then I sit, wrapped up, on Porthmeor beach with Alice and Mutton each side of me and watch Matt surf until the sun begins to set, a huge, incandescent orange, sliding over the horizon behind him, leaving apricot and black streaks. Magnificent, reflected in the huge circular window of the Tate Gallery behind me.

The black blobs of surfers rise, like smooth, silky-headed seals from the swollen surface of the waves, up, up up, then down with a crash and thunder of spray, shooting in, in, to the shore as fast as an express train.

The sun goes quickly and we trail home to Matt's flat, shivering, his bare feet making little wet marks on the staircase. He pours more wine and I sit in the window as contented as I can be, and Matt comes out with a towel around him and kisses and kisses me over and over to the sound of the waves.

I take his face between my hands in the dark. 'Matt . . . Matt . . . I don't know if this is such a good idea . . .'

'OK,' he says cheerfully, and stops kissing my mouth and goes on to my neck while his fingers undo my plait. He smells of soap and aftershave, and the sea is still in his hair. He stops, is very still, and the lights beyond his head blink over the black sea and the world seems such a lonely place now he has stopped. I put my mouth to the pulse on his neck just to see how it feels and I feel him sigh . . . And then he takes me to his bed and makes sweet love to me and I feel safe and protected, quite forgetting I was going to keep this relationship platonic. We lie in the dusk finishing our wine, becoming childish and giggly.

I love his lack of intensity and power and technical know-how. I love the lack of obsessive passion and its isolated aftermath. This, this feels normal and comfortable and very, very good.

'Matt?' I whisper.

'Ssh.' He puts a finger on my mouth. 'I know what you are going to say. I risk getting hurt . . . it's too soon . . .' He knots his fingers through my hair. 'We're friends, mermaid.' He tucks me into his shoulder. 'Very good friends . . .'

I feel him smile and then we fall asleep and when we wake it is dark outside his window and we watch the small lights of fishing boats out on the black sea. We do not speak. I feel safe and golden and loved.

We get dressed and walk slowly back up the hill to Huer's Cottage and we sit around the kitchen table and have a last drink with Beth and John, talking about the plans Beth and other Virginia Woolf Society members have for a festival in Bloomsbury.

'By the way,' Beth says to me, 'your solicitor rang. Jake flew to Cyprus today. He had to leave his address there with the police and his own solicitor. Your police lady checked on his flight number for you.'

The surface of my skin is warm to me, a sort of glow, a sudden rush of joy to be here with these people, to be happy. I cannot speak, only sit, silenced by gratitude.

I wonder if Beth let the police know I was jumpy.

Eventually I say to Beth and John, 'You can both go off together now, can't you, and organize your Woolfy festival, and leave me to look after Mutton and Talland House for you.' I know they have been reluctant to leave me here alone, because of Jake.

'We'll see, Siggi. It's a kind thought, but it might be a bit much for you.'

'John,' I beg, 'I want to do this for you, so much. I want you to both go off together for once. I can so easily look after Talland House, the flats are empty and you said yourself what a quiet time it is, before the season starts. I will enjoy looking after Mutton and the twins. Please . . . let me.'

'We'll see, sweetie, we'll see,' John repeats, grinning at me.

Matt says to him, 'I'll be here, remember. Sigrid won't be on her own . . .' He stops as Beth and John exchange glances.

'We're just good friends!' Matt and I say together, indignantly.

'They're just good friends!' Beth and John say together, mimicking us.

'The matter is settled,' I say, crossly. 'You can both take yourselves off.'

Beth blows me a kiss. 'OK, Si, that would be wonderful . . . if you're really sure. But we'll take the twins with us. Introduce them to a bit of culture while we have the chance to be in London. With two of us we can probably manage them, just! It's very sweet of you.'

We sit for a while longer, the candles Beth loves reflecting the four of us in the panes of the conservatory, which links the kitchen to the small garden behind. The conservatory is full of resting geraniums and pots of non-hardy shrubs and dried falling leaves and Mutton's bones and children's bikes.

As I sit there, full of wine, with laughter and gentle banter filling the warm room, the shadows flicker and move and sigh to the rhythm of my happiness, and it feels suddenly as if I have come home after some long strange journey.

Chapter 13

Huer's Cottage feels so empty without the twins and Beth and John that I spend more and more time at Talland House, sketching and painting. The days are beginning to get warmer. Spring comes early in Cornwall and I want to capture the camellias and blazing azaleas that lie bordering the gardens.

It is a magic place to paint. I move around, inside and out, throwing open French windows, going out on to the wrought-iron balconies to feed the squirrels and watch the birds against a great backdrop of purple sea.

I have only had two lots of Woolfies to take round. One was a lecturer from Cardiff. She was fascinating and I spent two hours with her and wrote down everything I learnt from her to tell Beth when she comes back. The others were sixth formers from a local school. They were giggly and uninterested, and their teacher looked as if she itched to slap them.

Matt joins me often in the evenings before the sun sets, when he isn't in the gallery. Tonight, we're staying here late because there's a full moon we want to see from the balcony of Virginia's room and from the top flat, which has a wonderful bird's-eye view of the bay. We're both completing a series of paintings from the house, which we thought would be interesting as our work is so diverse.

The other reason we plan to spend the night at Talland House is that we suspect from the state of the lawn that there are badgers here. Badgers and a full moon are something we cannot miss.

I come and paint in the peace and stillness of Talland House in the window of the drawing room or upstairs in the empty flats with Mutton at my feet, and my contentment grows and flourishes as I get more and more involved in my work and more excited as I see the way I'm painting is changing subtly, almost without my being aware of it.

There is an influence here that I can't explain. It's not just the huge curve of the sea filling the windows, glittering in the distance where it meets acres of pale sand; it is the house itself, standing square, solid and different in its own little world above the town, the sounds below muted, the moving figures small and insignificant.

I feel so often I've been guided to various spots in the house or garden with a strange or arresting view, places I might not easily have chosen for myself. Everywhere I move in the house or garden, I catch a flash of blue sea or feel submerged in the deep waxy green foliage.

Standing here in late afternoon, waiting for Matt, I see as dusk comes, that the texture and atmosphere of the approaching night changes in the house. I turn and catch a flutter of a dress moving slowly out of the room, a rustle of silk moving to stairs no longer there.

Out in the hall, near the curved front door, there is a faint sound of laughter and the shadow of a small boy jumps down the last two stairs.

As a child I used to lie and imagine time like electricity, humming along wires, strands all parallel – past, present, future. What might be. What might have happened if you had had those parents. Met that person. What could happen if you made that decision. All shimmering along independently, side by side.

Matt brings fish and chips and a bottle of wine, and we sit outside on the steps in the dark watching this incredible moon rise huge and incandescent over sea the colour of cast iron, so still it looks like oil. We feed Mutton and Alice chips, which will ruin their already indeterminate waistlines and we sit huddled together, talking, cold and happy as the lights on the horizon rise in little arcs of settlements over the water. Then we move to our different places in the house to sketch.

I work for a couple of hours in Virginia's room, then cold despite the electric fire fed with fifty-pence pieces, I lie on the bed and pull blankets and the eiderdown over me and fall into a deep sleep with the moon streaming in the room, ivory-white making shafts of pale light across the floor.

When I wake Matt is sitting up in the bed beside me, very still, watching the sea. I stare at his face before he knows I am awake. It is a lovely uncomplicated face and I suddenly see that he is like Dan.

In profile, his face is sad and I wonder what he is thinking about. Then, in the dark silence of the night, broken only by the shush and slap of waves below us, I hear the whispering, the gentle whispering coming from the walls, circling the room, rising and falling as if the sounds are coming from a distant room.

I sit up slowly, my skin prickling and Matt turns and puts his arm around me, hoists me to him without speaking and we sit and listen as the whispers rise and fall, hover like the breath of moths above us in the air, then fade away and are gone.

Silence fills the room, heavier than whispers, and a melancholy, a deep ache of loneliness, like listening to Mahler at dusk in an empty garden, catches the back of my throat; an ageless angst that is part of the fabric of the room, hung in time like dusty curtains waiting to be shaken, triggered by premonition or unacknowledged sorrow. A room filled with unfulfilled and suddenly interrupted lives.

We move down into the warmth of the bed, Matt and I, and we hold each other tight and we weep and do not know why we weep. Perhaps for the knowledge held cold in the heart of all of us that each one of us is alone in this world and will die alone, even though the two of us hold each other tight against this sudden consciousness of death and darkness.

It will happen. One day we too will be old and lonely and our laughter and youth will fade and be dulled and forgotten.

Matt's body is Dan's body. His taut, young and healthy body wrapped around mine is part of me in this room, on this night, where the moon shines through a sudden frail shiver of cloud like creamy muslin; hangs in a navy sky full of high tiny white stars scattered across the universe like icing sugar.

Across the bay the lighthouse flickers amid the black rocks and nothing really changes, except man. This house will still stand square to the wind. The sound of the sea, muffled as horses' hoofs on a windy night, will still turn in flaring, phosphorescent waves long after we are dead, Matt and I.

Other people will lie here and our ghosts will murmur like faint music from the secret places of the house and someone quite else will lie and watch this sea and weep for they know not what.

'You are right,' Matt murmurs in my ear. 'This house is full of ghosts.'

We lie quite still, disturbed by the sudden sadness in the house. 'If you think,' I whisper, 'of all the people passing through this house, all the galaxy of emotions, it's not surprising we hear them all talking sometimes, is it?'

I feel Matt smile in the dark. 'You would have thought Woolf would have frightened them all off with her witty and sometimes scathing tongue, wouldn't you?'

'She was only a child here, a clever wistful child.'

Matt yawns. 'This is what this room reflects, I guess. Children always fear the ending of childhood, don't they?'

I didn't.

'Come on, my fey little friend, we should go and let the dogs out of the car.' Mutton has been keeping Alice company in Matt's car because she is unreliable in the house.

We gather our things and move out into the cold night and let the dogs out into the garden.

'The badgers didn't come,' I say, disappointed. 'I listened for them all the time I was painting.'

'They might have come when we slept, of course,' Matt says.

We get into his car and drive down the hill to Huer's Cottage. 'Are you surfing in the morning?' I ask.

'I plan to. Why, Si?'

I am looking at Huer's Cottage, which is in darkness because I forgot to leave lights on. Suddenly, unaccountably, I don't want to be left alone.

Matt ruffles my hair and says gently, 'I can stay if you want me to.'

'Please . . .' I turn to him and he smiles and raises his eyebrows at me.

'It's not a hardship, exactly . . .' He makes a provocative face and I laugh.

We settle the dogs in the kitchen and climb up to my attic room. We are both tired and Matt falls asleep instantly with his arms wrapped round me, but I can't sleep. I lie thinking about the lives lived, jostling and moving like displaced people in Talland House. Lives of success, happiness, sadness and tragedy. And hope. The fragility of hope in futures unknown.

I think about that other house in another place where I could never sleep. I move Matt's arm gently from around me and get out of bed, trying to be quiet in the dark. I pull on my dressing gown and shut the door behind me so I don't wake him, and sit on the stairs in the dark. It is as if those strange, disturbing murmuring voices have followed me home. Or is it me? Am I the cause of disturbing something deep in the fabric of a house which lay sleeping? Is the disturbance me?

I used to do this as a child, sit on the stairs. In the dark and narrow terraced house in Edinburgh. I used to watch the sliver of light under the door of the sitting room where my mother sat long into the night. I used to think, she will come out in a moment and she will see me and she will ask me if I am all right. She will hug me and make me a warm drink and take me back to bed. But she never did. Never.

Sometimes I used to go into the kitchen and make myself hot chocolate and a hot-water bottle from the tap if I couldn't stop shivering. Then I would go back to the same stair and wait some more. It was as if she knew I was there, but resolutely refused to come out. When I finally crept back to bed I would hear her go to her room.

It was not as if she had ever come to me so I should not have expected it. It was just that once, when I was staying the night with a friend and I was having nightmares, I got out of bed and sat on their stairs and my friend's mother came down and found me and took me back to bed, and then made me a hot drink and a piece of toast, and sat with me while I ate it, talking all the time about ordinary things. Then she hugged me hard and wished me sweet dreams.

I slept right through until morning, and I woke safe and warm and happy. I never forgot that feeling and something perverse in me willed my mother to acknowledge me in the same way.

The moon in the landing window is so huge, so near, I feel I could reach out and touch the dark places with my fingers. I go downstairs to the kitchen and the dogs push cold wet noses at me and I sit and stroke their smooth heads, one so wide and flat, one so tiny and angular.

Mutton suddenly stiffens and turns towards the door of the conservatory, his hackles rising, and starts to growl low in his throat like a warning, and Alice takes up the refrain.

My heart jumps. I look up into the conservatory and think I catch a fleeting movement, a shadow, then it is gone. I scream and the dogs throw themselves hysterically at the door and I scream again. Matt comes flying down the stairs. 'What the hell . . .?'

'There is someone in the conservatory, Matt. The dogs are going mad. I saw something . . . Oh God . . .'

'Stay there,' he says. He pulls on the sweater he obviously grabbed, over his boxer shorts, and shouts at the dogs to calm down. 'If there was anyone out there, they will be long gone by now.'

He opens the door leading to the conservatory and the dogs fly out and jostle and fuss amongst the fallen geranium leaves and dusty plant pots. The far door to the garden is shut, but cannot close properly because the door is so old the wood has warped. Matt pulls it open and peers out into the moonlit garden. The dogs go out too but they are no longer barking or agitated.

'John should really fix this door so it locks,' Matt says.

'The garden gate from the road is always kept locked. It is so high, and with houses each side no one should be able to get in,' I tell him.

Matt comes back for a torch, pulls on some of John's old shoes lying in the conservatory and goes out into the garden. When he comes back, he says, 'The gate is firmly locked, Si. There is no sign of anyone breaking in. I honestly can't see how anyone could possibly be in the garden unless they abseiled in from the cliff above!'

He leads me back into the house, makes the dogs go back to bed and turns the light off. When my eyes are accustomed to the dark, he says, 'What can you see out there?'

I feel chastened. Beth's geranium, hanging from the ceiling, swings in a draught, making flimsy shadows in the lightening day.

'What about the dogs, Matt? Why would the dogs go berserk if there was nothing there?'

'Look.' He points to the gap in the door and the hole in the rotting of one window frame. 'Small scurrying things, my spooked one. Shadows. Mutton isn't exactly Mensa material, is he?'

'Steady!' I object. 'He knows the difference between mice and burglars. Anyway, your Alice made as much noise.'

'Oh, she's just a biddable little hussy trying to impress a handsome Labrador hunk.'

Matt succeeds in making me laugh. I turn and put the kettle on. He comes up behind me and, crossing his arms round my shoulders, lays his head on mine.

'OK now?'

I nod. 'Sorry.'

'Sorry enough to come and warm my cold feet?'

I laugh again. 'Yes, go on, I'll bring the coffee upstairs.'

At the door Matt turns. 'Si, you thought it was Jake, didn't you?'

'Yes . . .'

I can never forget the hospital. Jake has a way of getting through doors. He has a way of suddenly appearing. Jake loves games.

'Why,' he asks gently, 'for your own peace of mind, don't you ring his parents in Cyprus? However awkward the call, at least you'll know if he's there or not.'

Matt goes upstairs and I make the coffee and take it up. The bed is warm. Matt is warm. When he gets up to go surfing, I listen to him whistle cheerfully for Alice, shut the front door. I hear the Volkswagen start up and Mutton's heavy paws coming up the stairs to me. I relax into sleep with the first flush of a new day.

All sounds, real and imaginary, mingle in the high screaming of the gulls hovering in a clear blue sky.

Chapter 14

While I am up at Talland House waiting for two German journalists who are writing a book about places Virginia Woolf once lived in, Beth rings.

'Everything all right?' she asks anxiously.

'Fine,' I assure her. 'Everything's fine. There haven't been many people round and I've made sure that the Woolfies who've come on spec have your telephone number. Most people have asked for details of the flats, which I gave them, of course, and two retired school teachers wanted the address of the Virginia Woolf Society. A Dutch couple you spoke to on the phone were disappointed you weren't here, but I explained I am just filling in for you for a couple of weeks . . .'

'Dearest Si, I'm not ringing to check up on you. I wouldn't have left you if I hadn't thought you would do a good job. I just wanted to know you were all right, not lonely. Matt still around?'

I laugh. 'Yes he is, and I'm not lonely, but I do miss you all. How's it going?'

'Surprisingly well. There is definitely a resurgence of interest in the Bloomsbury lot. I've given two lectures in small literary clubs to women's groups, and our bookings are definitely up on last year. If we persevere, I really think we can get on the map. Make a profit one day . . . refurbish the whole house, just as I see it in my head . . .' She laughs. 'John is worried I am getting too involved. That I won't be able to take a back seat when the owner of Talland House returns and I don't have such a free hand. It's just I'm having so much fun, Si. It's a job of a lifetime before I settle into wet nappies again!'

I smile. I love Beth's pragmatism. 'He's terribly proud of you. Has he made any remark about *working* women asking intelligent questions afterwards?'

Beth laughs. John can never get his head round Virginia Woolf's appalling snobbery.

'Beth, Mrs Morton is cleaning the top flat tomorrow. She says you asked her to do a spring clean on the whole house and her daughter is going to come and help her. But there's no need for her to come to Huer's Cottage. I can clean there, for heaven's sake.'

'Si, let Lettice come, she loves to be needed. Her one terror is getting too old to "do". I'm sorry, I know she will want to mother you, but Lettice is a dear old soul and the fact that her eyesight is so bad she can't see the dust is neither here nor there!'

I smile. I had noticed.

'What else?' I ask. 'There is something else, isn't there?' I know Beth, I know when she is gathering courage to say something she considers important.

Beth is silent, something that doesn't happen often. Then she says slowly, 'Si, I've been awake all night wondering whether to tell you or not. It may mean nothing at all, but John says I must say something. Do you know Jake has an exhibition here in Cork Street with a Chinese artist? It opened two days ago and is on until the end of April.'

My stomach lurches sickly. 'No, I didn't know. But he does exhibit there.'

'Does he always attend his openings?'

'Usually.'

'I should think it highly unlikely that he would fly back so far, just for an opening . . . but maybe you should check, Si?'

'Beth, two weeks ago you told me I was becoming obsessed with Jake. You said he was highly unlikely to jeopardise the court case by contacting me. He's high profile and if he has an exhibition, he's not going to risk his reputation by adverse publicity. He's much too proud, and we're talking big money.'

'Yes, I did think that too . . . I just felt if there is any chance of him bothering you, John and I ought to be home.'

'No, Beth! You are *not* coming home early. Matt is still with me nearly all the time. Honestly, I'd tell you if I was worried,' I lie. 'You have another five days to enjoy. It's your one chance to visit all your family and friends. I really would be upset if you came home, Beth.'

'It's just . . .'

'What?'

'We went to the exhibition yesterday to have a look, steeling ourselves in case Jake was around. There are so many paintings of you, Si. Brilliant. Clever. Sad and . . . obsessed. That's what worried me. They had such a strange and haunting effect on us both.'

Now I am in pain. I double up. Caught. Something pierces my heart with remembrance of love. I see through the window of his studio a man bent, his fair hair flopping over his face, ageless. His concentration is so great he is aware of nothing, neither me nor the day nor the cold. Hours and hours bent and standing back. Bent and standing back. Like a private dance. Then one day he will call, 'Darling, come and look . . . come and look . . . I'm pleased, I'm quite pleased . . . I've got you . . . I think.'

He will stand behind me with his arms around my neck as I look. As I stand still and look at a likeness of myself that is so true, I reel. For he has captured my silence and my secrets, my youth that is marred by what I hold in my eyes. How can one man capture more than I know myself?'

'Si . . . Si. I've upset you. I shouldn't have told you.'

I take a deep breath. Sound normal. 'Beth, you did the right thing. Will you relax if I find out whether Jake is still in Cyprus or flew back to London for this exhibition?'

'Yes. Will you ring us tonight?'

'I promise.'

I put the phone down. I go to the mirror in the hall and I look hard at my neck, which still has a slight discoloured yellow patch. I look at the still red scar over my eye. I feel my arm where it still aches. I lift my plait, heavy in my hand and remember how he wound it round his hand before he pulled. Then I look into my own eyes which might swallow me up with the enormity of my conflicting emotions.

I must never forget how he hurt me. I must never forget his cold and clever cruelty. I must never forget his mood swings and the terrible feeling of loving a stranger.

As I meet my own eyes in the mirror, a dark shadow passes behind me in this hall and I shiver. I suddenly remember Virginia Woolf as a small child being lifted from a mirror in this hall by her half-brother, George, and touched. Something which affected her for ever.

I turn quickly away, lock up Talland House and walk down the hill back to Huer's Cottage. I think about last night in the conservatory and about how haunted by ghosts living and dead I am becoming.

Mutton greets me as if I have been away for a year. I go upstairs and find my address book and Jake's parents' number. I quail at having to do this. I have met them only once, at our wedding, and I found his father much easier than his mother. Jake rarely mentions his childhood, which seems to have been mainly spent in boarding school. I try to work out what time it will be in Cyprus, but if I wait I will lose courage so I go downstairs to ring. The telephone rings and rings but no one picks it up. No one answers.

I try again in the evening, but there is no one in that house in Paphos. Beth rings me because they are going out. I lie to her. I tell her everything is fine and Jake is still in Cyprus with his parents.

I lie, because even if Jake is back in England, I feel safe, because of that London exhibition. Jake is ambitious and he needs his agent and he needs to exhibit. He sells a large amount of work abroad; he won't risk a sniff of a scandal at the moment. He needs to support his lifestyle. Jake has never been poor. Jake very much likes the good things of life.

Out of his sight I can no longer incense and enrage. Something in me provoked his cruelty, his moods and his passion. And I am out of sight now.

Lettice brought me a bunch of anemones and left them on the windowsill and she put a small pie in the fridge. She thinks I need feeding up. She is old and she works so hard for so little, yet she seems always happy. I asked her if I might paint her and she was thrilled.

Such a small thing to warm me. Yet it's not a small thing, this hugeness of the human spirit. Lettice in her shabby coat and uneven skirt lengths, sitting in the kitchen at Huer's Cottage, banishing shadows and ghosts and useless guilt and angst quicker than a flick of her duster.

As I climb into bed, I suddenly think, Lettice was one of those working women Virginia Woolf would have been so patronizing about. Yet Lettice won't have had a moment's mental instability or self-questioning. Neither could she have written sentences which stay in the heart and mind likes notes of music.

'I've done a full circle of contemplation on the meaning of life,' I tell Mutton, who has decided he will sleep up here with me tonight. He sighs, grunts, does two circles before he collapses, dreaming of breakfast and the long walk to Zennor tomorrow I have told him about.

Chapter 15

I wake to frail grey light filtering into my room and Mutton's nose in my face, gently nudging me. He wants to go out and whines when I open my eyes. I get up sleepily and go quickly downstairs, open the front door and let him out. Beth likes him to go across the road, not in the back garden where the children play.

I put the kettle on the Rayburn, go back upstairs, pull on my dressing gown and return to the front door to make sure Mutton doesn't disappear. It is cold and damp, and a watery sun is hanging over a grey sea. One small fishing boat chugs out of the harbour looking very small.

I can hear Mutton snuffling about in the garden below me, sounding like a baby elephant in the undergrowth. Through the mist the sea fills my ears with its shush and thump.

I cannot see down the overgrown garden, which is hidden by the sprawling buddleia and small trees that cast shadows across the road. I look at this view every morning from my bedroom window. Is there a difference in the shadows, the collection of skeleton branches sprouting transparent new leaves to the right?

Mutton starts to bark. He is running down the garden, clumping through the undergrowth towards the gate at the bottom, barking and barking at something. Suddenly he gives a high-pitched yelp, and as I peer into the half-darkness a shadow seems to dislodge itself from the bushes and slender branches to the right of the wall and move swiftly away down towards the gate.

I shiver, turn back into the house quickly, fetch a coat and pull on some old wellingtons and run down the front steps. I don't need to call for Mutton – he is at the door waiting for me, tail between his legs. I shut the door behind me and bend to comfort him. 'Poor old Mutton, what happened to you, then?'

There is no one around. It is still early, no one is up, and the houses are still in darkness or empty holiday homes. But it is light enough for me to see. I am afraid, but a slow anger is overtaking that fear. I walk down the garden, Mutton behind me, through the damp grass to the gate at the bottom. I can see no footprints and any disturbance in the undergrowth could have been made by anything.

The gate at the bottom is ajar, the padlock broken. Near the gate there is a torn dirty quilt lying in the dew. I shut the gate, and turn and walk with Mutton back up to the house, glad my anger brought me out here. It is not Jake, but it looks like someone is sleeping rough in the garden, which I will have to stop somehow.

I go back inside and make some coffee to take upstairs. My hands are shaking. With relief. The trouble with fear is its face is everywhere and I see a threat in every shadow.

I pull on two sweaters because I am meeting Matt early for the walk to Zennor. I make a flask of coffee, collect my pad and pencils and move quickly out into the early morning, hurrying down to Matt's house and the sweet comfort of him. Hardly a day goes by when we don't see each other now.

Down round the harbour we walk in the deserted early morning, Matt and I, with Alice and Mutton dotting between us through the mist. Just us, it seems, ranging the empty streets. The smell of the sea, strong and pungent, brought in by the rain, which is mostly sea mist, touches our faces with damp fingers.

Matt says the mist will lift and above the grey blanket a warm day lies crouched and waiting. We both carry small rucksacks; we are going to sketch if the weather clears.

I tell Matt about Mutton finding someone in the garden and the quilt and broken padlock. He says we will get a new padlock and lock both gates until John gets back. He says Rob's father will see to it for me. I have already decided to let Mutton out into the back garden in the mornings.

'Were you worried it was Jake again?' Matt asks.

'For a moment. But Jake would have had a Harrods camp bed and hamper down there!' We both giggle at the thought.

We walk silently through the mostly sleeping town, round past the harbour wall where the seagulls collect, past the ice-cream and fish-and-chip shops where they wheel and scream and demand food with menaces.

Outside the small chain stores delivery vans are being unloaded. I love the sight of a small town waking up. Usually all the shops are open by the time I get down here.

We walk up round the Island and the dogs begin to get excited, sniffing a long walk. We skirt Porthmeor beach and take the coastal path to Zennor. Matt points vaguely up to a cottage nestled high into the cliff. 'My Aunt Jo used to live up there. It was holidays here with her that made me fall in love with St Ives.'

Virginia Woolf used to take this walk to Zennor and I smile to myself with pleasure at the continuation of things, the small happinesses that do not change. I have walked here once before with John and Beth, in high summer, to the Tinner's Arms at Zennor – the only way we could get John to come with us. That day it was baking and adders sunbathed on top of the Cornish hedges like exotic necklaces.

Today the walk is wild and bleak, and we bend against the wind in single file, unable to talk against the irritating gusts. Then suddenly, as we round the point, the wind begins to drop, the mist fades away magically like a stage set and we can feel the sun behind the clouds ready to erupt into a beautiful day.

We sit on a large damp rock, look down at the sea swirling over the rocks below and drink coffee. 'I used to come to St Ives and stay with Jo each summer. It was wonderful. I ran wild all day long, I was totally free, no one hassled me. I was completely alone to do as I pleased. Jo used to go off and sketch or paint for hours and that's how I began to paint.'

I watch Matt's face, how it lights up at the mention of his aunt. 'Who hassled you at home?' I ask.

'Oh, my stepfather. I loathed him.'

'Why? Was he unkind to you?'

Matt snorts. 'Sarcastic. He bullied my mother too. I could never understand why she married him. Or stayed with him. Certainly not for me.'

'What happened to your own father?'

'I don't know. My mother always said he died before I was born. She never would talk about him, so I know nothing at all about how I came to be. It's not hard to assume she was never married to him or that he could be as alive as you or me.' He grins at me. 'Why am I telling you all this?'

'Because I asked. Because I'm a nosy cow.'

Matt laughs and tweaks my nose. 'Anyway, my stepfather died when I was fourteen. I sat in my bedroom and silently cheered with relief.' A stone under his foot rolls down the cliff, over the edge into the foaming sea below. 'My mother and I had three great years together before I left for university. I think they were our happiest.

'Then she married again while I was still at university, a lovely guy who dropped dead two years later. I thought she would go to pieces but she didn't, she enrolled with the OU and now spends her time qualifying for things she is too old to ever work in.'

'But she's doing stuff she's interested in, so it doesn't matter, does it?'

'Not a jot.' Matt packs the coffee away. 'But if she hadn't married that bastard she could have done it all before and really achieved things. When I was young I never even realized she had a brain, patronizing little prick that I was.'

We walk on and the sun comes out, and the view is so stunning I gasp with pleasure: deep green fields shivering with dew, against a vivid purple sea stretching out for ever to the horizon. 'If your mother had worked, concentrated on a career during your child-hood, she wouldn't have been there for you, and you wouldn't be you and I happen to think you're pretty jolly damn special . . . What?'

'Idiot!' Matt laughs and links arms. 'The trouble was, she wasn't really there for me. She was too afraid of my stepfather to protect me from his tongue.'

Matt stops and turns me to him suddenly, watching me intently, his hands holding my shoulders. 'Si, what is it? What is it that makes intelligent women love men who hurt them, either physically or verbally? What on earth is it that makes a woman go on and on trying to please a man who despises her for being a doormat, for being afraid? I want to understand why women let men like my stepfather bully them. Why they throw away their lives.'

Does he think I have an answer? Does he think I can solve patly the conundrum of his childhood? I pull away. 'I don't have an answer,' I say, and I walk on ahead and watch the heather spring up under my feet. Amongst it are small carpets of violets, hidden and protected. I walk fast on the small path and my breath comes quick and fast too, and my heart hammers against my chest with the pain of what I don't want to remember.

I don't have an answer. I don't understand either. I don't understand the magnetic pull and surge as strong as the sea and as powerful. I don't understand how or why it is not possible to let go, move on without a backward glance. To move forward confident of reaching anywhere meaningful.

How can I say to someone as straight and gentle as Matt that in the dark of nights, in places where he could not be, his mother would have had another life? She was not just his mother, but a sexually active young woman with a powerful man who could make her believe she was the most beautiful, the most precious being in the world. Who could activate acute feelings heightened by fear, to a place beyond reason, beyond an intellectual appraisal.

A man who told her often, in the fear of his own darkness, that he could not live without her. That she must not ever think of leaving or ceasing to love him, for only he could love the flawed creature that she was. Only he would have taken her on board, with a child not his – women shackled to control and obsession, gratitude and amazing sex. Calling it love, never daring to call it anything but love.

And this is only a part of it – one tiny portion of a vast complicated nasty jigsaw where pieces are for ever missing because women do not understand themselves.

The sun is warm. I am growing hot with walking so fast away from Matt. I pull off one of my sweaters and hear him calling gently, puzzled. I have upset him and it is not fair. I turn and wait for him to reach me.

Despite the beauty of the day, and the dogs and Matt, the grey cloud enfolds me, holds me tight in its suffocating grip. It is much more real than the man walking quickly towards me.

We stand facing each other on the path. I see that he dare not come too near. Something in my face forbids it. He is afraid suddenly to touch me. Afraid of how I might react to any more unthinking words of his. He is as lost and afraid as he was in childhood.

'Sigrid, I'm sorry . . . I'm sorry, I'm so stupid. Please forgive me . . .'

I look at him. I want it to be all right. I do not want to spoil the day. It is not his fault. He needed an answer, and he thought I might have it – that I could stand away and make an objective appraisal of women like his mother. Like me. It is not his fault, it is mine.

'Sigrid, don't look like that. I'm a shit for upsetting you. Come here.' He snatches me to him, holds me, rocks me backwards and forwards and the dark place slowly begins to recede.

I can smell the heather, and the sun on the back of my neck is warm. The sea in front of me is turning pure aquamarine. I want to sketch.

I joke, 'This is what happens when I get up too early. Come on, let's find a sheltered place to sit.'

Matt looks relieved and we walk on towards Gurnards Head, find a little spot protected by the cliff, and sit with our coffee, idly sketching.

'My mother was Norwegian,' I tell him. 'I get my occasional gloomy moods from her.' I am drawing him sketching the small beach below us.

Matt looks up. '*Was* Norwegian? Is she dead, Si?'

'She died eight years ago.'

'What about your father?'

'He's alive. He remarried. He lives in France.'

'What about your childhood? Was it happy?'

I pick my words carefully, examining them slowly like bruised fruit. 'It should have been. I was an only child and my parents loved me. My father longed for a boy and I always knew this. I tried hard to be the boy he wanted but of course I couldn't be. He was a Scot, an islander, and he loved hunting, shooting, fishing, those sorts of things. Such a shame his one child was a girl.'

'If he'd had a son, he would probably have wanted to be a ballet dancer!' Matt says.

I laugh. 'He was an engineer, my father. Mostly rather dour. Always careful to keep his feelings well hidden. I didn't realize it when I was a child, but my parents were hopelessly ill-matched. They were always perfectly polite to each other, in front of me, anyway. I can't remember any rows, but I can remember awful atmospheres without understanding what it meant. Probably worse than rows, actually.'

I have become so good at this, I almost believe it myself. I watch Matt and my pencil moves swiftly across the rough white paper, my hand a small shadow like a bird.

'Neither of my parents could ever discuss their feelings, either with me or each other. Silence was the order of the day. Emotional responses to anything were just frozen out. Maybe if they had been Italian they would have screamed and shouted at each other and all their resentment or disappointment would have been in the open. But my mother, especially, was a very cool and distant person. There seemed no passion, no real emotional involvement in their marriage. I hardly ever saw them touch. Like you, as I grew older I wondered what on earth had made them pick each other. The one mutual love they had was skiing.'

Matt turns slightly towards me, as if he senses half-truths.

'Don't move,' I say quickly. 'I haven't finished.'

There is a silence filled with insects in the grass and a cow calling for its calf somewhere. I have not thought of my father for years and years. He is shut firmly away. He is not the man I have just described. That is a man I have made up. A man who is not too good and not too bad.

There is a man who lives in France with a new wife and family, a man who was once my father, a man who started again. I hope he had sons. I really hope he had sons. But maybe he is different now. Matt is asking me something.

'How did your mother die, Si?'

I finish Matt's face and blur the outline with my finger. I do love the contours of his face. They hold so much. More than I shall probably ever know.

'She committed suicide when I was sixteen years old.'

Matt stares at me. 'God Almighty, what a terrible thing to do.'

I move on to his hands, which are difficult to get right as he keeps moving them.

'Yes. I thought it was a shitty thing to do at first. Selfish. Leaving so many people with that terrible, inevitable guilt. Her family. My father. Me. I still needed her and I wanted to understand why she had done it. Why she had wanted to leave me, even if she had wanted to leave my father.'

I smudge his thumb because my hands are shaking. 'Then, slowly as I grew up a bit, I realized suicide isn't a personal condemnation of those left behind. It is a horrible, terrible, overpowering, irrational depression and need to escape. To be free of the power of thought and the realization of failure, or whatever it is that torments.'

Matt puts his sketchbook down and comes over. He takes my head in his hand and kisses my face. 'What a mature and lovely little person you are. I hope I am not going to fall in love with you.'

I cover his hands with my own and grin up at him. 'You can't fall in love with me, you nincompoop, you're still in love with Lindsey.'

'Oh, that's all right then. It's a bit cold, shall we walk these bored dogs home?'

I want to believe one day that Matt will see through my cant. I want to believe that one day I can say to another human being: I know exactly *why* my mother committed suicide. But I will never understand *how* she could leave me alone with my father.

It seems a long walk back into St Ives, even with the wind behind us, and I am tired by the time we reach Matt's gallery. Someone has opened up for him and there seem a lot of people inside the shop.

Matt makes a face. 'I better get in there. Can I take you out to supper tonight?' He takes my hand and kisses it, his eyes laughing. 'I thought we would try the new Italian.'

'Great.'

I drop Mutton back at Huer's Cottage and walk up to Talland House, which is full of sunshine.

There is a message from Beth on the answerphone, telling me the telephone number of her sister in Hitchin where they have gone for

96

a couple of days. She warns me that the editor of some interior design magazine might ring with a view to photographing the interior of Talland House, and adds a cryptic comment about my rarely being at home.

I lie on the sofa in the sun and fall fast asleep for an hour. Then I look at my sketch of Matt. It's not bad. I paint all afternoon, listening to music. The drawing room is flooded with sunlight and the sea glints away in the distance. There are so many different photos and small pictures of Virginia Woolf on the walls. The Beresford one is my favourite. They watch me paint from all angles of the room, and as I dab paint on to the canvas I talk to her in my head, as I always do, and the room fills up with warmth, and filtered sunlight from the panes slants across the polished floorboards.

When it is time to go and feed Mutton I walk down towards Huer's Cottage as the most incredible sunset fills the sky. The colours are so extraordinary that people stand in little clumps staring at the sky.

I can hear Mutton barking as I open the front door. Somehow he has got himself stuck in the kitchen and the door is jammed, with him on the wrong side, by a wellington boot. He is highly indignant; his only consolation when he is left is to make for the sofa in the sitting room.

I feed him quickly, then try to capture the brilliance of the sky. I have a bath and Mutton and I both walk along the beach path to the town to meet Matt and Alice. The sky is still flecked with orange and purple lines to the sea. I think I have caught it.

I feel excited, on a high, because I am painting well and the joy of it makes me want to dance and sing.

Chapter 16

We are lying, Matt and I, on a mattress pulled right up to his enormous bowed window. The sea lies below us, the stars above. We are suspended, out on a limb above the ocean. The noise of a rough sea crashing against the rocks underneath the polished boards of the extended window and swirling and sucking up the walls, in bursts of dramatic spray towards where we lie, is sensational.

We are full of pasta and friendship and wine. We have placed in the circle of the window small candles, which reflect flickering light over and over everywhere and smell like the inside of a church. The flat is warm and we lie naked touching each other and talking and making love and laughing.

I don't want to love Matt. I don't want to fall in love. But it is impossible not to feel close to him. It is like it was with Dan. It is like having a best friend. I love the beauty and the shape of his body without it necessarily being sexual. I love the easy person he is. Our bodies respond gently and instinctively to each other, as if they are as familiar to each other as children who grow up naked, bath together, romp together and think nothing of the intimacy of skin touching skin, the warmth of body against body. Like small puppies who wriggle comfortably together in a basket.

Matt finds this very funny. 'Brother and sister? Little fat-bottomed puppies wriggling about in a basket! Very romantic, I don't think!'

He starts to tickle me. 'Stop it . . . stop it . . . You know what I mean, you know you do . . . Stop making me laugh . . . it hurts . . . It's wonderful to me, Matt, we are friends, we're such sudden and complete good friends.'

Matt rolls me on top of him. 'Of course we are. We always will be, my little Norwegian mermaid with your pale hair and your strange Scandinavian eyes full of blue stars. But your passion is for another type of man. I'm your friend, but I don't make you tremble. You would never sit, sick with longing, by the side of the phone waiting for me to ring. You don't shake with desire when I touch you.'

I watch his face, which suddenly looks young and wistful. I start to say something but he puts his finger over my mouth.

'I am the man who will sit in the kitchen cooking you a meal or pouring you wine while you cry your heart out over someone else. We, you and I, *are* as familiar as if we had grown up together, but perhaps that's why we will always be friends rather than lovers. Maybe there is not enough mystery for you. Maybe both of us are drawn to people who hurt us. Heaven knows, Lindsey was complicated enough.'

I bend and kiss him. I know what he is doing. He is insuring himself against being hurt. My hair falls over him like a curtain, hides him from the night sky full of stars. 'I think you're talking about sex, not love, Matt. There is a difference.'

Slowly his hands come up and he holds my hair away so that he can see my face and says so softly I can hardly hear, 'Don't they go together? I am talking about passion, Si.'

I stare down at his face. I don't want to hurt him. I don't want to lose him. I don't want passion. He smiles suddenly, tired of being serious and pulls me into his shoulder. 'My fault, anyway, getting involved with a mythical little siren.'

I kiss his nose. 'Oh, I'm going to seduce you on to the rocks by singing to you, am I?'

Matt rolls me over. 'Sing away. Sing your siren song. I'll risk the consequences because you are a very rare and beautiful mermaid.' He moves his hand gently over my breasts and down over my hips. 'Stay just like that, Si, I am going to draw you.'

He hops out of bed, his neat little bottom disappears into the gloom of the room. He plugs in an electric fire, then hops back into bed and begins to sketch me.

I lie on my side, head on my arm and watch the quick deft movement of his hand. Behind him the dark velvet sea meets the sky and brave little lights of fishing boats move on the surface of the water. I feel as if I am out on the sea in a boat too, floating, near sleep.

Happiness comes in moments, I've learnt that, not in great chunks. Tiny moments of searing joy, so strong, so profound it is why people weep, because they are so perfectly aware of it.

I watch Matt. Hear and feel my breath slow down for sleep, my body becoming languid and heavy as I relax. Everything he has said about loving the wrong people is true – for me, anyway. Yet in this moment I know we both have something which can grow. There are hundreds of different ways of loving, comfortable and uncomfortable. I want comfortable.

'I'll sing a haunting, eerie little siren song to you, Matt, but I'll never let you get near my rocks,' I whisper.

His fingers do not stop their quick movements, he doesn't raise his eyes from his work, but his mouth twitches with amusement and arousal.

'Baby,' he says, in a terrible American accent, 'you are the rocks!' He drops the accent and says more seriously, 'You silly bitch . . . I'm already in deep, deep love with you. And you know it. I talk utter balls most of the time, but I'm not stupid. Jake is inside you, hidden and waiting. Until you can get him out, you're not free to love anyone, and I am vulnerable.'

'At this moment, I feel more love here than I have felt for years, Matt.'

He looks up quickly, smiling. 'Because here is safe. I'm safe. And the shadows have retreated for a while . . . Don't move, one second more.'

He finishes, throws his pad aside and reaches for me. Cold now, we curl up under the duvet. 'Somehow,' he says into my hair, 'somehow, Si, you must leave Jake behind you, out of here . . .' He taps my heart. 'He's gone, it's over. You can move on . . .'

I can hear his voice is thick with sleep. He folds me into his shoulder again and almost immediately his breathing changes, becomes heavy and slow. It is always a wonder to me how people can be talking one minute and asleep the next. I am deeply envious of it.

I lie for what seems a long time watching the lights on the sea. I grow warmer and warmer against Matt until I too fall asleep . . .

The water of the pond is so deep, so dirty and muddy. I peer in, try to see down, down into its depths but I cannot see anything. I cannot remember what it is that I have to find in there, and anxiousness overwhelms me.

I lean lower and lower over the still water. I hear someone call out urgently, yell a warning, and suddenly the snake rears up out of the water, just missing my head. It is huge, huge, its fangs curved, razor sharp and covered in blood.

I open my mouth to scream and no sound comes. I can make no sound. I dream. I dream. I know I dream the terrifying snake dream.

I am running, running for the sea's edge, for the red dress floating out in the shallows . . . I turn her over. My face, my face a mask, a white drowned death mask . . .

I want to wake . . . I cannot wake.

I am being shaken hard, someone is yelling at me, holding me, shaking me. I hear my own screaming now and it frightens me. I cannot stop. I am being pulled up out of the bed, across the floor and eventually I hear a man's voice over the screaming. I stop.

Jake is going to be angry. His voice fills my head. I keep my eyes tight shut so I cannot see his anger.

'You are happy here with me, do you hear me? You are happy. You do not have nightmares in my house. I love you and you are happy. Do . . . you . . . bloody well hear . . . me?'

I nod. I nod. 'Yes, yes, I'm happy . . . please, please don't hit me.'

'Jesus Christ, Si, open your eyes. Please wake up . . . for Christ's sake, wake up . . . Don't look at me like that. It's all right. It's Matt, not Jake . . . It's Matt.'

I come from a long, long way away. I come from another country whose map is like a jungle, where the snake has my father's small, dark impenetrable eyes.

Matt is standing before me. I see it is Matt and I shake with relief. I wake. Oh, how good it is to be awake. 'Sorry . . . sorry . . .'

He winds my hair in his fingers and I see he is white and shocked as he clutches me to him and lifts me back to the bed. He goes away

102

and brings two brandies back with him. We both down them in one. He moves away again and puts the kettle on.

'Try and tell me, Si,' he says quietly when he comes back. 'Why on earth you are still so afraid and haunted by Jake?'

Matt places my hot tea by the bed and gets in beside me. The bulk of his body touching mine is comforting. Is vital. I lie against him for a while, then I try to tell him how it was, living with Jake. But all truths have layers of duplicity.

I tell him about Dan and his death. I tell him how good Jake was to me when it happened, supporting me in so many practical ways over the shock and my terrible, overpowering grief. Helping me limp through the rest of the term. Just taking over and being kind.

It was Jake who explained the following year that my work was not good enough to continue with my course. I had fallen too far behind and he persuaded me that it might be an idea to take a sabbatical and review my situation later.

He used to have weekend parties at his cottage in Dartmoor. He started to invite me. A few of us would go down together and we would just walk and talk and it was good. Then, somehow, it began to be just the two of us and he seemed so concerned about me all the time, so caring.

I was lonely. I was so lost without Dan. Dan was the first, the only person in my life who had really loved and liked me and made me laugh. And I didn't have anyone else really but Jake. Beth was still in Zimbabwe.

Jake was very different from Dan. He was older, exciting, flattering. He would tell me wonderful stories of his life in Hong Kong. I admired his work, accepted his judgement of mine. Sex was . . . well . . . good, and I mistook lust for love, I suppose.

This sounds so feeble, but I think I married Jake because I didn't know how not to. Married him to feel safe again. I married him not knowing he would make the dark moments grow and breed and multiply.

Matt touches my hair. 'What dark moments, Si?'

I cannot answer. I have been silent for too long. My silence is denial. My silence has been my survival.

After a moment, Matt says, 'Go on.' His fingers in my hair are

103

like hope and I take his other hand and press my lips to his palm, hold it to my cheek.

'After we were married he wanted me to live on Dartmoor all the time. After we were married he seemed to change almost overnight. He would suddenly criticise tiny things. He would ask me what I was thinking and if my answer was not what he wanted to hear, he would hold my face between his hands, "I-want-to-know-what-is-in-your-head. Do you hear me? I need to know what goes on up there." He would tap my forehead.

'He would go through my books and private papers constantly. He read my diaries, riffled through my drawers as if he would find secrets there. He would read all my letters, and I would have to tell him exactly where I had been whenever I went out of the house. He even used to put a dip stick in my petrol to see if I had told him the truth when I used the car.

'I was in trouble if I asked anyone back to the house and there was always a reason why I could not invite friends for the weekend. I wasn't allowed to have a bath by myself or even shut, let alone lock the bathroom door, whatever the time of the month, whatever privacy I needed.

'I was swamped, suffocated. I could not breathe, Matt. After about a year I knew I had to leave. That's when he began to hit me.

'He would tell me what crap I was and how I was lucky to have anyone even look at me, I was such a miserable apology for a human being. He would tell me I could not paint to save my life and even my boyfriend had jumped over a bridge to get away from me. He would say, "Haven't you noticed you can't keep friends? You don't have any lasting friends." "But I do," I would cry. "I have lots of friends." And I would name them and he would smile and say softly, "Ah! But they don't know you like I do, do they, darling? If they did, you would have no one, because I have discovered you are not a very nice person. You are a very selfish and hopelessly unbalanced human being."

'When he had reduced me to a gibbering wreck, and I was almost catatonic with isolation and misery, he would suddenly switch dramatically. He would tell me how utterly amazing I was to put up with his moods. He would say I must know how he adored me. He would whip me off to exotic places. We would start to do things I really enjoyed. He could make me feel as if I was the most incredibly gifted and beautiful woman in the whole universe.

'He would sparkle with wit, throw parties. People would love him, be charmed. Beth was. He would assure me again and again how much he loved me and apologise over and over for sometimes being moody and difficult. He would tell me how good I was for him. How well I understood his artistic temperament. What a little saint I was to love him.'

Matt goes on holding me in the dark, rhythmically stroking my hair. Outside in the lightening day the little lights of the fishing boats head past the window out into the bay. I cannot say to Matt what is true and which I wish was not.

Jake knew my body and what I liked and I despised myself for how he could make me feel. He could blot out all the hurts and wrongs and humiliations of weeks in a couple of hours.

Matt is so still that it is possible to imagine he knows my treacherous thoughts.

'I would think I had imagined everything,' I say. 'That Jake was right, I was a little mad, unbalanced. Then . . . then just as suddenly, when I was lulled into blissful normality, when I thought things were really going well between us, I would turn and say something that would make him unaccountably furious or jealous and the whole cycle would begin again. Twisting every meaning of mine until he felt he had an excuse to hit me. Once he started he seemed unable to stop and I would go crashing to the ground, totally unaware of what I was supposed to have said or done.

'But the worst times were when I tried to leave. Beth rang one night when he was in the middle of a terrible rage because he had found my packed rucksack in the wardrobe. He nearly killed me. I ended up in hospital. That's when Beth and John brought me here.' I turn so I can see Matt's face. 'The police are fed up with me because if he is charged I've said I don't want to testify.'

'Why not?' Matt asks quietly.

'I couldn't bear the thought of having to face him in court.'

'Are you still so afraid of him? When he can't touch you?'

'Yes. He would try to humiliate me in court or at least get his barrister to do it for him. You don't understand, Matt. He can make you feel you are all the things he says you are . . . I am, I am afraid of him. Just to see him makes me shake . . .'

Matt stops stroking my hair. He says quietly, 'I think you are ashamed because you enjoyed brilliant sex with someone who hurt and abused you.'

I raise my hands up to the night with the pain of his words.

'Si, Si, don't . . . don't . . . don't . . . You've done nothing wrong.'

'But I have. I have. I hate myself. I loathe myself, Matt. I could have left – he didn't chain me to the chair. He didn't lock me up. I was terribly frightened of him, but I felt grateful, grateful when he was nice to me. I kept thinking, if I was careful and tried harder it would all be all right. When he was nice, Matt, when he was fun . . .'

I think about that soft voice, his beautifully shaped hands, his body kept fit with running, the way he touched me . . . I shiver . . . I shiver. Matt's right. He is right.

'You loved him. Sigrid, you loved the bastard. Do you still?'

'Of course I didn't! Of course I don't!' I cry out.

'Come on,' Matt says suddenly, his face tight. 'Neither of us is going to sleep again tonight. Let's go out and watch the sun come up.'

In the dark we walk in silence for a long time on the deserted beach, watching the sky lighten. Matt does not take my hand. Eventually he says, throwing an arm round me, 'Thanks for telling me. It must have been hard . . . a hard thing to talk about . . . It was brave . . . I'm trying to understand.'

'Matt, I don't understand myself. Please, oh please, don't walk away from me. I need your friendship.'

'You've got it, Si.'

'But I've hurt you.'

'Yes. Because I'm jealous. Because the man is still your husband. Because I'm so fucking afraid I'm going to get hurt again. And because I'm out of my depth. That's what I was going on about obliquely earlier.'

'I don't mean to hurt you, Matt. If I hurt you, it is not because I don't care. It's because I'm damaged.'

Matt looks down at me. 'Si, I think I'll go to Newquay to surf for a couple of days, maybe with Rob. I need to breathe. Maybe things have moved too quickly for us both. Maybe we are in too deep, too soon.'

I freeze. I feel the blood drain away from my face. He is going to walk away from me. I am going to lose him too. Every good thing I touch . . .

Matt, watching my face, suddenly pulls me to him. 'God, how can anyone go that pale? I don't know what I'm saying. I don't mean it. I can't walk away from you . . . even if I wanted to, Si.' He holds me so tight it hurts but I hold him too. 'I'm just so afraid I'll lose you . . . that you'll go back to that bastard . . . Go home and get some sleep. We are both tired. I'll ring you later on before I leave.' He takes my face in his hands and presses his mouth to my forehead. 'I'll see you in two or three days.'

I walk quickly away across the heavy, wet sand. I turn my back on the sun coming up and my friend standing miserable in the cold. I walk with Mutton lolloping beside me, mindless of my moods, back up the path and winding hill to Huer's Cottage.

It is *not* better to talk about some things. It is better to leave them be, to keep silent or they go on and on destroying.

Haven't I learnt this already?

Chapter 17

The daffodils are out, yet the weather is bitter, like midwinter. I huddle in front of the Rayburn. Huer's Cottage is freezing, I don't know how Beth and John survive.

I miss Matt. I miss him being in the gallery. I miss knowing I can wander down into the town and find him. There is a small sick place in my stomach in case he will decide to give up on me.

I miss Beth and John and the twins so much. For the first time since I came here I am alone with my own thoughts and they frighten me. Loneliness settles like a cold place. The mist and the rain make a cloak around me that seems to separate me from the rest of the world. The cottage is full of the constant smell of wet dog. This cold house, which I can no longer settle in, is not mine and has none of my possessions in it.

Devoid of the people I love I suddenly feel like a refugee.

The presence in my life of this family, of Matt, has camouflaged the fact that I am cuckooing in other lives. I have to make plans soon. I can't stay with John and Beth for ever.

Mutton and I stand in the conservatory looking out at the sodden garden. There is a constant drip-drip from the trees up on the bank. The conservatory smells of gently rotting wood and of something vaguely sweet, like ripe apples, that reminds me of childhood, of houses visited, faded and still, full of the slow movements of someone old making tea, which seems to take forever.

Tubs full of straggly geraniums and pot plants stand next to bicycles and garden furniture, and a faded garden umbrella lies like a memory of distant summer, gathering cobwebs like dusty lace.

On the far side of the conservatory there is the sliding door to an annexe that Hanna and Amy use as a summer playroom. I go slowly in there, wishing I could hear two squabbling, chattering little girls. Hanna's recorder stands on an old piano next to a glass of congealing orange drink.

A chipped chest of drawers squats with the drawers hanging open, dressing-up clothes spilling out. A school sock and straw boater lie where they were thrown on the floor . . . Hanna with her smooth shiny bob, just like Beth, and Amy, furious that she has inherited John's dark wiry hair that stands out like a halo. The rooms looks as if the twins have just left it and an overpowering sense of loss and dislocation swings in as I look at the comforting detritus of lives I have shared for a while and from which I now realize I must soon move on.

I look up as the sound of a sudden scurry of rain hits the glass roof full of tiny dark pouches of moss scattered like soft green pebbles over the sloping glass panes. Mutton sniffs around happily at the comforting smell of his twins and swings his tail, knocking toys off the small sofa in the corner.

I must get out of the cottage. I must walk somewhere. I will drive to Zennor and try to find the cottage that Virginia Woolf once rented. Katherine Mansfield lived in Zennor too for a while, but disliked it and moved on to Mylor, which was sheltered. According to one of the books Beth lent me, she later forgot she had hated Zennor and tried to persuade Virginia to buy the cottage next door. If I can't find Virginia Woolf's cottage I will look for D. H. Lawrence's.

I get Beth's car out for the first time, load Mutton and towels, and drive the winding road to Zennor with John's maps. Everything is grey: huge dark grey boulders hang in small sodden fields; blanket-closed grey sky and gusting, misty rain slanting on a vast expanse of slate-grey ocean.

I park next to the Tinner's Arms, whose doors are closed against the rain. The village seems deserted even by the inhabitants. Reluctantly, I get out of the car at Mutton's urging, clumsy in my waterproofs, and we make for the cliff path with the wind pulling and tugging at my clothes, whipping my hair into my eyes and stinging my cheeks.

Cows stand in the farmyard as I pass and there is a comforting sound of a milking machine somewhere but I am the only one on the path and I bend against the wind, thinking no wonder the Lawrences had blazing rows and incipient depression here. I am unlikely to find my feet, let alone a couple of literary cottages.

It is so unlike the beautiful morning I came with Matt. This is like being in an entirely different country. I march on, miserable, unable to see or enjoy anything, but reluctant to turn back. I am unsure I am even going in the right direction but keep to the narrow cliff path, high with bracken and heather.

I walk fast, keep moving, push my body against the wind. It is hard suddenly to confront this awful cowardice in myself. Not to feel overpowered by that persistent pernicious little voice that sounds like the echo of Jake. I quail at the thought of what I am going to have to do soon. I won't testify against Jake if it gets to court, but I will have to make contact in some form. Money from my parents is tied up with Jake's. I am going to need somewhere to live.

After a while I stop at an inlet of rock to get my breath and stand in the shelter of great boulders that hang like teeth over the cliff edge. Below me the sea roars, churning up angrily over the rocks and swirling forward in great greedy white froth that eats into the roots of the cliff. I stare down, hypnotized by the power and suction of that sea and awed, almost swamped, by the bleak aged strength of the landscape.

As I stand there, gazing down at the sea, I have a clear and terrifying sensation of something shadowy creeping stealthily towards me from behind. Dark, crouched, so real in my mind that I whip round with a sharp cry, my heart jumping, clutching the edge of the rock.

I peer out into the mist and rain and see shapes moving, nebulous dim half-glimpsed silhouettes back on the path. Walkers. There is nothing, no one anywhere near me. Yet Mutton stands quite still, nose in the air, sniffing and growling monotonously under his breath like slow thunder. I move quickly away from the rocks back on to the path and follow the disappeared walkers.

According to the map, at some point the path branches inland and

111

down into a hamlet of cottages. I trudge on in the wind and the relentless slanting rain for a minute, then stop and listen.

But is it not what I can *hear* or *see*, but what I *feel*.

I am scared. The creeping sensation of someone behind me is still there. I cannot understand what induced me to come out to this stark place in this weather. It suddenly seems totally stupid, but as I start to turn back, and face what lies behind me, I see the path down the valley, which must pass the cottages or at least lead inland, and thankfully I begin to walk away from the sea and downhill.

I pass a row of small cottages and eventually reach the car park, having completed a circle. I towel Mutton down and even he seems glad to go back in the car. As I stand hesitating, wondering whether to shed my waterproof trousers and go into the pub for a coffee, a walker comes round the corner by the farm, muffled up in yellow sou'wester, walking awkwardly in too many clothes. He stops for a minute by the pub as if he too is wondering whether to go inside, then he walks to an old blue car parked down the road and gets in.

Mutton, watching, growls under his breath. I turn to him. 'We're not the only ones allowed out in this, you know.'

But he won't stop, he growls like a slow monotonous swearing under his breath. Suddenly jittery, I stare across the car park to the road, peer at the muffled, almost invisible figure sitting there with the engine running to clear his windscreen. Then I see with relief that yellow sou'wester has been joined by a woman coming from the direction of the pub.

'Don't be silly, Mutton.' I start the engine, move out of the car park and past the blue car. 'You're starting to growl at everyone.'

As I drive homewards the sky begins to clear.

When I get back to Huer's Cottage I leave Mutton tucked up in front of the Rayburn and drive up to Talland House with a painting I want to complete and a couple of new canvases. It's more than possible in this weather that people will come, wanting to see round the house. The answerphone is flashing. I forgot to check at Huer's Cottage. It is Beth and John and the twins to say 'Hi' to me. It is also Matt, to say he is coming back tomorrow and will be round about seven.

'I've missed you, mermaid,' he says. 'I've missed you.'

I laugh with relief. It will be so good to see him. I go and light the fire in the drawing room, which Beth likes me to do every so often. Visiting Woolfies love it and it gives extra warmth to the room. Extraordinary how two voices on a telephone can completely change my mood. I am embarrassed now to think of my stupid imagination at Zennor.

I lay out my paints and I paint from memory that small cottage on Dartmoor. I want to paint it out of my being.

After a couple of hours, I curl up on the sofa in front of the fire. Looking into the fire, I am reminded of the house in Scotland. I daydream of my mother, as I so often do . . .

I walk in the front door from school and call out her name. She does not call back. The silence is heavy as treacle. I stand in the hall with the late afternoon sun shining through the stained-glass window of the front door, listening, listening for my mother to answer, to call back, 'Si? Si, you're back!'

But there is no sound at all, of radio, cooking, teacups or movement.

My heart thumps. I notice the dust on the small table. Has she finally left my father? Has she done a runner back to Norway?

I call out again, afraid, my cry urgent and high as a bird at sunset and again there is nothing, only this terrible overbearing stillness in the house. Heavy as lead. Heavy as an unsaid reproach.

I stand rooted to the bottom of the stairs, straining for any sound, however slight, to indicate that my mother is still inside this house. The door of the sitting room is open and a breeze from the top of the open window lifts the beige curtains covered in cream and brown flowers so that the lining separates and flutters. On the carpet lie fallen petals from a rose bowl.

I turn back to the stairs and start to climb leadenly like an old person. My hand makes small sweaty fingerprints on the mahogany banisters. The door of the bedroom is closed. My mother never closes her bedroom door during the day and my legs start to shake as I climb those steep stairs.

I know that I am going to find her room empty, for the house is surely devoid of her. I know I am going to find her empty drawers and gaping wardrobe and her neatly made bed with a note of goodbye on the pillow. I know it.

I had watched the cold fog of depression reach out and envelop her in the past week. Clutch her in its cobra-like grip. I had watched her face almost change shape and her eyes dart here and there, searching for help or an answer.

It had not come from my father. It had not come from me. We were gentle with her but evasive, for we had been caught in her desperate moods too many times and we did not want to be drowned in its wake.

I had exams – my excuse for avoiding her. I do not know what excuse my father had.

I can smell again the scent of my own fear as I reached out and turned the shiny glass knob of her bedroom door. I could see her in my mind's eye sitting on a plane to Oslo, having finally had the courage and the will to leave us both.

As the door swung open and I saw her lying on her side, facing away from me towards the window, I felt a moment's elation and relief. I smiled fondly at her fair hair lying across the pillow, her small white neck exposing a slight and tender crease.

Then, with a start, I noticed the terrible stillness of that small body. I rushed forward, calling out her name, reaching out to touch, to shake her shoulders. Wanting her to turn, turn with a smile, still full of sleep, her voice croaky and her mind fuddled, like she always was if she slept in the afternoon.

Instead, my hands found her shoulders, already stiff with death. She must have taken the pills even before my father and I had left the house that morning. She was thirty-eight years old. The following day was my sixteenth birthday.

Even now, almost nine years later, here at Talland House in this drawing room, the loss swings in, drowning me like a gigantic wave and throwing me up on the beach.

I draw my knees up to my chin and I moan like a hurt animal with the hopeless pain and guilt that I let my mother sink to such a pitch of depression that she took her own life at thirty-eight years old.

I feel a sudden, strange sensation across the top of my head, like an insect moving over strands of my hair. I reach up to feel my hair, but there is nothing there. As I raise my fingers, although my eyes are still closed, I see clearly a hand with long fingers stroke my hair slowly and with infinite tenderness.

I shiver, open my eyes, sit up, my skin prickling. It is an eerie sensation. I meet the eyes of Virginia Woolf in the small double-headed photo of her on the wall. She meets and holds my eyes steadily as if she is trying to tell me something I should understand.

For a moment, a moment only, the window behind me is no longer plain glass, but full of small coloured gothic panes. There is no tall building in front of Talland House, but an uninterrupted view of cloudless blue sky and sea.

Outside, where the car park is, there is a white wall in the sun, full of pale, ripening peaches. There is a garden full of secret places and walls of shrubs to hide amongst. And here in this room, as the sun sets and fills the sky and is reflected in the sea, a small girl in a white dress tucks herself up on a sofa and scribbles and scribbles her heart out. Writes her soul out for posterity, in long days of sun and happiness that, like all children, she believed would never end.

But they did. Her childhood ended when her mother died.

I glance again at the photos, at Virginia's beautiful and sad face. I see the river near her garden in Sussex slowly rise and swallow her up.

I get up slowly. The fire has died, but I make quite sure it is safe, then I lock up, put my painting, uncompleted, on the back seat and drive down the hill to Huer's Cottage.

I take a torch and go through the conservatory into the back garden and let Mutton out. I am so looking forward to Matt being back tomorrow. I feel like a child. I want to ask and tell him so many things. Mutton is ages scrabbling about in the undergrowth, there must be a fox about. I see the trail they make across the bank from the railway. I whistle. I don't want him to roll in anything and he comes bounding back, licking his lips, pleased with himself, and jumps into his basket. I bend to say goodnight, surreptitiously sniffing him. 'Sorry to be rude, Mutt, but I know fox is Jo Malone to you . . .'

But he smells all right. I am so glad I have him for company. 'What did you find, you old dustbin, a scrap a seagull dropped?' I drop a handful of biscuits into his bowl to get him through the night.

I lie in bed, planning and dreaming, watching the twinkling lights across in the harbour. Before I fall asleep, I have an idea about what I would like to do this coming year.

I wake to silence. Thick silence. Only my heart, the unsteady beat of my heart and the soft velvet stillness of a clock ticking night and the hum of inanimate things.

An empty house and yawning darkness that is like a blanket I struggle to fight my way out of. I cannot get my bearings or quite remember where I am because I come from such a deep sleep and the room is so completely black.

Then . . . then suddenly the blackness moves silently an inch and I glimpse a strip of glimmering sea and star-filled sky, and my heart lurches painfully in utter terror because someone is standing blocking the light from the window. Someone is watching me, holding their breath. Someone is watching me.

I must not blink an eyelid. I must not move a muscle. I must not flinch or cry out. I must feign sleep or I will be hurt. I know this as clearly as if someone had whispered in my ear. The hammering of my heart drowns all sounds. If I am in the middle of a nightmare I want to wake now . . . now. My nightmares are so real, please God, I am dreaming . . . Suddenly a rushing of blood fills my head and real darkness comes.

When I come to the window is full of sea and the sky is back and light catches the mahogany dressing table, and the mirror glints and reflects light from beyond the window. I lie still, bathed in sweat and shivering. I strain to listen for any sound in the house but I can hear nothing. A bad dream? I don't know. I just don't know.

Mutton? Where is Mutton? He is usually here with me, snuffling and snoring, pottering up and downstairs but always sensing when I am awake. I lie there for minutes and I hear no sound.

Light is filtering into the room and as dawn comes my fear begins to subside. Slowly I realize I must have been dreaming because Mutton would have set up such a barking if anyone had broken in. Half of St Ives would have been alerted.

I get up, switch the light on in my bedroom and on the landing, and pad down the stairs, calling him, but he does not come. I go into the kitchen and as I switch the light on I see he is lying out of his basket, quite still on the cold floor.

Something is wrong. I rush to him, calling his name, touch his silky body. He does not seem to be breathing, but he is still warm. I lean over him and see he has yellow froth all over his mouth and his teeth are drawn back in pain. I see now where he has been sick all over the kitchen. His food bowl is empty. What on earth could he have eaten other than the biscuits I gave him to make him this ill?

Suddenly, as I sit beside him, he jerks into life, heaving and vomiting, whimpering pitifully, then collapsing again, his breath coming in great painful gulps. He did not bark because he could not bark.

I rush to the phone. On her board Beth has left all the telephone numbers and I ring her vet, get through to the emergency night vet and beg him to get here quickly for Mutton is dying, there is no doubt about that. I tell the vet this. He asks me my address. I am crying now as I give it to him, watching Mutton in such pain. 'I'll be ten minutes,' the vet says, and slams the phone down.

I go back and sit with the poor dog, talking to him gently, telling him to hang on, and I think he is conscious of me because he gives a great sigh as I talk. The vet really is only ten minutes – 'Luckily, I live round the corner.'

He bends immediately to Mutton. 'Oh, poor old chap, what have you been up to?' He peers in Mutton's mouth. 'He's eaten something. The trouble is these dogs are such walking dustbins. Any idea what he could have got hold of?'

I look around the kitchen; all the cupboard doors are shut. 'No,' I say. 'I left him some biscuits in his bowl when I went to bed last night, that's all. He was fine yesterday. The only thing I can think of is something in the garden. He was ages out there last night and came in licking his lips.'

The vet bends and listens to his chest, then looks at me. 'I'm afraid he's in a bad way. It looks to me as if he has got hold of something poisonous out there, but it's too dark to look at the moment. I am going to give him an injection to calm him down, but I need to find out pretty quickly what he has taken. So when it's light enough, would you take a look around and give me a ring?

'I'll take him in my car now and do some immediate tests, and I'll ring you as soon as I know . . .' He hesitates. 'I'm sorry, it doesn't look too good for him at the moment. I have my doubts about whether he can pull through this one.'

I try not to cry again in front of him.

'I know.' He smiles briefly at me. 'It's especially awful when you're looking after someone else's dog. I've been here before, though. Mutton is a one-man disposal unit. I'm going to back my car to the door and lift up the back because he's a heavy lad to lift.'

I wrap Mutton in his favourite blanket and hold his head as the vet lifts him and staggers down the steps to his car with him. 'Sorry, sorry,' I say, 'to get you out at dawn. But thank you, thank you so much. Please ring as soon as you know anything.'

He smiles at me. 'I will. Go back to bed with a hot cup of tea. Try not to worry. I'll do my level best.' A nice man.

He drives away and I shut and lock the front door and put the kettle on. I put the light on in the conservatory and, shivering, I go out there and look round, and into the children's annexe. I go upstairs and I check all the windows. All shut and locked. I go back downstairs and make a hot-water bottle and take some tea back to bed.

I can see no way anyone could have got into this house. Even Jake. I am shivering, not with cold and misery, but with a rising hopelessness, a jumpy fear. My dream last night. A dark shadow blocking the light from the window.

I watch the sun come up, but I do not see it. I see a lone figure in a car park, hidden and wrapped. I see a blue car and I remember Mutton's odd relentless growling. I watch the rain begin again in a heavy stream that becomes a deluge, shutting me up again between sea and sky.

I am hanging on to a thread of hope because I also know fear can make one deluded.

As soon as it is light, I get up and go into the garden and search and search the lawn, the flowerbeds, the garden shed and all around the bottom of the conservatory. I can find absolutely nothing.

At eight o'clock I ring the vet. Mutton is still alive.

Chapter 18

At lunchtime the vet rings me to say that Mutton is still holding his own but is heavily sedated. They have sent some contents of his stomach to be analysed. They're pretty sure he's eaten some sort of poison and they want him to stay put so they can keep an eye on him. I just pray he pulls through and is home before Beth, John and the twins return on Friday.

I feel slightly cheered. Dear old Mutton isn't dead yet and he is a strong dog. But I am worried that he got hold of something poisonous while I was looking after him.

I check the conservatory again but all the insecticides are up in high cupboards. I go once more into the garden where he was scrabbling about under the trees but I can find nothing and I'm unlikely to. Mutton has been known to swallow food in plastic bags. I look up at the bank, wondering if anything could have been thrown down into the garden.

I stand with my cup of coffee, thinking about yesterday. It was such a strange unnerving day, which ended in a terrible nightmare. I get my address book and go to the phone. This time I let it ring and ring and a Cypriot girl in Paphos answers it, but she sounds very young and she speaks hardly any English.

'May I speak to Judge Watson or Mrs Watson, please?' I ask.

'No here. No here,' she repeats.

'Their son? Is their son there?'

'No, no. All go Troödos. Holiday. Maybe two week.'

'Judge and Mrs Watson are on holiday with their son in Troödos?'

'Yes. Yes. All holiday. Back next week, I think.'

'You are sure? They're not in England?'

'No, no, they not in England. They Troödos, then Nicosia, then home, Paphos.'

'Thank you. Thank you very much.'

I put the phone down and sit heavily at the kitchen table. Relief makes me feel dizzy. I can't trust my instincts or judgement any more. I sit looking at my hands for a while, quite still. It dawns on me that Jake has probably been right all along: I am unbalanced, and paranoid. Perhaps there really is something wrong with me. Perhaps I should have taken the hospital's advice and had counselling.

I shake these thoughts away. Things are going to be all right. I just have to learn to believe this. I have been too much on my own.

The cottage is awful without Mutton. I walk down into St Ives to get something to cook Matt for supper. It seems like a hundred years since I last saw him and I'm surprised and amused at my own excitement at the thought of seeing him again.

The sea is still grey and rain hangs in great gloomy clouds over the harbour. St Ives is a colour-washed black-and-white today, like an old sepia photograph. When I look back on this spring, I will always see it through a constant curtain of sea mist and rain, like watching old black-and-white films on a Sunday afternoon, in which everyone dashes through rain-puddled streets, clutching umbrellas.

Halfway back home the rain arrives in great blowing torrents. The sea has disappeared into an anomalous, cloud-ridden purple mass that is forbidding. Soaked, I fall up the front steps and drop my bags while I find my key. On the top step is a bunch of purple and yellow irises beautifully wrapped in Cellophane. I take them into the kitchen and open the message. 'So looking forward to seeing you!' No signature. Matt. I smile with pleasure. I can't wait.

Lettice must have been and I am sorry to have missed her. She has worked hard; the kitchen is spotless. She obviously doesn't trust me to have the place up to Beth's standards by the time she gets back. I put the irises in water. I think they are the most elegant and dignified flowers in the world. I have always loved painting them.

There is a strong smell of Dettol. I have to admit the kitchen does smell better. Usually, Lettice puts everything up on the table while she cleans and then forgets to put them back and I have to go around putting things in their right places. Mutton's food and water bowl have been tidied away into the conservatory – my heart lurches sickly – as if he has died. I stare at them. What if the vet rang while I was out?

I quickly phone the surgery. Mutton is no worse, but his condition is still very serious. They do not have any results yet. No, they don't think it is a good idea for me to go and see him. It would just upset us both.

Perhaps I can catch Lettice at Talland House later. I plan to spend the afternoon cooking supper. I have never cooked for Matt before and I want to show off. I want it to be a little celebration, a sudden moving on and an acknowledgement that I can no longer pass him off in my head as just a platonic friend.

All afternoon I listen to the radio and cook while outside the rain slants across the beach in a steady depressing stream. If it wasn't for Mutton I would feel perfectly happy. Here inside, the kitchen getting fogged up, I feel warm and domesticated, cooking for someone I am so glad to be seeing again. I realize I can no longer bear being too much on my own. My thoughts will swoop and flutter in panicky circles, invade my life like dust in corners, getting everywhere, spoiling the present.

I invest into this meal an importance that it should not have, just so that I can prove to myself a skill, a usefulness. I spread Beth's bright plates over the table and fill them with my ingredients: prawns, slices of smoked salmon, rice, cheese, cream, salad, crusty loaves, pastry, strawberries.

At six the phone goes and it is Matt. For a horrible second I think he is going to say he can't come but he is just shaken and very cross.

'Sigrid? I'm going to be late. Some prat has just cannoned into me on the dual carriageway. Bloody idiot was going too fast, cut me up overtaking in this sodding weather. Then . . .' I have never heard Matt angry before, '. . . he didn't even *stop*. I'm furious. He was going at a hell of a pace. I think the Volkswagen is a write-off.'

'Matt, I'm so sorry. Are you hurt? Are you all right?'

'Yes, I'm all right, just mad. Robbie was with me, luckily. We are

121

just finishing with the police. But neither of us saw a thing. The police think it was probably a stolen car. Rob's girlfriend is going to pick us up in a minute and drive us home. She's just finished work in Truro.'

'I could have come and got you, Matt. Are you sure you're OK?'

'I'm pretty angry at the moment. Mel's on her way home anyway or I would have rung you. Look, I'd better go. I'll go home first and shower, and see you about eight, if that's still OK . . .? I promise I'll have calmed down by then. I'm sorry I went on, Si. I don't often swear and rant, but I was uncommonly fond of that car.'

I smile. 'I know you were. I've cooked a meal. Matt, would you mind coming up to Talland House first? There's a photographer coming at about six thirty and Beth wants me to light the fire and capture the atmosphere. We could have a bottle of wine up there.'

'I feel better already!'

'See you at eight, Matt. Take care. Relax, don't rush.'

'I'm very much looking forward to seeing you again, mermaid!'

He is smiling, I know. I can hear he means it.

I wash up, set the table, put the irises back in the middle with candles each side, and go upstairs and have a bath. I forgot to thank him for my flowers. I don't put a dress on; it's too cold and I don't want to seem too romantic.

Matt and I have only done casual things together. I want to get it right. I want this to go on and on, this special friendship that is turning into more. I could not have got through the days without him. But he is right, I have learnt this, these last few days. My mind throws up the past and I cannot let go of it yet. I have to get Jake and the power of him out of my system before I can honestly love Matt.

It is not fair to be so afraid of losing him that I hurt him by my affection and dishonesty. Affection is not love. Matt deserves more than this. I want one day to say, with no shadows to cloud my words, 'I love you, Matt.' So I am going to be honest. Because Matt is so easy to love and too easy to hurt.

I put tight white jeans on and a black sweater and let my hair loose for once. I walk up to Talland House carrying the painting I want to finish if I have time. The rain has stopped as it always seems to in the evening, and the colours are mellow. A faint gold aura hangs over the harbour and the mass of boats pulled up on the beach.

I light the fire in the drawing room. I love the feel of this room, love the feel of lives past, time arrested. On my knees I turn to look at the photo of Virginia Woolf. Today she is subdued. Today she is just a photograph in a pretty frame.

And yet, as firelight flickers and catches, as it reflects in the small-edged paned windows through which lights are beginning to shimmer across the sea and in the surrounding houses, I wonder. I wonder, with sadness that is curiosity too, how many times Virginia looked out of these windows and if she ever, with the years stretching like elastic before her, for even a second, saw how her life would end.

A sudden rush of water, a beating in the ears. Lungs full. Then nothing.

I shake the sudden mood away, get up and go to the window where my small easel stands, and I put the unfinished canvas of the Dartmoor cottage on it. I peer at it, startled. I cannot remember that I put in this much detail. It is finished.

How very strange I have been these last few days without people around me. Like my mother, so introverted and inward-looking that she was totally unaware of what she was doing half the time. It is a better painting than I remember.

The photographer for the interior design magazine turns up, complains about the weather in Cornwall and takes a reel of photographs, of the drawing room mostly.

'Pity the staircase is gone,' he says. 'Will you tell Mrs Elliot we'll be in touch if we think the house is right for our magazine?'

He disappears quickly out into the night, probably making for the pub. I wish I had retorted that Beth would see if the magazine was right for the house.

It is a quarter to eight. I put some music on, then I go back to the fire and start to read one of the many articles about Virginia lying on the table.

Eight thirty comes and still Matt does not appear. I wonder whether to go back to Huer's Cottage to turn the oven on, start the rice. At nine I ring his number. It is engaged. At least I know he is there. I wait five minutes and try again but it just goes on ringing.

He must have been trying to ring me. He must be on his way. I turn the tape over and put more wood on the fire. But he does not come.

Out of the drawing-room window the lights fan out like fireflies. The wind has blown the clouds apart and the moon sails out startlingly and is reflected in the coal-black sea. This room shivers with something intangible. I stand very still, listening. I catch the edge of a whisper, the sudden rustle of a dress like dry leaves. Firelight catches Virginia's wistful face. The room fills with tension.

I hear the soft, almost muffled sound of a young girl weeping as if from a faraway upstairs room. It goes on and on and on. The moment is as thin as a blade of grass casting a sliver of shadow on an open book. As fragile as the shiver of intuition hovering in the stillness of dusk. I just catch it.

It is then I know.

I throw on my coat and lock the door behind me. I run through the car park and down the hill, slip down the steps and take the steep little lane towards the water. I cut down the little alley and down more steep steps until I get to Matt's gallery where the window is always lit up.

I run round the side to Matt's front door. It is open. It is ajar. But there is no light on in his hall. I call out. I call out his name. There is no answer and Alice does not bark.

I rush up the stairs and my fear flaps around my head and makes my legs leaden. I push open the door of his flat and moonlight shines in from the huge window, the moon enormous, invasive, the sea moving and queasy so that it is like suddenly entering the hold of a moving ship and I sway before I can get my bearings.

The bed is ruffled, untidy and Matt lies quite still face away from me in the middle. Like . . . just like that other time. So still.

I cry out, run to the bed and feel the warmth of his body. Thank God. Oh, he is only sleeping. I kneel on the bed, call his name over and over. The car accident . . . he must have been hurt. I turn his face to me. His eyes are rolled up into their sockets, his face ashen. There is a thin line of foam in the corners of his mouth, spilling over his grey lips.

On the pillow near his head there is an empty syringe.

Frantically, I feel for a pulse but cannot find one. But he is still warm. He is still warm. He still breathes. I rush for the phone, drop it in my panic and dial 999. It seems to take ages – for ever – to tell them, to make them understand. I am screaming and shouting at them to be quick.

I go back and cover Matt with his duvet. I spread my arms over him to try to keep him warm. Matt did not take drugs. He never touched them. I can't understand it. Nothing makes sense . . .

It is happening all over again.

I hear a faint noise in the corner of the room and I freeze with fear, but it is only a cowed and shaking Alice limping towards me from under the table. I reach for her but she bolts for the door and down the stairs.

I am shaking too. I don't know what I'm doing. I get up, I sit down, I pray. I touch Matt. I talk to him. I can't think. Shock and fear are making me dumb and slow. I sit beside him, warm him, warm him with my body. 'Matt . . . Matt . . . what's happened? What's happened here? Don't die . . . please . . . please, oh God . . . please . . . don't die . . . You can't die.'

On the far side of the bed I catch sight of the sketch he did of me before he went away, when I lay naked, before my dream ripped the night apart.

It has been torn neatly into four equal pieces through my face, and placed back on the bed. I uncover Matt's hands. They are scratched and his arms are red. They feel so cold. I place my face against his face. It too is turning cold.

'Matt,' I whisper. 'Oh dear God . . . Matt . . .' I look at his face. There is a bruise coming out on his forehead. His lovely open face is distorted with pain and fear. I watch him stop breathing. I watch him become quite still.

He is dead.

Chapter 19

I turn and run down the stairs and out into the night. Blindly I run, so fast my breath catches in my throat, painful and raw. I run. I run. Away into the night, down the narrow alleyways, away, away, flying, flying from this nightmare. I cannot stay and wait. I cannot speak to anyone of what is dawning on me. Not yet. I must think, I must be sure. I must . . . What must I do? 'God,' I scream, 'tell me what to do.'

Run. Run. Past the harbour and the great inky black water breaking over the wall on a high tide. Past the ambulance racing down the hill, siren going. Past the people spilling out of the pub at the sound. I stop, my chest bursting, legs aching, leaning over the railings, leaning over the black sea. How did I ever think I could get away? The bastard. The ruthless, mad, obsessive bastard. He has killed Matt.

Did he kill Dan? Is this what I have always known? The possibility throbbing under a layer of skin like a vein, sensed but buried deep. A hidden mantra silently howled into the night air and out over the crests of the waves rising in white plumes of spray, to haunt me for ever.

Too late.

A few feet away people laugh and sing, chatter and call good night in circles of light streaming from the pub. I stand there shivering, clutching the railings, cold, grainy iron to my touch.

'Sigrid? Sigrid? Are you all right?' I turn. Rob detaches himself from a group of people and stares down at me. 'What is it? What's happened? You look terrible. Where's Matt?'

I open my mouth and try to speak, but no sound will come. He shakes me gently, alarmed. 'Sigrid, for God's sake, what is it?'

I clutch him. 'Matt . . . Matt's dead . . . he's dead . . .'

Rob grabs my arm. 'What do you mean? What's happened? What do you mean, Sigrid? Where is he?'

I wave back towards the gallery, my eyes fixed on Rob's face. As if he can make the image go away, as if he can change what I have seen. 'In his flat. I found him. I called the ambulance. I . . . I must . . . know . . . I have to find Jake . . .'

'Jesus Christ . . . He can't be dead. Come on . . .' Rob turns sharply and pulls me into a hobbled run back towards the gallery. I don't want to go back. I don't want to see Matt's body lying on the bed, framed by the moving green swell of the sea and that vast creamy moon, hanging sickly in the sky like an omen.

We run, back down the narrow streets and alleyways, windows like yellow slits between badly drawn curtains, where people sit like any other night watching television, arguing. Back, back we run, Rob clasping my arm, past the ambulance slewed sideways as far as it can get in the narrow street. It is empty, the radio is cackling . . . Past the gallery window where a small sea scene is illuminated by a bar of yellow light. Up, up the steep stairs, where two men in green bend over Matt, working to resuscitate him. Hope leaps. My arm aches where Rob is gripping it. Our breath is held in shivering suspension. Dear God. Please, Oh please.

God does not hear.

Exhausted, the two men shake their heads, stop, lean back and let out a sigh. 'No good . . .'

There is a cackle of static and one of the ambulancemen speaks into a handset. 'No. Afraid not. Too late. Male, early twenties. Possible overdose . . . Yes . . . Suspicious death. They are on their way? OK.' He turns to the other man. 'The police are just behind us.'

I cannot see Matt's face. Only his square brown feet scattered with dark hairs, toes turned slightly outwards like a child sleeping. A sound escapes from somewhere so deep inside me that I am as startled as Rob and the ambulancemen. I hardly know it is coming from me.

The men turn and seem to freeze for a moment at the sound, then

I am turned away from the still figure on the bed and the window full of sea. The tiny flat is suddenly full of police and the voices rise and fall. 'Sigrid found him, she rang for the ambulance . . . I don't know . . . I don't know what happened . . . I was with him a few hours ago . . .'

I stare at them all. Nothing feels real. It is like a dream sequence.

'I know what happened. I know who killed Matt.' My voice is wavery, strange. All eyes look my way.

'OK, let's clear some space here,' a policeman says.

Rob and I are led downstairs, out of the way. Out of the flat where the sea reflects small lights and a moon can fill the panes. Away from the bed where Matt held me so gently and lies growing colder and colder.

Rob's father stands by the ambulance, talking to a policeman, and he takes us slowly through the clumps of curious people to Rob's house where his mother makes me sit by the fire and brings me sickly sweet tea. She stands and hugs Rob, who is ashen and repeating over and over: 'I don't understand . . . I don't understand . . .'

I sit very still and look into the fire. Behind me the room fills and empties, fills and empties.

Rob's father pulls a chair up next to me and says gently, 'Remember me, Sigrid? Bill Symons. I came and mended John's gate? I'm a special constable, which means I'm a part-time policeman. Now I know you are in shock, but I'm afraid there are going to be a lot of questions tonight.'

'I know who killed Matt,' I say, watching the flames leap and form sizzling patterns on the back of the fire. 'It wasn't an accident. You know Matt didn't take drugs.'

The room is very quiet. I do not know how long it takes for it to empty. I am left here with two policemen who do not wear uniforms, Detective Inspector Trelawney and Detective Sergeant Miller.

I tell them about Jake. I hear myself gabbling, jumping from one thing to another. My words sound hysterical and paranoid. Even to me there does not sound enough substance to accuse Jake of murder.

I think he has been following me. I think he may have poisoned my dog. I think he has been watching the house. I think he may have been in the house.

They watch me carefully. They are polite. My husband is a very well-known painter? His father is a judge? One of them goes away to check the house in Cyprus. I don't have the number with me.

What exactly did I touch in the flat? Did I try to move Matt? How exactly was he lying when I found him? No, I did not touch or move the syringe. Did I notice anything else? Did I pass anyone as I approached the gallery? How long had I known Matt? Did he ever, to my knowledge, take any form of drugs? What were my exact arrangements with Matt for supper? What car accident? This they are very interested in. One of them goes to find Rob. No, there was no argument. No, Matt had been shaken up but not so much he needed a fix. Yes, I would have known.

In and out. People come in and out of the room and whisper and confer.

Am I absolutely sure Matt never took any sort of drug? Yes. Of course I am. Ask Rob, they are friends.

Did my husband know of my relationship with Matt? Was he formally charged for assaulting me? Had he, to my knowledge, ever been violent outside the home? Why did I ring for the ambulance and then run away? Did I remove any illegal substance from the flat? Have I ever taken any form of drugs? Does my husband take drugs? On and on.

I am so cold, despite the fire, and my teeth are starting to chatter.

'Why don't you get out there and look for him?' I shout, and Rob's mother comes in and gets annoyed with them.

'Can't you see the girl's in a terrible state? Can't it wait until the morning? She is in shock and who can blame her?'

The policeman leans towards me. 'We are taking everything you say very seriously indeed. But it will help our inquiry into your friend's death if you are honest, Mrs Watson. Apart from the drug which killed him, we have found a quantity of drugs hidden in the flat so it appears Matt did take drugs occasionally. It is obvious your friend's death is not an accident, but at this early stage we do have to keep an open mind as to who killed him. It would help us if you are honest about illegal substances. Until the evidence has been gathered from the flat and there is an inquest we will not know how Matt Tregonning died for sure. What we do have is a drug-related death. So, I ask you again, why did you run from the flat after you had called the ambulance?'

'I don't know . . . I panicked . . . I thought my husband would be out there, waiting for me. I wanted to confront him, get it all over with.'

'If your husband had wanted to kill Mr Tregonning there are easier ways of doing it.'

'Except if he had wanted it to look like Matt took drugs.'

'We'll take a break. Have a cup of tea, Mrs Watson. Let's see if we can establish if your husband is back in England.' He smiles a foxy smile, which I think is supposed to reassure me. 'You are still afraid of him?'

'Yes.'

'Even though he has been nowhere near you since you left him?'

'I believe he has.'

'You believe he means to hurt you?'

I look the policeman right in the eyes. 'Yes. Matt is his way of telling me this.' The policeman stares back and for the first time this evening I think he believes me. 'In the morning, we can go over Huer's Cottage if that will make you feel better. Meanwhile, you are safe here with your friends.'

Both policemen go away for a while. I will have to answer the same questions all over again tomorrow at the police station. Rob's mother, Mary, runs me a hot bath. She brings me a voluminous candlewick dressing gown to put on and insists I stay the night.

I throw my clothes in a corner and slide into the hot water. Slowly the shivering, which is making my teeth chatter, begins to subside. There is such horror inside me. I have made a terrible, fatal misjudgement. It seems I have not understood anything at all about what my violent marriage meant.

Jake has been in St Ives all the time and I have had so many clues. The changing of shadows in the garden in early morning, an instinct of someone there. Mutton barking, warning me . . . I let the hot water trickle constantly from the tap, but I cannot get warm. Mutton knew, though. He was the barrier between Jake and me.

It wasn't Matt who sent me irises, it was Jake. Jake who knows they are my favourite flowers. And, I wonder now if it was Lettice cleaning up the kitchen in such a sterile way. Jake must be delighted. I was far too stupid to pick up any of his clues. He even finished my painting. But, most unforgivable of all, his shadow fell over me and I wanted to believe it was a dream. I believed he was in Cyprus because I wanted to.

Matt is dead because of me. Because of me. And I cannot bear it. Matt, I am so, so sorry. I cause death by my own omission, my selfishness, my self-delusion. I seem dominated by death. It is a theme, a threnody, a hymn that links my life like a chain.

The pain is coming. It is like an avalanche. I pull myself out of the bath, wrap myself in the dressing gown Mary has left me, and go into the cold little spare room where she has plugged in an electric fire. Outside the rooftops of cottage upon cottage stretch out like a small shanty town to the sea, just glimpsed between buildings.

Mary is calling me. The police are back. I go downstairs and wonder why they are looking at me in such a strange way. They are silent for a moment, then one of them says, 'Mrs Watson, we were able to contact your husband's solicitor. Your husband did return to England. For his mother's funeral. His mother died suddenly while they were on holiday in the mountains. He returned with his father to bury her in the family grave in Devon.' The policeman is searching my face as if he has been vindicated in his original assessment of me. I imagine him talking to Rob's father about my fears that someone had been in John's garden. A woman who sees the shadow of her husband everywhere. A woman who possibly takes substances she should not.

'You will be very relieved to know that both your husband and his father are on the evening flight back to Paphos. We checked. We also checked when the coffin was brought into England for burial.'

I can say nothing. I feel that familiar and overpowering quailing of the spirit which acknowledges that there might after all be something wrong with my mind.

'So, you have no reason to be afraid. Your husband cannot be in

132

two places at once. We shall be in contact with him in the morning. I suggest you get a good night's sleep and a police car will pick you up at around nine thirty tomorrow, and we will go through your statement in detail.'

They go out into the night and I hear that they're talking to Rob's father outside the door.

Rob says bitterly, 'They seem determined to believe Matt was into drugs. And do you know why? Because of Lindsey. She was bad news. He got his flat busted because of her last year. They couldn't prove anything, but she disappeared mighty fast.'

Rob's father comes back into the room. 'Come on, son, let's all get to bed. This is all shocking enough without speculation. The police want to get to the truth, that's all.'

I wait until the house is silent and all creaks have subsided, then I dress and creep downstairs and leave a note by the phone to say I will be back in the morning to go to the police station. I open the door and I run down the silent dark streets. I cannot stay in that claustrophobic little cottage full of kindness. Only a hunting cat flits shadowlike down the narrow road ahead of me. There is a high tide and the fishing boats turn in the harbour in a small night wind smelling of fish. I have reined myself in, suspended thought, and now I stand and listen to the quiet deep place within me. The only sound is of water lapping with a little slap against the side of the boats, and up the harbour wall at my feet with a small sucking sound.

The silence of the night reaches into me with a steady voice and clears my mind. Jake killed Matt. I know this. Wherever he is he will be back for me. I know this too.

Chapter 20

I walk back along the sea path and up the hill to Huer's Cottage. I walk up the steps to the dark cottage, quailing at the thought of the supper I started for Matt still lying spread out on the kitchen table. I get out my key, but the door is unlocked and it swings open before me with a bang. I stand in the small hall, listening, my heart jerking about, but the house is silent.

I walk slowly into the kitchen. The kitchen table has been cleared. All the food has been put away. The big pine table is empty. Empty of food, candles and flowers. There is no evidence at all of the table I set for Matt.

I call out, my voice high and frightened in the silent house. 'Jake? Jake? Come on! Enough. Just let's get it all over with . . . Come out.' But there is only silence and my slow-burning anger, which for the moment leaves me past being afraid.

I look quickly into the conservatory and out into the garden. I look into the annexe. No one. But for the first time I see that the children's curtain frieze has been moved and hides a door. The other side of the door is a tiny dark room that John uses as an office between kitchen and hall.

This is how Jake gets into the house. So easy. From conservatory to annexe to the hall. I didn't even know there was a door there. It doesn't matter how many times I locked front, back or kitchen door, he could still get in.

My heart begins to pound again. I look in the sitting room, run up the stairs, making a lot of noise, my anger only just keeping my fear at bay. I look into the twins' bedroom and John and Beth's room, expecting any moment to turn and find him there, a shadow behind me. I look in the bathroom, the lavatory. I throw open every wardrobe.

I look up the last flight of stairs to my room. Of course . . . this is where he will be silently waiting for me. Fear is back; my legs start to shake. I go up slowly, holding on to the banister rail, listening, straining for the sound of his voice, which will loom suddenly out of the dark.

My bedside light is on. My bed is turned down. There is a lump under the duvet where my nightshirt is wrapped round a hot-water bottle. Two books are placed on my pillows. A glass of water is on my bedside table.

I know that if I begin to scream I will never stop. I will become the scream. The silence swells and fills the room, the house. There is no one here. He has gone. To be here now, tangible, would be too easy. Jake has always liked games.

The emptiness enfolds me. This terrible silence is as deafening as it was the afternoon I found my mother cold, her skin waxy and drawn tight with death. I crumple on to the top step, my arms around myself, rocking backwards and forwards.

What is he playing at? When was he here? Before or after he killed Matt? Is he on his way back to Cyprus, having shown me what he is capable of? Or is he somewhere waiting? I don't know.

I get up and stumble downstairs. I've got to get away from here before he hurts anyone else. I see there are two messages on the answering machine. I begin to shake again as I play the first message, I am so afraid I will hear that mad and credible voice. But it is Alan Rowe, the vet.

'Hello. I'm ringing about Mutton. He's definitely been poisoned. This is a serious matter as the contents of his stomach are not something he could have picked up anywhere, so the poison must have been given to him deliberately. Please contact me first thing in the morning. Oh, Mutton is recovering, against all the odds. Good-bye.'

Jake has been so near, near enough to touch me. Near enough to poison Mutton. Kill Matt. My flesh crawls.

The second message is from John.

'Hi, Siggi. Thanks for your telephone message yesterday. Sorry

136

we keep missing each other. We will be home tomorrow afternoon. Getting into Penzance at three fifteen. Looking forward to seeing you then. Lots of love.'

I have to be away from here, long gone before John and the family get back. This I know. If Jake is here, he will follow. The phone rings suddenly, making me jump. I cannot answer it. I cannot. I wait until the machine clicks on. I wait for Jake's peachy, insidious voice to fill every corner of the kitchen. But there is only silence and the click of a phone being replaced. Who else but Jake would ring here at two o'clock in the morning?

I have to tell my body what to do. I make a mug of tea. I go upstairs and change my clothes, pull on old blue jeans and an enormous sweater of John's. I pack some things into my small rucksack. I try not to look at the neat bed, my hot-water bottle under the covers, books on the pillow, water on the bedside table. The message is clear. He always did all these things for me when he had beaten me up.

There is no doubt in my mind that Jake means to kill me. Matt was punishment only, far more effective than killing me first. That would have been too easy. I would not have suffered enough.

I go back down to the kitchen. I go to the rack on the wall where John keeps his cooking knives and I select the sharp one he always carves with. I take it to the twins' room, clamber up on to the top bunk and climb under the duvet covered in small rabbits.

I lie there in the dark and wait.

Chapter 21

I lie in Hanna's top bunk with her little mushroom lamp on. It is comforting lying in a child's bed, being in a child's room. The small lamp glimmers and casts shadows on the dolls' house, the box of dolls and toys; the Beatrix Potter books and brightly coloured children's paintings on the walls. The sea is like thunder as it crashes down viciously on the beach below Huer's Cottage.

I lie very still, as if to move would hurt, would be impossible. Some part of me still hopes I have just woken from another recurring nightmare, that I will wake up with such relief that it is only a dream. I think about the times I have peered in at the relaxed, sleeping children, taking comfort in their safety, their sweet just-bathed smell.

I think of the horror of Jake looking down at them. I know that he did not come while they were here, but I am suddenly so aware of what he is capable of. The implication of my flight from Dartmoor suddenly seems like a pack of cards collapsing horribly inwards.

The knife is under my pillow, but I do not really believe the shadow will come here tonight. He has punished me, hurt me far more this way. If he does come, I do not care if I use the knife on him or he on me. It really does not matter.

I lie, listening to my own breathing in the glow of the lamp, and Hanna and Amy's voices fill the room.

'Kirsty Farmer's mother died in a car accident.'

'I know. Miss Polenski cried and so did Mrs Brownlow.'

'Will Kirsty come back to school?'

''Spect so, but how will she manage without a mummy? I couldn't live without Mummy.'

'I couldn't either. I couldn't live without Mummy or Daddy.'

'No . . . Poor Kirsty. But she's got her daddy.'

'Yes . . . Hanna, nothing'll happen to Mummy or Daddy, will it?'

'Course not, silly. Let's put the telly on. I don't want to talk about it any more . . .'

I must make sure they are all safe. I must leave first thing in the morning. I will leave a letter. I will get a taxi to meet them all at Penzance station tomorrow. I must draw Jake away from this house. I am the cause of two deaths already.

What made Jake pick me, single me out amongst all the other women at university? There were so many interesting and talented women students. What imbalance did he immediately perceive in me that would respond to his needs, perhaps mirror his own?

Could he really have murdered Dan to get to me? Why did it never occur to me before, in the face of his obsessional behaviour? Or was it an aberration, a sudden drunken whim on Dan's part, that made him take drugs, just once, and enabled me to drop into Jake's lap, giving him the idea for Matt's murder?

I try to conjure up Dan's face and his voice, but they belong to another life I lived long ago, when I was a quite different person. But, as I lie in the dark, I suddenly remember his shout of laughter, his love of rowing and rugby and all sports, and I realize how simply impossible it was that he would kill himself. Impossible not to admit to myself that Jake killed Dan in the same way he has just killed Matt.

It is terrifying, this sudden understanding. I have always been aware of his cruelty, his ability to hurt. But murder?

I hear Jake's slippery voice. 'Darling, I have to tell you, you really do have the most weird imagination. Is it childhood stuff, something hereditary, that makes you such a paranoid personality?'

'Jake, I am not paranoid. You really did say that.'

'I happen to love you. Why on earth would I say something like that?'

'I don't know.'

'I know you don't, sweetie. Come here. I'll hold you and hug you. You are fine here with me. I'll always, always look after you, you know that. But would it be an idea, do you think, for you to see a psychologist, darling, with this history of your mother's mental illness?'

'She was not mental. She just suffered from bouts of terrible depression.'

'Clinical depression is an illness, my love, that's what worries me. Why I was so concerned for you when Dan died.'

'You twist everything, as if you want me – are willing me – wishing me mad.'

'And you, my darling, assure me you are not paranoid. I rest my case!'

Oh God. Those terrible, circular conversations. He got a real buzz pushing me to the edge, watching my fear. Once I had shown it, he would change to being loving and kind. He would stress how much he enjoyed my company. He would ask my opinion on his work. He would charm me and everybody else with his witty observations. He would make me laugh about the idiosyncrasy of various well-known painters we knew, and the preciousness of the two partners who ran his gallery.

He would take me up to London, fly me for a weekend to Paris. Surprise me with another trip to Venice just because I was spell-bound by the place. He would take me to wonderful exhibitions, where he patiently explained and taught me about obscure Italian painters, fired me with his knowledge and enthusiasm.

Those were the times I believed, in the middle of many nights, that I was the one with a screw loose ever to have doubts about this attractive, vibrant, loving and popular man.

Huer's Cottage seems very still tonight, as if it is hushed and listening too, not to the familiar creaks and whispers of the night, but for noises and sounds which might disturb the laughter of the twins, caught in a drift of their mobiles or floating abstractly in falling dust motes. I seem to carry my ghosts with me.

In the early hours I doze, but a part of me cannot sleep, is still and alert to every sound. I know that Jake might well be on the flight back to Cyprus, but I also know there are internal flights back into Newquay and Exeter.

If my mother had taken me back to Norway I would be safe now. Why wouldn't she? Why wouldn't she make me safe?

My whole childhood seemed to be listening for clues. Neither of my parents ever talked to me; everything seemed to go on behind closed doors. I learnt to try to find out for myself.

Every month or so my parents had a dinner party for the people who worked for or with my father. It always surprised me that my mother could throw off her inertia and plan so precisely what they would eat and who came.

She was immensely house-proud, obsessively so. She spent hours lovingly polishing the furniture, changing the position of a vase of flowers, so perhaps these dinner parties were a chance for her to show off her home to people.

I noticed that at these times my parents always seemed happier; they were connecting and doing something together. They spoke to each other more.

Hearing the music I would sometimes creep down the stairs and watch for a while through the door. I would see the beautifully laid table I had helped my mother lay. I would see the people sitting round it chatting and laughing. I would see my mother and father and I would not recognize them. It was as if I had pushed the door open on to a life they had that I did not know even existed.

There was this tall, dark, good-looking man with his arm thrown over a beautiful pale woman with her long fair hair caught up in a slide. The woman wore a grey woollen cashmere dress, a sort of grey-green like a winter sea, with a leather belt showing off her tiny waist. Her painful thinness, disguised under that dress, made my mother look like a model and I would notice everyone looking at her.

My father, looking down on her, had pride in his eyes. Or was it love? Was it? In front of people it was safe for my mother to acknowledge it and she would smile lovingly up at him. Or were they just both playing happy families to an audience?

I would go back to bed and lie in the warmth of laughter and voices, and wonder if it was like this all the time in some homes. It was such a great feeling, as if the world was full of people liking and chatting to each other. Talking. And yet as the people filed out of the front door, so did the laughter and the music, the affection and the safe feeling in the house.

The next day all would be exactly as it always was. Silent.

Once, I came down the stairs because I heard my father's voice. They were both sitting at the kitchen table facing each other. My father was begging my mother to stay. I had never heard him sound like that before. He reached out for her hand and she did not pull it away. She stared as him as if trying to come to a decision.

'I need you,' he said. 'Please, Kristian . . . Please don't leave . . .'

So, my mother never took me home.

I think of John and Beth living down here in Cornwall, trying so hard to give the twins, and the new baby to come, a safe and secure family life, a childhood to look back on. I think of Virginia Woolf's father discovering St Ives on a walking holiday, discovering Talland House, built for nobody knows who, by the Great Western Railway.

I think of long journeys from London. Safe and secure summers. Blackberries and Cornish cream. Narrow little streets, seagulls screaming, the sound of the sea. Talland House, like 'a child's drawing', the garden broken up into rooms, filled with visitors . . . Thoby sailing a small boat in the bay. All safe and happy. All to be snatched away so suddenly and cruelly. Because that is life. I think of the twins and I ache with anxiousness and the need to protect them from anything that might change or still their laughter.

Night is slowly fading and I sense the colours of a new day. Through the open bedroom door, out of the landing window, the harbour lies below me, a myriad tiny lights. The wind is bending the small trees in the garden seaward. Flurries of rain hit the windows, which rattle like teeth. It feels like being alone on the bridge of a ship at sea. Or the last person in the world after a holocaust.

I see two small children in long white nightdresses stand by the window, staring out to sea. So still, watching the yellow lights like a rash of fireflies on the far promontory. A breeze lifts wisps of hair away from their faces as if the window is open.

Beyond them, I hear the soft chug-chug of the fishing boats heading out into the dark sea. The smaller child turns and looks at me with huge, sad dark eyes, caught in profile, merging in my mind into the adult photo of Virginia Woolf like a jerky echo.

The room is full of firelight, the flames flickering on fading wallpaper, and the older child takes the smaller one to the fire and they sit there together in front of a high fireguard, heads close, whispering, as if they should be sleeping. And the whispers of the children reach me, soothing and happy as the sound of the sea, the sound of the wind in the fir trees ... Virginia and Vanessa ... Hanna and Amy, still safe in childhood.

I close my eyes, warmed by that firelight and the rise and flow of secretive childish whispers, as if I live for a moment, wistfully, caught in the cobweb of their companionship, their long-ago childhood where things can be shared, written, talked about. Cornwall ... families ... summers which never end. Amy and Hanna ... Vanessa and Virginia ... I sleep, folded for moments in an illusion of safety, as if I might escape into another time and place in which I can begin again.

At dawn I get up and make tea. I watch the sky lighten in a thin band of red and navy blue, and I hear and see the comforting chug of the fishing boats heading in and out of the harbour in a sort of marine rush hour. The wind has dropped and the world seems suddenly stilled. I get dressed. I write a letter to Beth and John and leave it on the kitchen table. I fetch my rucksack and leave the cottage.

I walk slowly down the steps and into the road, peering in at the shadows of trees in the front gardens, but despite the jerking of my heart, nothing moves, nothing detaches itself away from the deep greenness of shrubs and becomes alive and threatening.

I walk down the path to the beach. I stand with a flood tide behind me, and turn and look back beyond the road to the top of the hill where I can glimpse the strange balconies of Talland House. A house that began to wrap itself round me, full of a kaleidoscope of juggling memories, happy and complex.

I have that sense of leaving. I think of all the people who came before me and who will come after me down the years and stay in that house. Stand with Beth by the fire in the drawing room and talk excitedly and discover more and more about lives lived there over the years. People who laughed and cried and put the world to rights.

I look up at the windows and it is as if I see the ghost of myself on the balcony, a flit of sunlight, a glance of shadow, an insubstantial movement of a branch of a tree in the garden.

Someone or no one. Just one more short memory, like the displacement of a falling petal or a sigh.

A movement of a shutter, the soft closing of a door.

Chapter 22

I take the coastal path away from St Ives towards Carbis Bay and Lelant. Larks rise up from the grass in front of me, diving and warbling, afraid I might tread on their nests.

I walk fast with the lighthouse in front of me and the stretch of sea changing colour as the sun rises. I do not know where I'm going or what I'm going to do, only that I must cover a great distance between myself and Beth and John.

The morning is beautiful, the day slowly unfurling. The path is steep, and I am still unfit and my breath comes in little puffs against the sound of birds and the dripping of the trees, and my footsteps making slippery marks on the muddy path.

The new leaves on the trees are the palest translucent green, and the sun shines through them, slanting in dancing particles on to the damp ground full of last year's mould. The smell of decaying leaves rises under my feet, strong in my nostrils.

Matt should be here to see this day. He should be walking here with Alice. There is an anguish inside me that is frozen. I know that Matt is dead, but something in me cannot bear to believe it. There is such a fear and loneliness inside me. Such dread of what lies ahead. John and Beth seem very far away.

I try to block out the memory of Matt lying dead on a rumpled bed. Block out the reality, making it into a nightmare that is not really true. But it is true and it hits me again on the path, in the first light of this new day, and I cry out with the sheer unreal horror of it and the sound rises up and mingles with the larks hovering like humming bees above the wet grass.

However much I twist and turn, Matt is dead because of me.

Because of me. I hear his voice, like I once heard Dan's, full of life and laughter. I see the movement of his muscular, fit body riding high on the waves in ecstasy. I see his dark eyes smiling at me with love and amusement. I remember the way his hair, streaked by the sun, blew away from his tanned face.

He had everything to live for in his life and his paintings. Oh, how can he be gone? How can he, on a day like this, so beautiful it catches in my throat, how can he be dead? His body, slack and cold, will never again rise up on the curl of a wave. Up, up, skyward, to sail in, exhilarated, bursting with joy and energy.

Words rise in me like an endless lament. All those things we meant to say to each other will never be spoken. We were just beginning, Matt and I. He was my friend, such a good friend, and I had another chance to love. I should have stood away. I should never have let him get involved with me. I should have kept it cool. Then he would be here now.

He was right that day on the beach when he said he was afraid of getting hurt. His instincts were right, just not in the way he thought.

He knew I wasn't free to love him. But it was impossible not to, and the knowledge made me want to dance and sing and long to tell him.

Oh, Matt, I thought I could make a life in St Ives . . . paint, have you and Beth. But we can never listen, hold or touch one another again. I can never smell the salt on your skin, watch your fingers paint, sigh with the sudden completeness of knowing you. It is over, gone for ever.

Nothing that happens to me now matters. I do not want to be safe. I have no right to be safe. I want to suffer as Matt suffered. It is only fair. I need to understand my guilt. My guilt in marrying and loving Jake. My responsibility for what has happened to two men I loved.

I stop on the path suddenly, wavering. I must turn back. I am conscious of behaving irrationally. I am running blindly this way and that, in order to mitigate something I have no control over. I don't really know where Jake is. I must think. I want Beth and John and the girls safe, but I should turn and face the police again. I should make them listen. Acknowledge what I fear, what I believe. I don't know. I don't know what to do.

146

I make my way back to the deserted early morning beach and sit in a corner by the rocks and watch the sun rise up in the sky and make an orange wake in the dark sea. I will wait. I will wait for an hour or so.

After a while, as I sit there, above the sound of the waves, I hear a strange, distant chattering coming down towards me, and suddenly a little procession of large middle-aged women in shorts and carrying small rucksacks appears down the coastal path.

I stand there and stare because it is still very early and the impression is surreal as they turn the corner of the path and reach the beach.

I hear the chug of an engine and turn to see a small motor boat heading from the harbour towards the beach. The women call out and wave and the boatman waves back. Perhaps they are from a cruise liner going back to their ship.

The first women have reached the edge of the water and are taking their shoes off. A large, dark woman smiles at me. She wears bright pink shorts and a red tee shirt.

'Hi, there,' she says. 'Timed absolutely right, huh? What a day for it. Like a mill pond!'

She is American. I nod dumbly without replying. The small boat reaches the shallows and the boatman jumps out and pulls it as near as he can, calling out to the women to come aboard.

Excited as children, they laugh and chatter, paddle in the shallows, hand each other belongings, heave themselves over the side of the small boat. Never for a moment do they stop talking. I watch amazed to see if they can all fit in.

They do, and as I watch the large dark woman calls out to me, 'Come on then, honey, the littlest last. All aboard for the lighthouse!'

It is then I notice they are wearing Ohio University, Harvard, University of Utah sweatshirts. They are Woolfies. They are some of Beth and John's Woolfies.

I hesitate only for a moment, then the thought of company and escape proves too strong. I wade into the shallows and climb aboard. The boatman grins at me over their heads.

147

'Hi, honey, I'm Maria,' the lady in pink says. 'I've organized this little Vir-gin-i-a Wooolf weekend. You must be from the tourist board. Now Daisy, over there, she is our world living expert on Virg-in-i-a Wooolf, so do you mind if she reads a little passage from *To the Lighthouse* as we leave the shore?'

I open my mouth to tell her I am not from the tourist board but no one is listening. They are all looking up towards Talland House. Daisy, the world living expert on V.W., is a striking-looking woman with her great thick, dark plait.

She stands up tall in the prow of the small boat, wearing, like a wonderful figurehead thrown up by the sea, primrose shorts and a purple sweatshirt. The tide on the turn, is pulling us out of the bay as fast as the idling engine would have done.

'For the great plateful of blue water was before her; the hoary Lighthouse, distant, austere, in the midst; and on the right, as far as the eye could see, fading and falling, in soft low pleats, the green sand dunes with the wild flowering grasses on them, which always seemed to be running away into some moon country, uninhabited of men . . .'

Daisy cries from the front of the boat, holding her battered Penguin paperback high.

'Daisy is a Sioux Indian,' the lady next to me whispers, proudly. 'A very clever lady indeed.'

The small boat turns and heads out to sea. I have a sudden, desperate desire to burst into hysterical laughter. It is so strong it could overtake me like tears and I bite my lip. I find the whole thing bizarre, like a dream sequence. A Sioux Indian, living a billion miles away in another culture is the world's living expert on Virginia Woolf. Brilliant, but strange.

'Over there, on the hill, that glimpse of white? That is the house where Virginia Woolf spent much of her childhood. Imagine . . . her view of this bay. Imagine the family on the beach. Imagine Virginia, Vanessa, Thoby, Adrian . . . on the balcony looking down on us! Later, we hope to make a visit there and see inside the house. The young lady from the tourist board is goin' to try and organize it for us.'

Daisy nods at me, her voice is being drowned by the engine. 'Right, now . . . to the lighthouse.' She points out to sea like a captain of a marauding pirate ship about to attack.

They settle in the small boat, earnestly marking places in their books and missing altogether the precise view Virginia saw on sailing to the lighthouse. They talk loudly in flurries and flutters. Two iron-grey women next to me, diffident and academic, gently try to top each other with their separate areas of research and reference.

There is something immensely endearing and unworldly about these women, with their knowledge and their excitement and rivalry in their own expertise. They remind me of my grandmother. Her generation seem so focused, so totally sure of themselves. They don't go in for self-doubt or introspection. Morals are absolute.

They talk about the influence the sudden death of Virginia's mother had on her fragile mental state. They wonder whether, if her bouts of mental illness had been treated, as they would have been now, with modern antidepressant drugs, whether it would have limited her genius.

I listen as they discuss her hallucinations and the drugs she was given with the result that it was difficult to determine which were the effects of her treatment and which were her own delusions. I absorb their words with the familiarity of an icy hand touching me. They discuss the distance family and friends inevitably make between someone who is mentally ill and themselves, forever increasing that shrinking feeling of isolation and despair.

I look down into the water flowing past the boat, dark and mysterious as night. Moving sinuously, like the body of a huge restless, green-flecked mammal. I listen to the voices rise and fall around me and my guilt rises up out of the water to haunt me.

I let my mother die. I let her slip down and away as coldly as if I had held her head under the waves. I shiver under my sweater and grief rises up in me, so overpowering, that I raise my shoulders to contain the breadth of it.

It explodes inside me like a burst of silver rain. I cry without sound. I cry without tears. I fight to keep the sound in, with my eyes firmly on the white lighthouse getting nearer and nearer with the sun shining fiercely on it.

Someone lays a gentle hand on the small of my back. And keeps it there. Fingers splay in a tiny movement over my spine until I have gained control. Then the hand is left there, a small reminder of the comfort of unexpected human contact.

I suddenly realize I am exhausted. I cannot remember when I last ate and the motion of the boat is making me want to sleep. We circle the lighthouse twice as I struggle to stay awake. Cormorants sit on the black rocks in rows like little old men, and stare back at us as we bob up and down in the choppy sea.

The noise of the engine begins to drown the murmur of women reading. I am giddy with the movement of the boat, purple and pink sweatshirts, bright ankle socks, and a sea of earnest grey heads. I wonder what Virginia would make of it.

The boatman grins at me and indicates it is time to turn back for St Ives. I turn to look behind me at the woman whose hand has been on my back. She smiles, meeting my eyes for a moment. She is a slight woman and I did not notice her getting on the boat.

I stare at her. I don't know if it's deliberate, but her dark, greying hair is pulled back into an old-fashioned bun so that she looks just like Beresford's picture of Virginia Woolf, the one I love in the drawing room of Talland House.

I turn away, again thrown into that strange, surreal dreamlike feeling. Rather as if I have been caught up in some extravagant practical joke.

Being with these content and intelligent women, who devote their lives to the literary past with such passion, makes me suddenly aware of the value of life. I don't want to die. I want to live, very much.

I long for sleep, I long for my own bed and the familiarity of my room, untouched by Jake. For the cottage filled with Beth and John's things. I am afraid to stay, but I am afraid to run too. I feel like a rabbit caught in the headlights, making small useless dives this way and that.

We all get out of the boat and stand on the still-deserted beach, a bright collection of women on a morning after a storm where the light is fragile and the sun lies as if behind a layer of muslin, making the surface of the sea an ethereal, water-washed green-grey.

On the horizon there lies a mass of dark cloud, like a bruise.

I make sure the women have both Beth's telephone numbers and I assure them she will be happy to take them round over the weekend. They call out their goodbyes, and turn and troop across the beach and up the steps to the coastal path, back to their hotel at Carbis Bay and breakfast. I watch them go until the last colourful figure disappears from sight, a strange, exotic procession.

I smile as I see them in my head moving excitedly through Talland House. Wandering through the kitchen, hall, drawing room and downstairs bedroom, exclaiming over the extraordinary view. Every woman, steeped in Woolf, seeing and feeling something different; in the photos, in the shadows and doorways and large windows, full of drifting, diffused light of Talland House.

I will go back now and phone the police. I won't even wait until nine thirty. This positive feeling that I am doing the right thing won't last. Why? Why am I so full of dread about doing what I should have done last night?

Because Matt's death will then be real. You won't be able to pretend it has not happened. You were so good at that as a child, weren't you? Pretending. So bloody good you could almost convince yourself.

I walk slowly from the beach up the hill and turn into the road to Huer's Cottage. I find my key in the small pocket of my rucksack and run up the steps and go inside and drop my bag by the phone.

The answerphone light is flashing. Tentatively I push the button.

Beth's voice fills the hall. 'Just give me a ring on this number, Si, will you? I'm sure you are all right, but it is odd that you are never anywhere when we ring. We can't get hold of Matt either . . . Anyway, darling, we've missed you. See you later . . .' Her voice is anxious.

Beth. Oh, Beth.

Suddenly, sickeningly, my heart lurches. I can smell cigarette smoke. In the china saucer on the windowsill is a small black cigarette end. Oh God! I have made a mistake. I should not have come back.

Frantically, I reach for the phone. Is he still here? Is he upstairs?

I hear myself making little desperate whimpering noises as I try to dial 999.

I feel, rather than see, the black shape that hurls itself from the kitchen and knocks the phone from my hand. I go flying in a strange slow motion and crash to the floor.

'Not a good idea, my darling. Not at all a good idea.' He stands looking down at me. His voice is as soft and dark as night. I stare back, hypnotized. He bends slowly to me and lifts me up off the floor. He bundles me into my jacket and picks up my rucksack. He opens the front door, peers down the empty street and pulls me down the steps and out into the road.

He stops for a moment and holds my face close to his, whispers, 'I don't think either of us will be on the wanted list quite yet, my darling, but don't think about shouting, or making any sound at all to anyone we might meet.' Out of his pocket he takes a syringe. 'There is enough stuff in here to kill a herd of elephants. You will die in absolute agony.' Gently, he kisses my mouth, pulls the hood of my jacket up. It is the casual, disinterested way he says this that chills me to the bone. He twines his arms around me and moves fast, practically lifting me off my legs down the hill. Fast, fast towards the coastal path.

Past the shut and deserted beach café, up the narrow path the Woolfies took, he does not speak. After a minute a terrible anger makes me brave. 'You killed him. You killed Matt . . . My God, you act as if nothing had happened . . . Why . . . why couldn't you just take me, without killing Matt?'

He pulls me on, up where the path forks and then widens at the backs of the large houses whose gardens lean down to the sea. 'Sigrid, I did not kill your boyfriend. I went to warn him off. After all, he was sleeping with my wife. He was preparing his fix when I arrived. I merely socked him one and tore up his bad painting of you, and left. If you will keep getting mixed up with druggies, darling—'

'You're lying!' My voice is shaking so much it sounds as if it is coming from underwater. 'I know you are lying. Why pretend to fly back to Cyprus? Why say you were at your mother's funeral if you didn't kill Matt?'

'I was at my mother's funeral. I am not supposed to come near you, remember? Who would believe me? I buried my mother at ten o'clock in the morning. I left my confused and shocked old father and my uncle Jacob Watson with a bottle of whisky afterwards. And I saw them both on to the internal flight to Gatwick, bound for Cyprus . . . Keep walking, Si.'

He is doing what he always does. I am numb with a terrible tiredness and need to sleep. He pulls me past the new villas perched on the cliffs, all windows facing the sea, protected by huge firs bent by the wind. Houses with their backs to me. Past the Balking House where the huer sounded his horn long ago, when the shoals of pilchards appeared, swift-moving shadows under the sea.

I suddenly feel faint and dizzy. I feel my legs give way, feel I am going to faint. Jake pulls me into the shelter of the Balking House, sits me on the wooden bench and pushes my head between my knees.

'You've had it, haven't you? You need food and sleep. Plan B, I think. Come on, not far now.' He sounds concerned. In front of me the roof of a bungalow stretches out flatly towards the sea and shimmers like a layer of tarmac. There is the isolating clack-clack of palms in the wind. In the distance the lighthouse lies surrounded by frothy white waves.

We move back on to the path. The small train chugs past, hiding the sea for a moment. A man passes us, walking his dog, and Jake calls good morning, but the walker hardly glances at us. The path separates again and Jake takes the left path down towards the cliffs.

Perched amongst trees is a drive to a small bungalow and Jake takes me down it. 'Horrible bungalow, wonderful position. Owned by a friend of mine, the painter I'm sharing an exhibition with, actually. Been very useful. I was going to take you straight home, but I think you need food and sleep first and travelling in the dark might be sensible.'

He takes out a key from under a small boulder and pushes me inside, into the one large downstairs room with a bay window and window seats facing the sea. He pulls my coat off and throws it over a chair, lights a gas fire. He sits me down and goes away and I hear him put the kettle on and come back.

I lean back and close my eyes, which feel as if they are full of sawdust and impossible to keep open. My hair has come loose and lies like a shawl over my face and shoulders. I would like to draw it like a curtain.

'I am going to make you tea and toast, then I will put you to bed. After you have slept you will feel better.'

He bends and moves my hair from my eyes. I open them without hope. 'I had almost forgotten how very beautiful you are, even when you are afraid.' His voice is tender. He lights up another cigarette and hands it to me. I take it, take a huge dizzying sickening inhalation of tobacco, and watch him.

He sits down opposite me, his strange violet eyes drinking me in. His fair hair flops over his eyes, his perfect, even white teeth smile at me like a fading, debauched film star.

I had almost forgotten how beautiful he was too. It makes evil so much harder to believe. I shiver. I begin to shiver uncontrollably. I am frightened. I am as frightened of myself as much as Jake. I am shrinking. Soon I will become servile with cowardice.

He reaches out and covers my hand with his own tapered fingers. He whispers. He whispers like a sigh, a breath on my face, so gentle I hardly hear it. 'Oh, darling . . . darling – my own special girl. What are we going to do, you and I? We can't live without each other, can we?'

Silence. Just the sound of our breathing. His and mine. Slowly, he gets up and lifts me up tenderly as if I were glass, holds me into his body to stop the terrible shaking, carries me away, away to a bedroom.

I can't fight, Too tired. Too afraid. I can't take any more. Please, God, no more.

The shadow has got me.

Mama, Mama. Help me.

Chapter 23

There is the sound of running water. *There is the sound of water running.*

He is having a bath. *He is having a shower.*

It is very dark in the room.

It is so dark.

He has closed tight my butterfly curtains.

The moon is behind dark velvet clouds.

Behind the butterfly curtains are rooftops spread out like a map.

This is where I fly.

Beyond the cliffs, on the oil-smooth shiny sea, lights begin to blink like glow-worms, small candles in the night.

No, Daddy. No.

Please, Jake. Don't, don't.

Mum. Mama.

Mother, who does not hear.

Jake is whistling. Outside the day is ending in a misty pale yellow over a dark grey sea, ruffled like birds' feathers. I have no idea what time it is, only that I slept as if I had died. And dreamt. My head aches and my mouth is dry. Jake comes into the room and puts a tray down with tea and toast. He does not switch the light on.

'Sit up, Si. It's late. We have to get going, we should have gone long ago.' He sits on the bed, reaches out to touch my face. 'My sweet, you haven't been crying? How can you cry when we have made such wonderful love?'

He pours me tea, butters my toast, lifts my fingers to kiss them, holds them to his mouth. Leans forward. A whisper. A breath like a faint burn on my cheek. 'How I love it, Si, when you cry out, when I give you pleasure . . .'

'*Hush . . . hush, my wee girl. Don't make a noise. You mustn't make a noise. It's all right. You know your daddy loves you so, so much.*'

I had forgotten. You see I had forgotten. A cry in the dark means everything they want it to mean.

I thought it was all in my head.

Mummy says it is all in my head.

Daddy is a good person and I am a wicked, wicked little girl.

'Si? Don't look at me like that. I hate it when you look at me as if I was not there.'

He moves the tray and holds me, pulls me to him. 'I will make your nightmares go away again,' he says, 'like I did before. I am the only one who can, aren't I, my darling?'

'Yes,' I say. 'Yes.'

'Eat. Come, I will feed you like a fledgeling . . . You must eat. You must be strong for me and then we will make plans . . .'

'*You must eat, you can't go to school without your breakfast, Sigrid. I am beginning to get bored with this every morning . . .*'

'Si, don't gag . . . You must swallow . . . chew . . . chew, drink your tea . . .'

'I want to have a bath . . . please.'

'No time . . . One more mouthful – good girl.'

'Please, Jake. I'll be quick.'

'I'll run it for you, like I always do.'

I lie in the deep hot water. I scrub and scrub my body, all of it. I wash carefully everywhere. Then again and again until I am clean.

In Venice, in that beautiful shabby villa with the peeling paint and the sound of water and the faded colours that shivered like soft silver inside me day and night, making me ache with wanting to paint again, Jake whispered one night, 'Tell me your secrets. Tell me what you have never told a living soul, ever. Tell me the dark maps of your mind.'

'I don't have any dark secrets. I told you I was boring, Jake. I had a dull, uneventful, quite happy middle-class childhood.'

'I don't think so.'

'Wanting me to be mysterious, doesn't make me so.'

He leans towards me. 'Why does your body know what your mind does not?'

I am startled. 'What do you mean?'

'Did you make love like this with Dan?'

'Well . . . not the same, he . . .'

'Was not experienced?'

'No.'

'But he was your first?'

'Yes. Yes, he was. What . . .'

'Then, darling, how do you know so much? How does your body automatically turn, adjust, move for a man, in the way you have just done, if you have never—' He stops as he sees my genuine bewilderment, stares at me, then laughs shortly. 'Sorry, darling, obviously you are a natural little whore . . . My beautiful, my own little private, whore.'

After that the nightmares started. What I had carefully buried all my life surfaced slowly out of a muddy pool. Rose slowly but surely, bit by bit like pieces brought in by the tide and thrown randomly up on the beach.

I learnt to relax and turn my body to avoid pain. Just as I learnt to make my mind fly free to snowfields and blue-tipped mountains. But passivity can be taken for compliance. Inertia mistaken for enjoyment.

I had a tutor once, who came to the house to teach me because I had glandular fever. My mother had gone back to Norway to help nurse my grandfather, who had been seriously ill.

This woman said suddenly, before she left, not looking at me, packing her books and belongings in an old holdall, 'I hope I'm wrong, child. But if I'm not – bury all remembrance deep as you can. Keep it as well covered as a body in a coffin. Never, ever air it to anyone. Never let acknowledgement of it surface for a second, even to yourself.

'It never happened. It happened to someone else, a friend, anyone. You will be away very soon, have your own life. Tell yourself, over and over, the happy but dull story of your childhood. Over and over until you believe it, until it becomes true.

'If I'm wrong, you won't know what I am talking about. If I'm right, do as I say and you will survive. Believe me, you can reinvent your childhood. You are a bright girl.

She was wrong. You can. You can reinvent your childhood for a long time, but slowly cracks will appear that grow wider and wider and memory leaks out and coats you with the truth.

I expect she found that out too.

There are always men or women like Jake, who specialize in prising cracks open so that a person can become exclusively, wholly theirs. That is how they thrive and grow strong and happy. On other people's dark secrets.

I get out of the bath quickly as I hear Jake moving about. I feel as if I have flu or I am moving through water.

I dry myself, see Jake has put some clean underclothes out. He is going to eat me up again. I want to cry out at the thought of him taking my things from the airing cupboard at Huer's Cottage. Riffling amongst Beth's jeans, John's shirts and the numbers of small pairs of shorts and tee shirts lying unironed on the shelf.

It seems like another life since we were all together.

I look in the mirror, I plait my hair. I see that my face is changing once more. Jake will rub out my features. I will become the anodyne, expressionless, appeasing person who lived in that Dartmoor cottage all those years.

I rub the steam from the bathroom window and look out on to a copse of trees. The sun is sliding away and in a while a Cornish mist will descend. I hurry back into the one main room in case I have been too long, and it suddenly seems to me as if I have carried the essence of that biddable anxious girl Jake married inside me all the time, buried only in a shallow grave, resurrecting herself now to conciliate, to avoid being hurt. She moves ahead of me a fleeting shadow, a sly glimpse, a mirror image. A horrible clone of what I became.

A dull but powerful anger resurrects itself inside me like a heartbeat.

Jake stands with his back to me, looking out of the window, smoking a cigarette, watching the sun fade like a burnished coin into the sea. There are a little pile of coats on the sofa, and the smell of coffee. He turns as he hears me. 'I would love to spend time painting here.' He goes to fetch me coffee and then looks at his watch. He no longer seems angry, but mellowed by the last burnt colours of the day. I take my chance.

'Jake, please, let me go back to Beth and John. What good is this going to do? Or do you really mean to kill me?'

Jake slowly puts his mug on the table. I know that suddenly closed face and I am silent. I must be very still. He lights yet another cigarette. He says so quietly I can hardly hear him, 'You, of all people, who know me better than anyone, believe I am not capable of killing you? Oh, I will kill you, Sigrid, I will kill you. Then I expect I will kill myself. But first I want a little time with you. Just you and me. Just us, together, like it used to be.'

The light is behind him. I can no longer see his face, which is merging into the dying day, but I catch the angry glitter of his eyes. It is useless to appeal to someone who has lost all rationale. The rain hits the window in a sudden angry little burst.

Why did he risk coming back, when he has taken so much effort to cover his tracks? A few hundred yards away people walk the coastal path, live in the surrounding houses. Such a small distance away. It doesn't make sense. Why didn't he just grab me and run like he is doing now, if he was not going to kill me straight away? Why kill Matt?

Because Matt was punishment for loving me. Or perhaps Jake did not really intend to kill Matt, but lost his temper.

Jake, watching me, says suddenly, 'I came back to fetch my wife. Sometimes it is better to do exactly what people don't expect you to do. Be in the last place people will look. Remember, darling, *I* am not a murderer. It was you who ran from the scene of a suspicious death . . .' He laughs and stubs his cigarette out.

I am incensed. 'It's just a game to you – life, everything. You don't care who gets hurt. You don't even care about yourself, do you? You feel nothing . . .'

Jake comes closer. Something changes in his eyes, a fleeting expression of pain, surprise – I can't tell. He says quietly, 'That's what makes a psychopath, isn't it, darling? Get your coat and shoes on. Get your rucksack and take out what isn't necessary. I've got most things you need. Hurry up, I want to get going.'

I pull my jacket on. 'Where are we going?'

'Home.'

'To the cottage?'

'No, to my mother's house, Sigrid. To *our* house.'

'Your parents' house on Dartmoor? Isn't someone renting it?'

'Not *their* house.' He laughs the laugh that always scares me more than anything.

I wonder how I can play for more time. I don't want to leave this house so near the coastal path. But Jake is right behind me and I can feel him anxious to be gone. I put my things back in my rucksack while he watches, then he pulls me out of the door and jerks up the hood of my jacket, and his own. We could be anybody walking at dusk.

The rain blows in a steady drizzle and there is no one on the path. We move on towards Carbis Bay; we will be soaked before we get there. The sound of the wind and the thunder of the sea on a flood tide drowns all sounds except our breathing. The waves crashing on to the rocks below us terrify me as we move down towards the cliff path.

'Where are we going?' I scream at him. 'For God's sake . . .' I pull away from him, turn back to safety.

He slaps me hard. 'I am not going to drown you, you silly bitch, but I warn you, I will kill you if you try to get away. I will kill you, Sigrid, as easily as I killed your boyfriend.'

He pulls me on and up into the darkness of the narrow coastal path, along the backs of the large houses where there are glimmers of light behind curtains drawn against the night. A thrush flies low into the undergrowth, squawking anxiously and the smell of damp rises up from last year's wet leaves.

It is so silent here at dusk, but beautiful, even in the rain. Pink and white rhododendrons grow over Cornish walls covered in ivy, and huge firs make dark bridges over the path. The bottom of the gardens belonging to the large Victorian houses up on the road, sold gradually over the years, now house a smattering of expensive, select, architect-designed houses set in the trees, perched along the coastline, private and aloof and somehow deserted as if waiting for summer. Their gardens are full of daffodils and dying snowdrops.

The path narrows and becomes muddy, and we slip and slide, following the railway line. Jake pushes me in front of him and we pass through an iron kissing gate. Startlingly, I suddenly remember walking with my father down the narrow paths of the estate for which he was Agent, back in Scotland. There were gates like these and the squawking and swoop of small birds in the shubbery.

I remember the sound of those songbirds and my anxiousness, as I listened to the firing of guns, that no small bird would be shot by mistake. I only went to a shoot once, to prove to my father that I was as good as a boy. I wasn't, and I cried as those flying brown and flashing colours were blown out of the sky.

In the dark of a wood, someone handed me two dead birds, still warm, and told me to carry them by their necks. They were nearly as big as I was. I hesitated, then saw my father watching me with a smile on his face and so I held out my hand and those soft broken necks were placed between my fingers.

I looked down on turquoise and green, brown and red, shiny glowing feathers, soft as velvet. I looked down on small hooded brown eyes. I felt the warmth of their lives in my hands, but no heartbeat.

I carried them back without a word, even when they grew heavy as lead, to show my father I was as good as a boy. In the dusk no one saw I was crying. Through the kissing gates, along the paths with a sun and a moon in the sky, freezing cold, to the gamekeeper's house where they were taken from me and draped in a pile on the wall like limp piles of clothing, necks dangling, colours fading as fast as the day. Cock and hen pheasants, duck, woodcock. Grounded for ever.

While my father drank whisky in a hot room with a roaring log fire, I went outside and was sick behind a tree. I still cannot bear the feel of feathers, or velvet.

The small train from St Ives rattles past, lights on, following the coast line. It hoots as it rounds the bend, a comforting childhood sound. The last train of the day. As it disappears the sea glints in the darkness below me. I stare down at a lone brave fishing boat heading out into the weather, a small light on its mast.

Beth and John will be nearly home.

I must keep all this, all that has been safe and beautiful, clear in my head, so that I can walk here in my mind when I need to escape what Jake does to me.

In childhood, I often travelled to distant places: the V&A, the British Museum. To long sandy beaches, to the shops. I would go in my head to see Dirk Bogarde in an old version of *A Tale of Two Cities*. I would catch the little flat-bottomed ferry across the fjords to lie flat on my back in Grampie's forest in Norway, where the pines make you dizzy when you look skywards.

In my head I can always escape. In my head.

Jake is silent. Wherever I am being dragged, it will be somewhere isolated, in the middle of nowhere. Jake loves places devoid of people.

An old iron gate, peeling paint like lichen, stands open at the bottom of one of the long gardens. I want to leap away, run fast from Jake, up the long path to a house with lighted windows. I want to bang on the door and scream to be let in. But I am afraid. I do not want to be pumped full of drugs. I do not want to die in agony alone on a coastal path in the dark.

If someone came on the path, I might be braver. I might have time to call out and jerk free. But no one appears in the rain and the dusk. There is going to be no shout behind me, no sound of voices and running feet. No one can rescue me, no one has seen me or knows where I am.

And that is my fault.

A pigeon dives suddenly out of the trees with a flurry and crack of bending branches, and we both jump. Jake holds my arm tighter as we cross the railway line, up the steps and over the bridge into Carbis Bay.

Lights of houses appear, and the hotel where the American Woolfies told me they are staying comes into sight, as we emerge from the coastal path and pass in the shadow of the tall wall in front of the hotel.

It is odd to think of those women up there in lighted rooms. Jake turns down to the beach, to the deserted seasonal beach café and locked public lavatories and small concrete car park that face the small sheltered bay where in daylight people park and walk their dogs.

Everyone is inside. Children are home from school. Suppers are being cooked. Why on earth are we here? Jake pushes me towards an old Daihatsu, takes out a key and opens the door. 'My uncle's car. Obviously I couldn't use my own. Down here these four-tracks are as anonymous as a London taxi.'

He laughs and begins to take off my wet things, pulling the trousers hard over my shoes as if I were a child, then he pushes me inside the car.

When he has taken off his own wet clothes he throws them in the back, gets in the driver's seat and starts the engine to clear the windscreen. He reaches in his knapsack and brings out a flask. In his palm he has two pills which he holds out to me.

'What are they?'

'Just something to make you relax. Take them.'

'I don't want them.'

'Take them, Sigrid.'

'No, I don't want them. I won't try to get away, you don't have to drug me. I won't take them.'

'I want you to take these pills.'

'No.'

Jake brings his hand back and slaps me hard; my head hits the door frame with a crack. Tears spring to my eyes, but I do not make a sound. I take the pills, swallow them with the coffee. I stare out at the black sea breaking in little white waves on the beach. A safe family cove, bounded by houses and hotels.

No person or place is safe. It is so frightening. I think about the people who make sudden discoveries of terrifying deeds done by someone they love. Someone who might always have been gentle or good to them personally. How, how, do they accept the sudden random violence in someone they thought they knew?

I knew quite early on there was a line beyond which I couldn't reach Jake or understand the dark places in him. Yet something horribly perverse in me continued to love him in a feckless childlike hope that love would warm the sometimes icy cruelty of his heart and change him one day for ever into the laughing, happy, exciting man he often was. I thought it was only me he wanted to hurt, a blindness that has caused death.

Jake takes a swig of coffee and screws the top on. He gets out of the car and with his back to me, he unzips himself and pees away towards the sea. Gives that little shake men give and zips himself up again. This casual, forced intimacy triggers such fear and repugnance that I begin to tremble uncontrollably.

A polythene bag blows across the front of the car and away across the empty beach, white in the darkness.

I think of Matt. Is this going to be my last journey?

Chapter 24

As we drive out of Cornwall I think of Beth and John and the twins about to arrive home. I think about what they are coming back to. Matt suddenly, inexplicably dead. Mutton poisoned, fighting for his life. Huer's Cottage, disturbed. A place that is their home. A place where Jake has prowled and left cigarette ends. And me missing.

All they have ever been to me are loyal and wonderful friends.

By now the police will probably know it wasn't Jake on the plane to Cyprus. They will start looking for me. But I left a note to say I was leaving Cornwall, heading for London. My first instinct, of getting Jake right away from people I love, was right, though. How good he is at watching me.

When I think of the possibilities of John and Beth coming home early, and finding him in their house, I feel sick.

The rain is coming down hard now and beats against the car in gusts. The windscreen wipers, pills and noise of the engine are beginning to make me heavy with sleep. I look at Jake's face, as if I might judge exactly what he could be capable of. Pointless. His face is set, concentrating on the road, unaware of me or anyone. The face of a stranger.

I desperately want to keep awake so I can see where we are going, but I keep dozing, then coming awake with a jerk. We drive over the causeway and out on to the dual carriageway. Cornwall will soon lie behind me.

Everything feels so unreal, like one of my sick nightmares, the really bad ones, when the dream is so detailed and real, you believe you are awake. I want Beth to wake me and tell me all this is just a nightmare brought on by my fear of Jake.

He has swooped again like a vast, dark-winged bird and I am enclosed, once more incarcerated with him in claustrophobic mist and rain while the rest of life moves safely on elsewhere.

I cannot even catch a glimpse of people in the cars swishing past in the dark, steamed up, back lights disappearing in water spurting up from the road by the heavy rain.

Jake drives through this fierce rain with concentration, not too fast or too slow; he will not want to attract any attention. I do not look at his face any more, only his hands on the wheel. I fall into a sort of half-sleep to the rattle of the diesel engine and dream I am with my mother.

One year we went to Norway together, just the two of us. My grandfather had been ill and my mother wanted to see him. My grandparents had a log cabin up in Voss and we went there with them for a month.

The log cabin was in the middle of a forest of vast pines. The snow was so thick around it, that we had to sit with all our luggage and skis in a trailer pulled by a tractor with snow chains.

The snow on the branches of the firs was so thick I couldn't understand how it could balance there. Every so often, day and night, as it thawed a little, there would be great thuds and swishes as it landed and the green branches swung back gloriously free and upright.

I loved my grandparents and I was sad I saw so little of them. They came to England infrequently and my mother would never allow me to go without her to Norway and stay with them, although they begged her to let me go in the long endless summers of my childhood.

I missed so much of a culture that should have been part of me and a place that was immediately home. I loved the mountains and the blue waterfalls that froze as they fell. I loved the deep mystery of the fjords, where the land rose sheer and crazily out of the water, but somehow did not frighten me. I loved the space and solitude of Voss, and the familiarity, warmth and safeness of my grandparents.

They taught me to ski, but I wasn't a natural. I had not started young enough and I envied the tiny children skiing to school with far more skill than I had at eleven. I envied my small cousins who skied before they could walk. Here, skis were like a pair of shoes, something you wore most of the time.

My mother was a brilliant skier and so was my grandmother. My grandfather had been too, but he wasn't allowed to ski all day and everyday any more, because of his heart.

Sometimes, in the evenings, my grandparents would tell me stories about the war as we sat round a huge fire that burnt the most enormous logs. I knew they had been in the Resistance and I knew they had saved many people from the Germans, although neither of them ever mentioned this. They used to laugh because all Norwegians could outski the Germans, and my grandparents knew every mountain top and valley round here. I would listen, rapt, at the adventures they told me. I couldn't believe how brave people were in the war.

One day, my grandfather took me to see an old woodcarver called Thor Palsson, who still lived up the mountains. We langlaufed across country all day, Grampie and I. We crisscrossed the glittery blue mountain, leaving a light, thin trail with our narrow skis, climbing until I thought we must reach the sky.

Thor Palsson lived in a small wooden house where the log-burning stove dominated the main room, and he carved the most beautiful figures of animals from one piece of wood. But he did not like selling what he had made and they were everywhere in his small cluttered house.

My grandfather had told me that he was the bravest man I would ever meet. He had organized and run the Resistance and he had saved more lives than anyone Grampie knew. Thor Palsson had been caught and tortured, but he had escaped and killed hundreds of Germans to save English soldiers and airmen.

My grandfather said that after the war he retreated up the mountain where he grieved for all those who had died, English and German. My grandfather told me something broke inside him because he was such a gentle person. All day and every day he carved.

The people in the village believed he was a healer and had second sight. My grandfather didn't know if this was true or not.

He had a very long white beard and piercing blue eyes and tiny hands. I looked and looked at his carvings that filled every conceivable space and asked if I might touch. He nodded, and with the smoky, raw scent of new wood in my nostrils, I tentatively touched small mountain goats, and rabbits, eagles and little songbirds.

I kept my finger on the rump of a horse going downhill with panniers on its back, the angle of its body, the muscles in its front legs so exact that its skin seemed to ripple underneath my finger. I felt the movement of that horse and the sweet smell that a working animal gives off. I could not take my eyes off it. I kept going back again and again to touch it.

I wanted it so much tears came to my eyes. The old man turned and asked my grandfather something in Bokmål – one of the official forms of Norwegian, although he spoke English. My grandfather looked shocked, glanced at me quickly and replied gruffly.

As we left and I was strapping my skis on, the old man bent to me and smiled, his incredible blue eyes crinkling at the corners, and I could see that when he was young he must have been very beautiful. He asked me why I did not speak any Norwegian – Bokmål or Nynorsk. He smiled, but he did not touch me. I liked him very much.

'It's too difficult for Daddy. Mummy says he feels left out if we speak either Norwegian language. When I was little we used to speak Nynorsk together.'

'And how old are you now?'

'I'm nearly twelve.'

'And you love horses?'

'More than people. I ride my friend's horse every weekend. When I'm grown up I am going to have my own horse.'

From his pocket he brought out the carved horse. 'Will you be so kind as to look after him for me? You see he has been waiting for the right person, the exact right person. You are that person.'

I felt myself go pale with pleasure. As he held out the beautiful carving to me, I put my hands out for it but they were shaking so much I could not hold it. The old man very gently covered my own hands with his around the horse. Automatically, before I could stop myself, I moved back, away from him and his small strong hands. His piercing blue eyes held mine only a second as he said very quietly so only I could hear, 'Sigrid, always be strong and brave like my horse. Never let anyone hurt you or do you wrong.'

He got up quickly, his movements fluid like those of a younger man, and he went to my grandfather, turned and led him away, bending to him, talking more than I had heard him all afternoon. I was left with the wonderful horse in my hands.

Skiing back down the mountain with my grandfather, fast, before the sun went, I wondered why he was so silent. The sun was blood red against the snow and falling lower and lower although it was only mid-afternoon. It coloured the sky the colour of peonies and tinged the snow in great dancing, glistening sparks.

We stopped for a second to admire it and I said, 'Grampie, are you sad because the old man is your friend and you don't see him much any more?'

My grandfather turned and looked at me with such love and pain in his eyes that I was embarrassed.

'Yes, I am sad because I don't see my wise old friend so much any more. But I am also sad because I do not see my beautiful granddaughter very much either and I know little of her life in England.'

Stricken, I said, 'Gramps, I will try and write more, I promise. I just wish Mama would let me come on my own for holidays. Why doesn't she?'

'I wish I knew, darling, I wish I knew. Come, we must get going again, or it will be dark, and your mother will be fussing.'

'Ginna won't be, though will she?'

'Ginna is sensible. She knows you are in good hands.'

Something in the way he said this made me ask, 'Are you cross with Mama?'

He bent and adjusted a ski, did not look at me. 'No, not cross, child, bewildered.' He added, almost to himself, 'Why make an art form of unhappiness? Why deprive yourself of all this and parents who love you?' He threw his arm out and upward to the mountain and the sky full of the deep dramatic colours of the dying day. He sounded very sad.

That night, when I had gone to bed, my grandmother came in and admired my horse again. 'You were very honoured, Sigrid.'

'I know. Why did he let me have it?'

'Because he liked you, darling.' She got up and fiddled with the wooden shutters, my counterpane, the small woodburner in my room.

I waited.

'Child, you are all right? Are you happy at school? Things are all well at home with Mama and Daddy?'

'Yes.'

'Why won't you eat, darling? You eat so little.'

'I do eat, Ginna, I just don't get very hungry these days.'

'You are far too thin, child.'

'Mama isn't worried.'

'Mama, it seems, doesn't worry about anything much these days.' It slipped out before she could stop it, I could tell. Then she said, 'And what about your daddy, does he worry about you?'

My face closed tight before I could stop it. 'I'm all right, Ginna. Can I go to sleep now?'

She switched off the light and bent to kiss my forehead. 'Good night, my beloved child, God bless.' Her voice fluttered in the dark as if it was coming out of a bubble, as if she was trying not to cry. She got up heavily and went out of the room.

I lay listening to the house creak as the wood contracted. It was a wonderful sound. The smell of wood burning, the plop of snow outside, the shine of the fire on the polished wooden floor. The warmth of my bed, the faint sound of music, the joy of tomorrow. The safety of tonight.

These creaks were only the house cooling down, the house slumbering for the night. These creaks were not the shiver of careful footfall on a loose board. Not a door opening and shutting. Not a sliver of light for a second on my closed eyelids. Not the sound of guilty breathing.

I almost did not want to fall asleep for the joy of being there.

I wanted to stay for ever. I ached to stay. My grandparents had five children, all daughters. Mama was in the middle. Down the mountains I had cousins and aunts and uncles, but Mama always liked to have Ginna and Grampie to herself for most of the time we were in Norway.

I found it exciting and intimidating to be with them all. I wasn't very good at mixing, but I loved the noise and laughter and chatter, the secure feeling of being with a large family. I longed with a terrible longing to live here for ever.

As the holiday drew to an end, I would weep and weep under the trees, now showing green as the snow thawed and summer began. I knew under the white blanket of snow lay all the wild flowers my grandfather had told me about.

Before my mother and I left to fly back to England there was an early thaw and spring began. I lay with my grandfather under the enormous firs on the softness of pine needles and looked up and up into towering cathedrals of spice-scented knotty branches, and recited after him, 'Purple orchid, wild pea, yellow gorse, Queen's bedstraw . . .' I loved that one and would giggle and repeat the name over and over while imagining a fat queen of hearts lying on a huge double bed of yellow straw.

My grandfather turned over on the rug, laughing with me. 'I am going to miss you, child, oh, so much.'

'Oh, Gramps!' I cried out, and moved to hug him before I remembered I mustn't. He sat up and took my hands. He was very serious, no longer laughing. For a minute I thought he was angry with me. There was a frightening flash to his eyes I had never seen before. 'Sigrid, why do you no longer think you may hug your old grandfather?'

I could not answer. I felt the colour come up from my neck and my heart beat in my chest and throat, painful, throbbing like a trapped bird. My limbs began to shake as if they had a mind of their own.

He let go of my fingers and took my face in his hands, knelt forward and placed his lips on my forehead. Hardly a kiss, so passing, so soft, so full of love it was. As if I were precious glass. His tears on my cheeks were like my own.

'My heart is breaking,' he whispered.

Then we gathered the rug up and walked slowly home.

That night my grandparents had the most terrible row with my mother. I lay in bed and listened to it blow about the log cabin like a violent storm. My grandparents wanted me to stay on in Norway. The anger, the things that were said that evening were awful. 'We will make her a ward of court . . .' 'She is our granddaughter . . .' 'We will not stand by and watch you make a sacrifice of your daughter to save a worthless marriage . . .'

'How dare you suggest . . .? How dare you . . .? There is absolutely nothing wrong with Sigrid. She is pubescent, for heaven's sake . . . growing up . . . self-conscious . . . Be very, very careful, Dad, before you start saying things you'll regret.'

'Your mother has been worried about you from the day you married him . . . wasted years . . . you are obviously very depressed, Kristian . . . you don't seem to care about anything, even your daughter . . . What makes you stay with him? Here you have a home, family, parents who love you . . . Sorry, I don't believe you love him. If you do, he makes you very unhappy . . .'

On and on into the night until my mother screams, 'Stop! Leave me alone. This is *my* life. *My* child. *My* husband. I don't have to share, explain, justify the way I live to you or my sisters, or their husbands and children. Just for once . . . this is mine. My life.'

The fact that my mother had been driven from her inertia made me pull the covers over my head. She rarely spoke, let alone shouted.

On the day my mother and I left Norway, my grandparents asked me if I would like to live with them permanently, or at least spend all my holidays with them. I looked up and saw my mother's beautiful and broken face. I shook my head and went to her.

'I must stay with Mama,' I said.

I never saw a spring in Norway. My mother never spoke to her parents again. I never saw my grandparents again either, although we wrote. When I was sixteen and my mother killed herself, my father had a huge row with them over my mother's body. They wanted her flown home to Norway. They did not come to her funeral. They told my father she had been dead to them for many years.

I never went back to Voss. Even when I grew up. Even when my mother was dead and I had no reason not to go. Perhaps I was angry

172

with my grandparents. Perhaps that last row lived on in my heart, spoiling the memories. Kristian was their daughter. They should have loved her no matter what. She was my mother and I loved her.

And she loved me. Of course she did.

Jake wakes me and hands me a lukewarm cup of coffee from the flask. He has pulled off the road. I come from a long way away. For a second I think he is my father. 'You've slept a long time. Another half-hour and we will be home.'

I feel bleary-eyed, dim-witted. 'Home?'

'Yes, home. You will love the house.'

I suddenly see out of the corner of my eye a cruising police car up on the main road. For a second my heart leaps, but in a moment the car is gone.

In twenty minutes we are on Dartmoor. The familiar mist reels off the hills in flimsy strips blown by a wind. We turn off on to a track and bump along it for a few miles. There are derelict outbuildings with sheep nestling in the broken walls, and the crumbling remains of small storage sheds for the quarry.

Eventually we turn off the track and Jake stops the car near what looks like a small barn. He gets out, opens the wooden doors and drives the car inside. I feel like crying. I have kept thinking all these miles that someone will find the car. Then it would only be a matter of time before someone found me.

I feel heady and disorientated. Jake is talking to me. 'Get out of the car, Sigrid. For heaven's sake, wake yourself up!' He has drugged me and now he is expecting me to walk across the moor in the dark.

'If you want me awake, why make me take tranquillizers, for God's sake?' I shout, not caring whether he hits me.

'Because I needed to concentrate on my driving, not to worry about you doing something bloody stupid, like throwing yourself out on to the dual carriageway.'

His mood changes suddenly. 'Come on, darling, it's not far now, just a little way up this track.' He gets a large torch out of the back and pulls me after him, shining the beam along a narrow path made by the sheep. On and on we stumble, into the middle of nowhere.

After about twenty minutes he points and I see a small white-washed house loom out of the dark. The house lies behind wooden gates, in a hollow near a small copse.

'Over there is an ancient oak wood,' Jake says. 'Absolutely amazing that it's survived.'

I glance past the house and shiver; the small bent trees look dwarfed and twisted, sinister in the dark.

Jake gets out a key, unlocks the gate and we go through. It shuts behind us with a clank. 'Look,' he says. 'You can't see in the dark, but it's such a pretty house.'

Misery sweeps over me. It seems more isolated than his cottage. Jake shine his torch over a small Georgian house with long square windows to the ground and an oak front door with a brass knocker which needs cleaning. The windows are all shuttered, but Jake has a key.

Inside it is dark. He switches a light on. The smell of damp rises up although it is not cold. We are in a hall and most of the furniture has dust covers on, but I am immediately struck by the small polished tables each side of the door. On them are silver frames, highly polished. Inside them are photos of a small blond boy. Jake? I look closer. Definitely Jake. I have seen photographs of him as a child. In an album and in his father's house. In one photo he is on a bicycle, wearing long grey socks and long shorts, fair hair flopping over his eyes, squinting at the camera.

Jake is watching me with unnerving intensity. I look at the other photo. He is with a slim woman with long fair hair, nearly as long as mine. I peer at her. She is crouched down to his height, smiling, looking at him, her face full of love and laughter. I am puzzled. She and Jake are so alike, but I have met his parents. His mother is small and dark.

'Who is the woman in the photo?' I ask, although I think I know the answer.

'My mother. I was adopted as a baby. Isn't she beautiful? This was her house.' Jake is radiating happiness and charm. 'Come upstairs, darling. I want to show you your room. I think you will be pleased. I have made you a Room of Your Own.

We walk up a polished wooden staircase the colour of pale honey, past a huge coloured glass window on the curl of the stair, which looks out on to the moor. Two more steps and we are in a big bedroom, very light, with a view over the garden and small sloping lawns.

The bed is turned down. There are books on the bedside table and nightclothes laid out on the bed. I walk slowly towards the bed. The books are all Virginia Woolf. *Moments of Being*, *To the Lighthouse*, *Mrs Dalloway*, Hermione Lee's biography, and a copy of the photograph I love of Virginia Woolf, which hangs in Talland House.

I sink slowly on the bed and pick up the photo and stare at it. The familiar long face and sad brown eyes stare back. I look up at Jake. He is watching my reaction. I open my mouth but no sound comes.

'Do you like this room? I thought you would like to face the garden, not the moor. Is this all right for you, darling? I have tried so hard to think of everything that you might need or like.'

He is as anxious as a small boy. Suddenly as vulnerable as the child in the photographs downstairs. I nod again and again without speaking and he comes and gathers me up, kneels by the bed and clutches me to him.

Over his shoulder I still hold the photo of Virginia. I stare at it, hypnotized. What is familiar in her eyes in this photo is her mental anguish, her madness. I recognize in her eyes the slipping away of reality, of truth. I recognize the blurring of boundaries where nothing is normal any more, neither people nor things. I have seen the same look in my eyes in the mirror. I see the same look in Jake's eyes now.

Chapter 25

I wake in the dark. Jake is asleep, fully clothed beside me. I too am still dressed and I am cold. The light from the landing shines into the room. I edge from the bed carefully and go out on to the landing. The house is very still, as if it stands waiting. Shadows of trees wave across the huge window. I shiver, hesitate at the shut doors leading off the landing, then go slowly downstairs.

The door to the kitchen is open and I go in without turning on the light, automatically making for a source of heat, a large green Aga taking up one wall. The warmth is like a womb; houses here absorb moisture from the granite like blotting paper. I lean against it, trying to get warm, my eyes adjusting to the dark.

Whoever lived here lived in the kitchen, like Beth. There is a soft chair in the corner by the window, a pine dresser full of bright pottery and a large scrubbed pine table.

My mouth is dry. Outside it is still black. I look at my watch: one forty-five. I long for a drink. I feel cold and dry and hungry. But Jake is asleep. This is my chance. My heart starts to beat with dread at the thought of going out there on the moor in the dark. If I found the torch, I could follow the sheep track we came on . . . I could get to the car.

The car. I go out into the hall. My jacket and Jake's are thrown over a chair. I put mine on and then look through his pockets for the car keys. Nothing.

I try to remember. How far off the main road did we come along the track? How long would it take me to walk if I cannot find the car keys? Once I am on the main road, I will be all right. If only I could find the keys. I look round the hall, on the small tables with the

177

photographs then I go back into the kitchen, shut the door and switch the light on.

I search on all the surfaces and I quietly open the top two drawers of the dresser. Nothing. I find the torch and go to the back door but it is locked and there is no key in the lock. Oh God. I move out to the hall again to the front door. No key there either.

I start to shiver again, with tension and the sudden chance of flight disappearing. Reluctant to give up, I lift the lid of a small mahogany tea caddy and the front door key is inside. I remember Jake's eccentricities.

I unlock the door. The large key turning in the lock sounds like a bullet in the silent house. I freeze, listen for any movement. Silence. I ease the door open. Outside it is as black as pitch and the hills rise up from the house, bleak and formidable. A wind like a knife whips round the side of the house and makes me gasp.

I whimper with fear and cold, and shut the door behind me. I put the torch down on the ground and pull my hood up. I don't have any gloves. Then shining the torch in front of me I move as quietly as I can across the square drive to the gate, trying not to crunch on the gravel and weeds.

The gate is locked. I climb over it and shine the torch at foot level. Then, head bent against the biting wind, I follow the narrow track in the dark, trying not to look at the small crouched oak wood with its twisted arms on my left.

I have always had this irrational fear about Dartmoor. I am in awe of it by day; at night, in the dark, it terrifies me. The weather can change in minutes. I know how easy it is to stray off known paths. Jake was always being asked to join rescue groups looking for army cadets, school children doing their Duke of Edinburgh Awards, lone walkers. Most people were correctly clothed and equipped, but they still lost themselves in weather that deteriorated before they were aware of it.

I am trembling, trying to keep the torch steady with fingers growing quickly numb. The wind, increasing as the ground rises, is icy. This is nearly April, but there has been freak snow on Dartmoor in early May.

The beam of the torch wavers in the dark as I shake with the cold. If I reach the barn where the car is it will be a landmark. I can go inside and it will be sheltered. I can warm up. Did Jake lock the door of the barn? Why can't I remember . . .?

I trip suddenly over my own feet and fall, and the torch flies out of my hand and rolls away from me. I get up, look round for its thin beam, see it and go to retrieve it. As I reach it, it goes out. I shake it desperately. It comes on again but the beam is weak, the battery is going.

I shine it down to my feet in a circle. I've lost the tiny sheep track. How could I have done? I shine it round me again in all directions. I move a few inches each way, but I can only see the tall thin reed grasses that mean boggy ground.

This is stupid. I fight overpowering panic. The sheep track has got to be just out of the beam of the torch. I have hardly moved. Again I move the beam round it. It is as if I have been lifted up and dropped suddenly on tufts of boggy grass.

I dare not move, I am so scared. I know the track is here, but is so insignificant I cannot find it again in the dark. I am not dressed properly. I will freeze if I don't keep moving. I can't survive in the open, I can't bear the dark . . . I open my mouth to cry out, and see the beam of a torch making a slow line towards me.

'Sigrid?' Jake yells.

'I'm here!' I shout, and start to run towards the beam of his torch.

'Stop!' he shouts back. 'Keep quite still.'

Too late. I scream as my feet are sucked downwards and I fall into muddy water which soaks my clothes in seconds. Jake is upon me, pulling me up hard until I come out of the mud with an aching painful plop, leaving my shoes behind me.

He props me upright, retrieves his torch and shines it carefully at his feet. Then he hoists me over his shoulders and moves quickly back on to the path. I wait for his anger.

'Stupid bitch,' he says, but sounds relieved, not angry. I hang over his shoulders, my head lolling. Bitter tears of relief at Jake coming after me war with the total indignity of being treated like a sack of potatoes.

In what seems only a few minutes, we are back at the house. My pathetic attempt at escape got me a few hundred yards. Jake carries me up to the bathroom.

'Get your wet clothes off, quickly.'

He runs the bath and I remove my sodden clothes, my teeth chattering, my fingers frozen and jerky. Leaving the hot tap running, Jake disappears and I climb into the hot water. He returns in a moment with a brandy. I can't hold the glass and he pours it down my throat until I choke.

He looks at me. 'You stupid bitch, you've lived on Dartmoor, for God's sake. You should know the score.'

I wait for his fury to grow at my attempt to escape, to leave him, but it does not come. You never know with Jake. You never know what's coming next.

He gets a large towel and rubs me dry, hard and painfully until I begin to feel my limbs again. 'When I was small, my father used to dry me like this, on the beach, when we had been swimming,' I say suddenly, inconsequentially, not knowing why I say it.

Jake glances at me and smiles without humour. 'Amongst other things,' he says, and goes and gets thick childlike pyjamas out of their Cellophane wrapper. My face burns. Is this the end of silence? I feel as if I am shrinking back into a child being put to bed for the night.

'Go and get into bed. Part of you getting so cold is that you have not eaten or had a hot drink for too long.'

I get into bed and I hear Jake running a shower, getting out of his wet things. Then he goes downstairs and I lie getting warmer. My feeling are confused and snarled: grateful for rescue and care, but conscious that but for Jake I would have no need for either.

As a child I utterly loathed *Alice's Adventures in Wonderland*. The book, read to us at school, made me feel as I feel now. Nothing is as it seems. People turn into different things. The landscape changes constantly. Every new chapter brings more disordered, more deranged and frightening people and things.

Jake brings me a hot-water bottle and scrambled eggs and scalding tea on a tray, and I devour them. He gets his own tray and sits and eats it with me in silence. He sits there in dry sweater and jeans and bare feet and drinks whisky.

'What time is it?' I ask.

'Two thirty in the morning. Not the ideal time to explore Dartmoor.'

I am silent. When he has finished eating I say, 'You never ever mentioned you were adopted.'

'No.' He puts both trays on the floor. I cannot tell what he is thinking.

'Is your real mother still alive?'

'No, she died last year.'

'She lived here, in this house?'

'Apparently. But I didn't know she did. I was totally unaware of it.' He sounds bitter. 'A year ago she died and left me this house. I didn't know that either. A concerned solicitor, an executor of my mother's will, contacted me. My stepmother was insisting it was kept from me.'

'Why?'

Jake smiles. 'The judge, apparently, made my mother an allowance all her life. My stepmother only became aware of it when my mother died, and was furious. She reckoned this house should go back to them as recompense.'

He runs his hand through his hair, agitated. 'Do you know, Sigrid, all the time you and I were living in the cottage, my mother was living here. She bought this house to be near me. She came to my exhibitions. She bought my paintings. She followed my career closely and I never knew. I wouldn't even have recognized her. Maybe I even spoke to her in the gallery without knowing it was her.'

I stare at him. 'You mean . . . the judge is your real father, but Camilla . . .?' I am beginning to wish I had left well alone. Jake has that dark brooding face I know so well.

He gets up and pulls his cigarettes out of his trousers pocket, lights up and paces round the room. 'I was seven before I discovered I was adopted. That I had a beautiful fair mother somewhere, instead of the small, dark, shrewish mother I loathed.'

He comes back to the bed and looks down at me. 'You are not the only one who circumnavigates the truth about their childhood in order to survive it.'

I stare at him, afraid of what he is going to say. 'I have always known. Those recurring nightmares of yours are childhood stuff. Who is it, Larkin? "They fuck you up, your mum and dad . . ."? I can't remember any more.'

He laughs and paces about the bedroom. 'My mother's name was Chloe. She was, according to my stepmother, an upper-class whore with a drug habit. My father met her at a pop concert. He told me once that she was the most lovely thing he had ever seen. Of course she wasn't a whore, she was just a young hippie singer my father fell in love with and bedded.'

All the sad bitterness of childhood is in his face and the curl of his bottom lip. 'Unfortunately, my father was already a barrister and ambitious, and engaged to the awful Camilla at the time. His family expected him to make a good marriage. Her family were steeped in the law. Her father was a judge and her grandfather had been. They were exactly the right family for an ambitious barrister to marry into.'

He looks down at me without seeing me.

'My father was told by his family to stop fucking about and marry Camilla, which he did. But my mother must have meant more to him than a casual screw, because when she became pregnant and asked for his help, he gave it.

'She had a drug habit and he couldn't possibly know if the baby was his or not, but he cared enough to try to get her dried out, make sure she had money . . .'

Jake turns away and throws his cigarette out of the top of the window and it flies away in an arc of sparks. The wind blows in and a great burst of rain hits the window, an isolating sound.

I start to get out of bed and he whips round.

'Not interested in my story, darling? I was so sure you would be. You see, you know all about make believe, don't you? You have lived all your life in never-never land, haven't you? The safety of silence. Aren't I right? It is not what our parents *do*, but what they are *seen to do*. Isn't that right? Children want to be just like every other child, that is why they collude in the misery of their own childhood.'

I stare back at him, suddenly angry. 'For God's sake, Jake. You were adopted, not sent to a children's home, adopted into a comfortable, educated, wealthy family.'

He laughs. The sound is harsh and painful. I see he is shaking. I cannot tell if his sudden coldness is because he got wet or there are ghosts walking over his grave.

'I have to sleep,' he says abruptly. 'You get some sleep too.' At the door he turns. 'Don't try any more silly stunts, Sigrid. I have the keys in my pocket. Next time I might be tempted to leave you to your fate.'

Chapter 26

I sleep. I sleep so heavily it feels like dying. I sleep and dream strange labyrinthine dreams of people and places I have long forgotten. The bed grows warm and I grow hotter and hotter. I toss and turn without being able to wake properly. My throat is dry, but my limbs won't do as I say and I can't get out of bed to find water.

I dream of Dan. I dream of a café in Spain where we waited on tables for the whole of one summer. We slept mostly on the beach and lived on nothing and were blissfully happy as we grew lean and brown and unkempt.

We had our first row there, over a Spanish boy who followed me around, touching the edges of my hair as if it was a fascinating species of seaweed. Dan was jealous. He accused me of enjoying all the attention I got from the locals and I laughed and said of course I enjoyed it. I was eighteen, totally in love with him, confident for the first time in my life. I had fair hair that reached my waist, and I tossed it and pranced about in the water, happy, happy as the day was long.

Dan made me cry. The first, the last, the only time he ever did. He couldn't know I was rejoicing in being free of guilt about my body. He couldn't know I was unselfconscious, exultant in this freedom for the first time in my life.

He didn't realize I had never been able to be silly, shallow, giggly in groups. Childish. Now, in hot, idle student days, full of the smell of suntan oil, chips, paella, the warm sea and baking sun, I could be all these things and I was. Because of him.

He knew nothing of my childhood. He only knew that day he wiped the smile off my face and made me cry. Once I had started I could not stop, for I thought he knew I loved him, only him.

I frightened him that day in Spain as I shook and sobbed. He grew pale and wretched at my extreme, over-the-top reaction. He was only nineteen and his feelings of jealousy were quite justified and normal. He watched me waver, quiver at his anger, dissolve hopelessly in a way that scared him.

I remember him so clearly rocking me in his arms. 'Sorry . . . I'm sorry . . . Please stop . . . Si, please . . .'

He never raised his voice or got cross with me again, and now, now I realize what a strain that must have been. He was an easy-going, gentle person, but everybody gets irritated, mad, at times. After Spain, did he feel he had always to be careful with me? What if what I perceived as a perfect relationship was something else?

I toss and turn and my throat burns. I become dimly aware of someone giving me sips of water . . . Dan and I *were* all right . . . We *were* good together . . .

I am running, running along the shoreline of a long stretch of beach. I jump over the slimy seaweed, driftwood and plastic bottle tops and old fisherman's ropes. The sea is like ink except for small perfect white waves breaking at my feet.

I cannot remember what I am running from. I turn to the right and there, there he is, the snake with his flat head held high, erect, holding himself out of the water like a periscope, high out of the waves, sliding fast along the surface of the sea, keeping parallel with me . . . I scream.

'Si, I'm going to sit you up. You've got a temperature. I want you to take some paracetamol.' I feel water slide down my throat then a pill in my mouth. I gag, open my eyes. Jake halves the pills, makes me swallow them . . . more water . . . I slide down the bed again.

Swiftly I fly, and the air beats round my head. Mutton – what happened to Mutton? Did he die? And Alice, Alice shivering. Who found and comforted Alice? Talland House is full of women in bright red dresses and the twins are doing handstands. Beth won't like it, she won't like it.

My body is burning. I am burning. A cold cloth is held to my forehead, the back of my neck, my hands. So gentle. Ginna . . . I love being ill when I am with Ginna . . . 'Just one of your fevers, darling . . . better in the morning.' My horse. I left my carved horse in the cottage. I have to get it. It was given to me . . . I must have it . . .

'Ssh, it's OK. It's all right, we'll get it . . . I'll get it for you. Come on, darling, drink. Jesus, I had forgotten these fevers of yours. Si, you're soaking, you'll get pneumonia. Into the chair. I'll have to do the sheets . . .'

Teeth chattering. Frozen. 'Sorry, Muma, sorry.'

'It is not your fault,' she says. 'You do not have these fevers on purpose, Sigrid.' She does not hug me. She does not stroke my hair. She does not love me or she cannot show it. 'OK,' she says. 'Hop back in. Call out if you need me.' She does not sit on the bed or kiss me. My mother.

I am aware of Jake helping me back to bed. 'You are cooler. Thank God for that.'

I sleep. My body cools as light filters into the room. I feel like air, as if I might float away. Someone strokes my hair very carefully away from my face. Oh, Matt. Matt, I had such a bad, a terrible dream . . .

When I wake the sun is high in the sky. For a few moments I do not know where I am. Then I turn and see Jake fast asleep in an armchair. My heart plummets. I am on Dartmoor. I close my eyes again.

When I open them Jake is gone.

Chapter 27

I have slept through a whole day. I cannot believe it. When I wake the sun is already low in the sky.

Jake puts his head round the bedroom door. 'How are you feeling?' He is genial, concerned. 'I'm running you a bath.'

'I am perfectly all right now. You don't have to wait on me, Jake.' I get out of bed and walk to the bathroom.

'Warm water has always been a palliative to you, hasn't it? It calms you. You are like a mermaid. Perhaps you were one in another life. Perhaps it's why you have difficulty coming to terms with Dartmoor, darling. But this house is better for you than the cottage, isn't it? Much lighter and airier.'

He leaves me and I undress and sink into the water. He talks as if we are going to live here, together, happily ever after.

'I'm very much looking forward to seeing you, mermaid.' Oh, *Matt. Matt.*

I lie in the water, trying to wake up from my long strange sleep. Jake seems to visibly relax in this house. I think about his mother. Did she live here alone? There is quiet evidence of her everywhere. No one has packed her things up, moved her on. It is as if she has just left a room.

Small, spare, rather odd pieces lie in this bathroom. Pottery, a tiny sculpture, a bleached branch, round granite stones. It is quite different from the judge and Camilla's house over the moor, crammed full of pieces from all around the world. Jake is like the woman who lived here. He chooses objects carefully and they all have an exact place.

I get out of the bath and into the pyjamas Jake has laid out. I am

189

glad of them. The house has the damp, musty feel of having lain empty. I brush my wet hair and leave it to dry and I go slowly across the pale pine floorboards, polished to a shiny warmth, and down the stairs. I have that light-headed, faintly floating feeling I get when I have had a high temperature. As if I am slightly to the side of my body.

The landing window is edged in red and blue coloured panes, and behind the low clouds rolling in over Dartmoor the sun is setting, lacing the edges gold. It is stunningly, hauntingly beautiful out there. I stand quite still, transfixed. I have lost one whole day.

I hear Jake coming up the stairs behind me. He stops and watches the sky without speaking. We are very still, arms just touching, side by side.

I cannot speak either, and the moment grows and swells and begins to tremble from our point of contact. As if the dazzling, intoxicating beauty of that flaming sunset touches and neutralizes all but the moment and the point my skin touches his skin.

It is not something I am able to control and I do not understand the feeling. I am ashamed and frightened by the sheer power of it, growing and seeking and beginning to beat like a pulse on the surface of my skin as if I am scorched.

I want Jake. I want him. What is this power? Can he, by the briefest touch, ignite his own desire in me? I don't know. I must breathe. He must not realize. The moment stretches to breaking point. The moment hangs and shivers, painful and raw, as haunting as the darkening sky, full of the fading colours of this day.

Jake says softly, 'This is what we missed in the cottage. Across the valley we missed the sunsets.'

He turns and smiles at me. The old smile, the beginning smile. The odd look has completely gone from his eyes. Cornwall has given him a tan and lightened his hair. His eyes seem almost violet. His skin is the texture of a polished apple. His perfect even teeth are white as white.

His beauty has always hypnotized me as if I am forever seeing it for the first time. When coupled with his cruelty, it reminds me of a fallen angel.

He is staring at me and reaches out to touch my drying hair. He looks wistful, sad. 'How lovely you are,' he says in that voice, smooth as the surface of the sea, 'with that strange, fey beauty that haunts me night and day . . . Come on, let's have a drink. I have a good bottle of wine.'

The kitchen is full of the last rays of the dying sun. It touches the table Jake has laid with white starched table napkins and wine glasses the thinnest, palest blue. I am glad of the Aga.

He opens a bottled of chilled, dry white wine and hands me a glass. He raises his glass to me, holding my eyes. I cannot smile, but I acknowledge him.

'Sit down while I look in the oven,' he says, and suddenly laughs. 'You look about twelve in those sexless pyjamas, and very sexy.'

I blush irritatingly, like a schoolgirl, and sit down at the table.

As Jake stirs a casserole he starts to chat about art in Cornwall, St Ives in particular. He asks me what I think of the Tate Gallery and the way they hang. He criticizes mildly the Newlyn Art Gallery, and says he was impressed by the wealth of talent in the small exhibitions and galleries.

It is bizarre. Anyone looking down on us would immediately jump to the conclusion we were a happy, civilized couple with lots to say to each other.

He brings two plates of chicken casserole to the table, gets a salad from the fridge and pours me more wine.

'How have you done all this? How have you filled the house with food, my books and clothes . . . everything, and been in Cyprus and St Ives?' I ask. 'I don't understand. It's as if you have been living here.'

'I wasn't in Cyprus for very long. I was in Troödos when my stepmother died, and my father, although mentally frail, wanted to bring her home to bury her, so we did. My father is terrified of being burgled in Cyprus, so he told the servants we would be in Troödos for another week.'

He looks at me, sardonic, as if smiling to himself. 'I have been getting this house ready for you for six months. Before you left. I knew you hated the cottage. I wanted you to be happy. That's the truth. I love you and I need you, Si. Simple as that.'

It is my turn to smile ironically. Simple as that?

He adds, 'Dartmoor is not another continent, you know. It is only about an hour and a half from here to St Ives.'

It might as well be the moon.

'Tell me,' he says suddenly, between mouthfuls of chicken, 'did you ever love me? Or was I always rebound material? Tell me truthfully.'

I am startled. His voice lacks any accusation. I sip my wine and look at him. I will be truthful. 'Like everyone else at Bristol, I thought your lectures were brilliant. I learnt a lot. I never really thought of you in personal terms. I was with Dan, and you were my tutor.' I pause. I don't say: Except, like all the other girls, I did fancy you from afar. It is true, I did. And I have never admitted it to myself. Because of Dan.

Jake is watching me intently. 'Later, when Dan died, you were kind, good to me. I was sad and miserable. I felt safe with you . . . and we saw so many lovely places together.' I put my fork down. 'I don't think I quite loved you when I married you. I was flattered . . .'

I look up at him and tell him the truth – and myself. 'I fell in love with you the first time we went to Venice. You had taken me to Florence for the day and you had bought *The Wings of the Dove*. We couldn't go out of the apartment because there was an enormous tide. We were surrounded by water and you sat reading it to me while the rain beat down outside. I fell totally, absolutely, in love with you in those moments.'

I falter with pain as I remember the utter joy of it. I look away. My chicken grows cold. Jake is very still. When I look up, he is watching me still, but he is crying. He is crying silently, without moving, without sound, and the sight of his distress is searing.

He gets up clumsily, comes round the table and pulls me gently to my feet, and holds me to him and we weep uncontrollably. We stand there holding on to one another in the candlelit kitchen, shuddering with our separate pain as if our hearts will break.

Then he gently wipes my face and his own. We turn away and blow our noses on our napkins, embarrassed. Jake blows out the candles and we go up the stairs together.

He undresses me in the dark. He makes love to me in the dark where we cannot read each other's face. Where we can both play charades with relentless, ruthless passion.

He has taught me to love his body. He has taught me to love all the things he does. To crave them. To cry out for them with the urgency of a swooping sea bird. He knows exactly. He knows exactly where and how. Every crack and corner of my body aches and burns, my skin hot and shiny with sweat as I arch and bend to him.

Move, we move with a musical rhythm. Together in one vast and aching, terrible needy climax that is more to do with pain than the remembrance of love.

It is not love. But something terrible and greedy. Hand-in-the-dark-hear-me-O God-Please-help-me cry of loneliness and silent terror against the threatening darkness. It is a fearful, hopeless, subversive power that haunts and destroys. Must be destroyed.

We roll away from each other and lie not touching. The distance between us is like an ocean. We lie very still. I cannot even hear him breathing. The silence in the room is like a note of music held too long, unendurable. The sweat on my skin cools and I shiver.

With an effort I get slowly, carefully out of the bed, not wanting to touch him, or for him to move. I pick up my pyjamas from the floor and I walk shakily to the bathroom and shut and lock the door. I wash myself. I wash myself again and again and I put the pyjamas on and slide down to the floor and crouch there with my head in my hands.

I am appalled. I am shocked and so sickened by myself I can hardly bear to acknowledge what I have just done. I rock. I rock and rock with this unbearable knowledge of treachery and perversity.

I am sick. I am a very sick person. It is one thing to be taken. It is another to enjoy.

I have felt this terrible despair before, so many times, after the footfall on the stair. After the reassuring words, after the pain and the shame. After the glass of water and my small, stuffed rabbit placed back beside me in the bed. In the darkness of endless childhood nights where I waited sure, always sure, this time, this time my mother would come and save me.

Are these the dark limbo hours that have distorted my mind to like what I should not have? Is my mother's sacrifice of me my own sacrifice of myself? What will become of the flawed thing that I am?

Like my mother before me, will I one day be so appalled by myself that I will decide it is better if I cease to be?

How can it be otherwise? I have just made love to a man who beat me almost to a pulp. I have just made love to a man who I believe cold-bloodedly murdered two innocent men I loved. Men who are dead because of me. I have just made love, and enjoyed it, to a psychopath.

And a small voice whispers, 'He is also your husband, and you once, briefly, loved and trusted him.'

Loved? Or lusted. Learnt to lust. As I learnt to pose.

Long, long ago, my father's camera. 'Sigrid, I want to take a photograph for your grandparents. Put on your little pleated skirt, your school uniform . . . Unplait your hair . . . hold it up, look at me sideways . . . Good girl, good wee girl, that's lovely . . . Now let's take a funny one to make your daddy laugh . . . Roll a sock down, get your hockey stick, pretend it's a horse . . .'

Mummy, Maman, Mutti, Mama, Mother.

Jake's paintings . . . Hundreds of them. 'Christ,' a painter friend once said, peering into Jake's studio, 'you are utterly obsessed with your wife.'

So when did my body become a commodity and something I ceased to take responsibility for?

I do not know where to go, or what to do next. I get up from the floor, I am awkward and cold. I unlock the door and go slowly back to the bedroom. Jake is sitting on the window seat looking out, smoking a cigarette.

He gets up as I come into the room. I cannot see his face in the dark.

He says, 'I will leave you. I am very tired. See you in the morning, Sigrid.' His beautiful voice is low and polite. Sad as the grave. As if I am a guest he vaguely knows. As if he too has reached a place without hope.

He goes out and shuts the door and I get back into the bed which still smells of him and his cigarette smoke.

★ ★ ★

Terror. A slow fear of the slide into the abyss.

Morality should mean the same to everyone. But how can it? The will to survive is immutable, incessant and corruptible. How can it depend on the recognition and acceptance of damaged lives? Something fleetingly glimpsed?

The damaged damage. But love endures, bypassing reason. Damage produces a crippled love. Real and searing. Powerful and iniquitous. Its form changed to something akin to hope, its shape willed into something normal, into something that can be more than endured.

Make *evil* acceptable to yourself if you cannot make it *right*. Understand the weight of silence. Sweeter than survival?

I recognized this man. I felt his pain, as hidden and unspeakable as my childhood. Pity surfaced, more poignant than love.

Passion without words to hinder the mysterious connection of body and being. The cry of life, so long abandoned in smothering silence, no longer stifled. Exciting and frightening. Furtive and dishonourable. Without hope. A chasm opens. Deeper, darker than taboos.

I must sleep.

Chapter 28

It is early morning. I lie and listen to the thick silence that is Dartmoor. No seagulls scream. No dull, soft roar of the ocean. No chug of small petrol engines on the water. I know exactly where I am the moment I wake. It is as if I have never left this place. I can hear no movement in the house, only the heavy sound of a clock ticking somewhere. I could easily believe I was back in Jake's cottage if I keep my eyes shut.

Has Jake left me here alone, locked in the middle of nowhere? The thought frightens me almost as much as being here with him. I think about him getting this house ready, for months, like a honeymoon suite. I think about the photographs downstairs.

A mother Jake fantasized about all his life – this perhaps holds the clue to Jake. I try to remember when he started to get seriously violent with me. Could it have been the bitterness of suddenly realizing his mother had been near all the time? Am I making excuses?

The silence was an illusion. Out on the moor I can hear sheep bleating now. I get up and go to the window. The sun is just coming up and the day looks as if it is going to be clear, the sky a perfect blue.

The hills are beige, gold where the sun is beginning to touch them. I know it is beautiful, but I cannot connect to it, feel it, as I do the sea. I must have been enchanted once – those first weekend parties when I came here with Jake. All my friends thought it wonderfully romantic.

I must have thought Dartmoor spectacular and full of space and light then, when Jake made me feel I was the only woman in the world.

I shiver. No one moves on the moor. Somewhere a dove is cooing.

I think about John and Beth and the twins in Huer's Cottage, all still sleeping, the twins tucked in their bunk beds, the sun rising over the sea. How sad they will be if Mutton has died. I wonder if Beth is awake, hands under her head, lying there, wondering about me.

I go to the bathroom attached to the bedroom and splash cold water on my face. I half expect the bedroom door to be locked but it isn't. I open it and listen. Filtered light is coming from the coloured window on the landing and there is a slice of light coming from underneath a door at the far end.

As I stand there, this constant, aching feeling of sadness rises out of the still house like a sigh. Did Jake's mother spend her last years living for glimpses of a son she gave away?

I walk towards the door with the light and tentatively push it open. It is a boy's room, small, full of books. Functional. A single bed, small desk, Airfix models.

In the narrow single bed, Jake is lying asleep, a book in one hand, his rimless glasses in the other. His fair hair flops over his face, hiding most of it. He is thirty-six but he looks about ten lying there. I have never ever seen him wear pyjamas before.

He wakes up with a start, as if he feels me watching him. His eyes are unfocused.

'Hello, Mummy,' he says.

I freeze. My skin prickles. It is hard not to turn and run. I stare at him and slowly he comes from a long way away, shakes his head, and, unsure on his feet, gets out of bed and comes towards me.

'Sorry . . . I was half asleep . . . dreaming . . .' His words are disconnected and slurred. I shiver as he touches me. Has he been drinking?

'You're cold,' he says. 'I'll make you coffee. Get into my bed, it's warm.'

'No. No, Jake . . .'

'Get into bed. Stop shivering, get in.' He pushes me firmly into the bed and pulls the covers up to my chin. 'Stay there. I'll be back in a minute. Don't move.'

I lie quite still, shocked again by the knowledge that Jake is not just an obsessive man who is capable of killing, but one who is disintegrating fast, perhaps going barking mad. The warmth of his bed, of his body, which has lain in this bed, makes me nauseous. The bed smells of him: Pears soap and a faint male heat. Attraction and repulsion are so close, so treacherously woven together.

I hear him moving about downstairs. The evocative, safe smell of toast rises up the stairs. The dichotomy of toast and danger are bewildering. I think I prefer Jake sane and violent. At least I had learnt the route maps of his moods. This slow fragmentation is far more frightening.

I have to get away. This time I must go when it is light and I must make sure I have plenty of clothes on. I would like to look at a map. I could get the exact position from the oak wood. All I need is to get to the main road.

I hear Jake coming back up the stairs and I hastily compose my face. He stares at me for a moment and then gently kisses the top of my head.

'You mustn't be afraid of me, Si, you know it upsets me. There is no reason to be afraid. I have everything I want now. I have you and this house.'

He takes a large bite of his toast and waves at me to do the same. I sip the hot tea and begin to nibble the edges of my toast. 'Good girl.' He smiles at me, then indicates the room. 'My mother,' he says, 'had this strange eccentricity, that if she kept a room ready, as if I, or a grandchild, might one day come, I would be safe in the world. So wherever she lived there was a bedroom for me. She never had any more children.'

He jabs the crumbs on his plate with a finger and puts them in his mouth.

'When I was born, my mother kept me. My father married Camilla and they both went off to work in America for a year. When he came back, he found that my mother had graduated to heroin and I was about to go into care. Camilla agreed to adopt me because she could not have any children.'

Jake is talking as if he is telling a story he has longed to tell, but never had anyone to tell it to. This is a Jake I don't know. All the time we were together he called Camilla his mother. I realized he

199

and Camilla were far from close. He did not talk about his childhood, but he would fly out to see them. He liked to name-drop, visit their friends, invite them to his exhibitions. I thought he had led a privileged and charmed life.

Jake smiles. 'Of course my father made sure I was his child first.'

'Why . . . why did they wait until you were seven to tell you Camilla was not your mother?' I ask.

'They didn't intend to tell me at all. My stepmother had agreed to adopt me as long as everyone believed I was hers. Can you think of a more ill-advised plan? A whole life built on lies. I was a year old and they set off for Hong Kong and a new life and pretended I was their natural child.'

He gets up and lights a cigarette from the packet on the table. 'Perhaps my wicked stepmother did love me when I was a little blond baby, but as I grew up, tall and fair, all I did was remind her that I was not her child, but a child of a beautiful woman who could have children. Who my father might possibly have loved.'

I think about Camilla. Small, dark, immaculately dressed. Polite, but cold. 'You call her your wicked stepmother, but she adopted *you*. She didn't have to.'

Jake laughs grimly. 'I have to have a drink,' he says.

'Jake, it's too early. Please don't drink.'

'Jake, it's too early. Please don't drink,' he mimics. 'I am not going to get drunk, Sigrid, I just need a drink.' He disappears downstairs and my heart sinks. He comes back with a glass and a bottle of whisky. I keep very still. I wish I had not said anything. I wish I could go and get dressed, but Jake has not finished. The tension in him is palpable.

He pours whisky into the glass and drinks. 'That woman I have just buried – I loathed her. As a small child I could not understand how I could loathe my own mother. I could not understand how I could be so repelled by the touch of her, by her dark body hair and sallow skin. I cannot bear dark women, they are repugnant to me.'

He sits on the bed and picks up my hand and curls his fingers round my thumb, holding them there. 'It took my father years to realize Camilla could not bear the child she had adopted. He came home one day unexpectedly. She had tied me to a kitchen chair, naked, ridiculing me. She was hitting me with a wooden spoon and screaming that I was an evil little bastard with a foul mouth.' His hands round my fingers tighten and hurt. Then he grins.

'I told her she was uglier than a witch, had hair like a gorilla, was far too ugly for my father to love her and I wanted to burn her skinny bones on a bonfire. My father carried me away to his study and told me Camilla was not my mother. I cannot tell you the utter, blissful, relief.'

He lets my hand go and pours more whisky. 'After that, my father packed me off to boarding school at seven and a half, for my own good.'

'You loved your father, though?' I say. I liked the judge. There was nothing cold about him.

'I adored him, you know that. And he loved me, and he tried hard to take care to protect me, but he was away so often. He was a circuit judge, and he advised in places like Singapore and Hong Kong. In the holidays he always employed a nanny or companion, so that I wasn't alone with Camilla. All the same, I dreaded the holidays.'

He gets up off the bed and goes and looks out on to the moor. 'I learnt well – a million ways to be cruel . . . as you know.' The wind rattles the window frames and a cold draught scurries through the room. The temperature is dropping and the house is beginning to feel freezing. Jake goes and switches a small radio on low. 'This weather – it's going to shut us in . . . I need to hear the forecast.'

He lights up and turns and looks at me. 'I was so unhappy, I asked my father if I could go back and live with my real mother. He told me it was impossible. She was drying out in a clinic actually. He begged my stepmother and me to try to like each other, to call a truce. And he planned as many trips abroad in my holidays as he could. To keep his love, we both, as we got older, played a clever game of let's pretend and social blarney to cover our mutual dislike.'

He gives that small laugh that I hate so much. 'My father caught me once, at thirteen, drowning Camilla's Siamese cat. He beat me while he cried and she yelled, 'I told you! I told you he is *evil*. Some children are born evil.'

'He caught her burning all the photos of my mother and the few precious letters he had kept for me to read when I grew up. He beat her until he cried. So we called a silent truce against his pain. The only thing we ever had in common was our unconditional love for him.'

I shiver, stare at him in silence. Into this silence I hear my name.

Jake swings towards the radio and turns it up. '. . . about five foot four, long blonde hair, of Scandinavian appearance. The police are anxious about her safety as she may have been a witness to the murder of Matthew Tregonning who was found dead in his flat on Thursday evening. They believe she could have been abducted by her estranged husband . . . six foot three, fair . . . Possibly somewhere in Cornwall or in the Dartmoor area. Anyone with any information, please phone . . . but do not approach . . .'

Jake switches the radio off. His face is pale and closed. 'Go and get dressed. I'll have to find you some more shoes. Go on, hurry up. Put as many layers of clothes on as you've got.' He follows me to the door.

'Si?' he says softly. I turn. 'No one else will have you, believe me, no one else.'

I feel sick. Outside the mist starts to descend, shutting me into the moor once again with Jake. I get dressed in as many layers as I can find and go downstairs. Jake is waiting in the hall with a pair of walking shoes and some thick socks. 'Try these.' I pull the shoes on. They are too big but fit comfortably with two pairs of socks.

Jake stands there waiting for me, looking at the photographs in the silver frames. I stare at them too.

'In those photographs you are about three or four. You said you were adopted when you were only a year old.'

Jake pulls his coat on and hands me mine. 'When I was about four, we came back from Hong Kong on leave and my father took me to see my mother. She had asked to see me just once, so that she could know for herself that I was well and happy. She was trying hard to kick the drugs and was about to marry, start a new life in Dublin.'

He hands me a woollen hat and pulls my hood up over it. 'I remember that meeting clearly, although I was only four. She was

202

the most stunning woman I had ever seen, with a soft southern accent. I walked through the garden of her home with her and I felt . . . right. As if some part of me instinctively remembered her. No one told me that this was my mother, no one said anything to me, but . . .' The pain in his face, so near to mine, is raw. 'When it was time to go I remember hugging and hugging her. I remember the smell of her and I remember the sound of her terrible crying when my father put me in the car, before we drove away. I never ever saw her again. I tried to find her when I left school, but I couldn't.'

His pain is darker than the day. 'My mother kept those photos of me, of that one day, all her life, in those silver frames. She was unable to have any more children.'

He goes to the door and throws it open and the hall fills with a bitter wind. 'It's not going to be pleasant out there.' He pushes me out and bangs the door shut behind him. He takes my arm and pulls me across the drive and through the gate, which he locks. We move down the track, our boots sliding in the mud. Into the mist which hangs like a flimsy cloud ahead of us. Away from the house that has lived so long on the memory of a small boy and a woman who waited for a son she knew would never come.

Chapter 29

Birds rise from the wet grass and sing against the sound of small waterfalls. The river has swollen with the constant rain and has overflowed into the fields and run down into the valleys of the moor, making the grass blue-green. As we reach higher ground the mist lifts for a moment.

Bog green, the ground. Sodden, squelchy underfoot, treacherous, sucking mud beneath our feet. Small pathways twist over desolate landscape, tors rise up in chilling spires like ghosts. Landmarks. I have never been able to read the map of barren paths, everywhere looks the same. Dartmoor, as nowhere else, makes me agoraphobic and dizzy. When we lived in the cottage I never ventured on new paths, only familiar circular ones.

But I am not alone. Jake is with me, firmly at my side. I am unsure why he has risked bringing me out again or where we are going, but the moor is deserted except for sheep, which cough in the hidden holes of the rocks and boulders and run out at our feet, making me jump.

The blue sky is disappearing again, the wind is rising and cloud is beginning to collect on the horizon in an ominous purple mass.

In moments, it will descend as mist, wet as rain, and it will suffocate us as completely as a blanket from the rest of the world. There will be no marker to indicate where I am on this earth. I will have disappeared, become invisible, evaporated into the air that touches my face like a clammy hand.

'Look at this mist coming in again. How can you possibly know where you're going? We're going to get lost out here.'

'Shut up. We are not going to get lost. I have a compass. I always know exactly where we are and where we are going, as you well know. Come on, Sigrid, keep moving.'

He pulls me after him and I see we are climbing uphill, travelling across country. Jake uses his compass in the fog. He has always been so sure of these moors. He will suddenly strike off the path and I always expect to end up in a bog, but we never do. We always finish up exactly where Jake has planned.

I fight a desire to scream out. However much I pretend I'm not afraid to die, there is terror when death draws near. I keep asking Jake where we are going, but he does not answer, just grimly grips my arm and leads me urgently forward. He seems hardly conscious of me, his mind somewhere else.

The going is tough and Jake moves so fast that breathing hurts me. There must be walkers out on the moor but I will never see them in this weather. I will never even know if they pass nearby.

Jake says, 'We'll stop in a minute and rest. I don't want to be long out here.' He starts to pull me downhill again and I realize we have circled, because the prison looms out of the mist in the distance and we are skirting the quarry. He must be making for his cottage.

Jake stops suddenly and makes me sit on a wet boulder while he rakes around in his pocket for his cigarettes. He stands in front of me breathing heavily, staring at me. He says, 'I killed her.'

Startled, I ask, 'Who?'

'Camilla. I killed her. She was foul to my father, she could not bear the fact he was going senile. I killed her.' His mouth is tight and cruel with anger.

'How?' I whisper. Jake closes his eyes for a second and I notice the black shadows under them, recognize exhaustion creeping into his bones.

'In Troödos. In the mountains. She used to like to swim in the hotel pool late at night when no one was around. I drowned her in the swimming pool. Or let's say I didn't help her when she slipped and hit her head going in. Silly, vain woman. I enjoyed every minute of the fear in her eyes. Every single minute of the knowledge of her own death.'

I begin to tremble uncontrollably. Jake finds his cigarettes and lights one. I watch him in horror and he suddenly looks up at me.

'Don't look at me like that. You have no right to judge me.' He too is shaking. 'She deserved to die. She tried to take my inheritance. She tried to take everything I ever had.'

'Please,' I whisper, 'can we just go back to the house? I'm cold. Please . . .'

'I want to get to the cottage. I need something from there. I need to know if it's being watched. I need to know how near they are.'

I am curious. He is taking risks and I wonder if he has a subconscious desire to be caught, to have an end to all this. I detect a terrible weariness in him.

'Jake,' I say cautiously, 'why don't we give this up?'

Furious, he leaps towards me and grabs me, pulls me to my feet and shakes me. ' "We"? There isn't a "we", is there? You lying treacherous little bitch. I should be in Cyprus with my father, but I needed to see what you were up to, and I was bloody well right to do so, wasn't I?'

I close my eyes against that face. He is working himself up to one of his terrible rages.

'You think your boyfriend was so pure, don't you? You are so gullible, Sigrid. Both your boyfriends were "user friendly" unbeknownst to you. They must just have had enough of you. I know I did. You are rather like the kiss of death . . .'

He draws heavily on his cigarette and laughs. 'The men you love have to be perfect, don't they? He wouldn't have dared take anything in front of you.' He grabs my coat suddenly. 'You know what the little bastard called me? A control freak. He told me I should back off and let you get on with your life. He said that to me . . . your husband . . . the little bastard.'

I open my eyes and stare at him, horrified. He had a conversation with Matt. Did Matt have time to know he was going to die?

Jake laughs at my face. 'Oh yes, darling, your boyfriend knew exactly who I was.' He hurls his cigarette into the wet grass. 'He should have watched his tongue. You are married to me.'

'He realized it was you in the car?'

'Yes, when I turned up at the flat. He was in a mighty temper about his car.'

I want to cry. 'You didn't have to kill him, for God's sake.'

'I did not go with the intention of killing him, I've told you. I meant to scare him off, in the same way as I rammed his car. I went to warn him, but he wasn't having it . . . He made me very angry. And the stuff he had lying about was very useful.'

I scream out at him, 'You're a liar! That's what you meant it to look like. You left those drugs in the flat. Why didn't you just come for me, leave him alone, you bastard? Just do whatever it is you are going to do. If you are going to kill me, do it, Jake, just stop playing games. You plan to kill me, don't you? Well, what are you waiting for? Just get on with it.'

Jake stares at me with contempt. Oh God, how I remember that look. He lets me go. 'Oh, yes. I am going to kill you. Of course I am. You deserve to die. There is no reason to let you live. You have no purpose on this planet. You have not made it better or wiser or more beautiful. You have just coloured it with your own paltry pain, tainted everyone you meet, as if no one else ever had a distorted childhood—'

'Shut up! Shut up! I don't want to hear your words . . .' I bring my hands up and grab his arms and shake his poisonous words away from me. 'Get on with it. Do it! Do it! Kill me if you are going to. Kill me, just get on with it.'

I am screaming at him now, out of control and he grabs me again and shakes me violently. 'Shut up! Shut up, will you?'

I stop as he reaches in his pocket again, but he brings out a hip flask and throws back his head and drinks from it. Then he listens. Nothing.

He stares at me and says coldly, 'Enough. Let's get moving.'

He holds on to my arm. We move on again down the valley where the mist is growing lower and lower. When the cottage comes in sight at the bottom, Jake pushes me under the overhanging rocks and gets his binoculars out. We crouch on the damp hillside, watching the cottage. It looks deserted.

I am puzzled. The police must surely be watching Jake's cottage, so why does he risk going back?

My eyes slide carefully over the countryside for movement, but I can see nothing. It is as silent down there as it ever was.

'OK,' Jake says. 'We'll go down slowly.' He comes very close and takes the syringe out of his pocket. 'Five minutes ago, I got very near to killing you with this. If you make a sound I won't hesitate, Si. You think you don't mind dying – well, I rather think you would.'

He pushes me down the hill slightly in front of him and moves warily towards the cottage, weaving away from the track to the back of the building. His eyes constantly scan the hillside. Small stones scud out from beneath our feet as we stumble in the wet.

The descending mist, blowing like fallen clouds, is a help and a hindrance to Jake. He cannot be seen so easily, but neither can he see. The cottage, as we approach from the trees abutting the bank behind the cottage, has an air of neglect, the windows dead, the back door in need of paint and full of weeds round the bottom of the door frame.

Jake has the key in his hand and he unlocks the back door and pushes me in quickly, closing and locking the door behind him.

'Stay there,' he says, dumping his rucksack on the ground.

The house is damp and cold, the Rayburn is out and the place smells of turps and drains. I go slowly to the doorway of the kitchen. Jake is on a chair unscrewing the ugly old-fashioned light fitting, which is like an upside-down soup plate with glass partitions. He takes from the light fitting two wads of money and a small white packet and drops them down on the table. Then he goes to the dresser and takes out our passports and two bottles of whisky from the top drawer. He must surely know we have no chance of using the passports.

He fumbles to unscrew the top of one of the whisky bottles and I watch his hands shake uncontrollably. He is sweating. He seems totally unaware of me standing there. He sits heavily on a kitchen chair and throws his head back and takes a long neat swig straight from the bottle. Then he folds into himself, eyes closed, legs spread-eagled outwards, exhausted.

I move slowly into the room. I lived with him for three years. He drank too much, heavily sometimes, I knew that, but this? Jake has always been such a proud man, contemptuous of drunks or drug addicts.

He has grown thinner, I suddenly realize. His clothes hang off his lanky frame, his limbs are no longer fit and hard. I suppose this is why he wore pyjamas. I see suddenly the beauty of his face is becoming dissipated. I pity him. He hardly knows what he is doing. Sad, fallen angel.

Conscious of my gaze, he opens his eyes. For a second I see shame. So desperate for a drink that he couldn't wait to hide and disguise.

'How long have you been drinking like this, Jake?' I ask.

'I am not an alcoholic.' His voice is sullen, defensive. He does not meet my eyes. 'We can't stay here . . . got to get home.'

'I want to go and get my horse carving.'

'I'll get—'

Both our eyes are drawn to the silent blue flash of a light moving slowly up the track at the front of the house through the mist and rain.

Jake claps his hand over my mouth and pulls me to the floor. We crouch there, listening to car doors slam. Jake pulls me in a bent run into the dark hall and we crouch near the front door, straining to hear. Then he peers carefully through the small window by the front door.

'Shit! There was someone out there at the top of the track.'

I hear footsteps coming nearer and Jake ducks down and pulls me right up against the front door, his grip tight. My heart is pounding. Oh God. Please, God . . . if I can just make a noise. I ease my weight slightly back to get my foot free to kick out at the door.

'Don't' Jake jerks my head back hard against him.

'Greg?' a man shouts.

'Over here!' There is a crunch. The voices are so near I want to cry.

'Where were you? You are supposed to be watching the house.'

'Trying to get radio reception. Had to get to higher ground. They think they have found the car in an old barn the other side of the moor, west of here.'

'Oh, that was all the crackling on my radio. Let's go. He was hardly going to come back here, was he?'

'God, this weather . . . This side of the moor gives me the creeps, too near the quarry, not enough sun.'

'There are a few empty houses near where they found the car. They've cordoned off the area from . . . Two Bridges . . . Ashburton road . . .' The voices and the footsteps fade. An engine starts up and there is the sound of tyres on wet slate and car lights, which disappear.

Jake let me go. 'Shit. Shit. Shit. We should have taken more from the house. We can't go back.' He looks at me in a sort of surprised daze, as if he thought no one would ever find us. He goes to the table and picks up the whisky bottle and waves it at me. 'Go and get your horse . . . if you still want it.'

I go upstairs to the bedroom. It is musty and damp. My things lie much as I left them, except the bed has been made. I feel shaky, disembodied. Did I really live here for four years, share a bed and a life with Jake?

I go to the windowsill and pick up my carving. Outside, where the hills rise up, small broken slate pieces, shiny green-black, lie on the surface of the ground, smooth and slippery as a lake. I go into the bathroom. In the distance the prison lies crouched behind the mist, tiny eyes blinkered by relentless rain. I shiver and go back downstairs.

Jake is making two black coffees. He hands me one and pours whisky into his. His eyes are bloodshot. He holds out his hand for my carving.

'I'll carry it for you, shall I, in my rucksack?' He folds his hands over mine for a moment as he takes the little horse, looks at me and smiles. 'Sorry I lost my temper out there, Si. It's just you and me now. You know that. Just you and me.'

He hums, moves away, puts the whisky and my carving in his rucksack, and the small white packet in his pocket and pats it. 'Insurance,' he says to himself. 'Sometimes buys you freedom.'

His hands shake; he is unsteady on his feet. Oh, how the mighty are fallen.

'Are you up to walking?' I ask, afraid of antagonizing him again. If only he would drink himself into a stupor.

'Course I am. In fifteen minutes I'll be singing,' he says sarcastically.

We leave the cottage the way we came. In a few minutes we have crossed the steep track and reached the high ground. In fifteen minutes Jake begins to hum.

Great boulders loom out of the mist, but despite the freezing rain and the wind buffeting us, making going slow, I recognize the landscape. I know the direction of the prison. I know where the river lies.

I look up and see a small patch of blue sky and a kestrel hovering on trembling wings before it dives. The mist is beginning to lift slightly. It swirls above our heads, vapourish, blowing away in hazy strips in front of us, over the moor towards the prison, squatting there with its tiny windows, watching.

Jake stops. 'I have to pee.' He turns slightly away from me, still humming. I am in front of him. This is it. This is my chance! I take off. Running, sprinting, pelting downhill, watching my feet. If I fall I've had it. I fly and fly, and hope flares. Small stones spin out from under my feet as I slip and slide and begin to gather speed as I career downhill.

I must not fall. I must not fall. I must find the track or the river. I can follow the river all the way down . . . There are police out there looking for me. I hear Jake's furious shout. I hear myself whimpering. But I hurtle onward, my breath coming in great aching gusts as I scud and leap downwards, my heart pounding, towards the sound of the flooded river, which I can follow downhill. To people and to safety.

Chapter 30

I can see the swollen river below me lying under a cloud of mist, bubbling fast over the rocks, the sound loud and comforting. The rain has stopped and I can see blue sky beyond flying grey clouds, which are pink-edged. I have longed for the mist to clear so I could be visible, tangible, rescuable in this desolate landscape, and now I pray for it to stay because I have far more chance of getting down river and away from Jake hiding within it.

I slow down, my chest aches, I have a stitch and I am coming to boggy ground. I turn and look behind me but Jake does not loom out of the mist above me and I move on again, trying to hurry and watch my feet, jumping from tuft to tuft of boggy grass, the water soaking my walking boots, until I get to a narrow sheep path leading down to the water.

Sheep run out from in front of me, startled and complaining, making my heart jump and I know Jake will hear the sound and know exactly my position. He does not have to hurry.

There is a stile somewhere near, I know this, where I can climb over the fence and then cross the river but I cannot see it. When I reach the fence, I turn up river again, thinking that Jake will expect me to follow the river down and make straight for the road.

With relief I see the stile and climb the high wooden steps and then cross the river on the small bridge to the other side where there is a hut. I stop and look both sides of the river bank, but I cannot see Jake. I cannot see anything but this extraordinarily beautiful mother-of-pearl mist hanging over the running water like an ethereal ghostly cloud.

If the sun comes out the mist will burn off in minutes. I shake with anxiety. I am suddenly unsure what to do. I crouch down by the water and lean against a smooth boulder. I am warm with running, but my feet are already cold and wet.

If I move up river I will be safe from Jake, but I risk being lost if the weather deteriorates. I am too thin and ill-equipped to last long out here. If I knew the weather was going to clear I could circle back up hill and down the valley again, back to Jake's cottage and the track to the road.

I will have to risk moving down river as I intended, and hope the mist will last to hide me until I have a chance of reaching the road. I suddenly realize Jake will have to stay the far side of the river until it narrows and diverts into a stream round the woods far below me. The river is far too swollen to cross before the next bridge, which is much lower down. So even if he can see me, he cannot reach me.

I look down at the water falling in frothy torrents over stones as smooth as eggs and I remember a time a hundred years ago, in another life, when Jake and I, baking in an Indian summer, took our clothes off and lay in the trickle of a stream, laughing and naked, trying to get cool.

I cannot remember if that day ended in happiness, or was marred by sudden angry words, a lightning turn of mood.

My eyes are drawn downwards and I see below me a flash of blue moving down into the mist the other side of the river. My heart jumps with trepidation, but at least I know where he is and which way he is going.

I get up and follow the muddy path down, into the mist that blows away in wet wisps in front of me. I walk as fast as I can, trying to get warmth and feeling back into my icy feet. I hear Jake's words in my head. '*Both your boyfriends were "user friendly" unbeknownst to you. They must just have had enough of you . . . You are rather like the kiss of death.*'

I smell the whisky again and see his pleased face. He is so adept at making me believe things, twisting and turning the sense of events or words. It is because there is always an element of truth in what he says, always a raw spot he is able to touch with utter skill and practised cleverness.

I know in my heart it is possible that both Dan and Matt smoked the odd spliff. But Jake is able to suggest so much more. *User friendly*. Words Jake would not dream of using normally. And he is right, I am like the kiss of death. With Jake, after a while, it becomes impossible to distinguish and unravel lies from reality.

I remember again the awful numbness that crept over me in order to get through some of the bad days with him and the gratitude I felt for that numbness. Anything to avoid the cruelty of his tongue. The effect of his words, like a dripping tap, can make a short circuit in my brain. My mind will fizz and dart this way and that to get away.

I must not forget, I must never forget the power he had in making me believe I was unbalanced. The suggestion of my frailty was always there. The truth of it is that it does lie there. I know this. I know myself. Frailty can lie hidden and dormant. Maybe with love and security it can die. But with the deft cruelty of Jake's tongue it was turned into a defect, to be brought to the surface of my skin, like an incurable and painful affliction.

It is the terror that Jake will take me, make me turn back into the shivering shame of an attic bedroom that lies level with the rooftops of a city where doves cooed into the warmth of the lead piping that clad the chimney. The fear that he will pull out from my being – like a tooth extracted without an anaesthetic – what I cannot bear to acknowledge without something central dying within me.

The pain has always been like a bruise, an ache, a sadness that lives on and on inside me. I can pretend. For ages and ages I can pretend, then suddenly grief will catch me unawares, it will burst from me. It will swamp me under the weight of his soft, silky, insidious words, soft as petals falling.

I glimpse myself in his words, a fleeting reflection he makes into truth. This, this is what Jake thinks of me. Is this what I am?

I would walk away from his voice, very straight, head high, away, as carefully as a drunk trying to leave the room with dignity, so that he would not see the shudder starting from somewhere deep inside me. So that he would not see his words hit their target.

Is this what made him angry? My refusal ever to break down, tell all? Would he have loved me more if he had known for sure what he suspected?

He stroked my guilt. He touched my wound, my private hell. He sensed my shame and my ignorance, my selfishness and deceit. He put a sure, deft finger on the amorphous place that I am.

Wet mud collects in great clumps on my shoes. The path bends round to another small bridge where the river becomes narrower. The mist is blowing away from me, will soon be gone. I look all around me, anxiously. No Jake. Below me I see fir trees. Under them it will be dryer. In that wood I will stop for a bit and be hidden.

The smell of the firs rises up with the damp as I move into the wood, evocative, full of childhood memories. I walk in to the thicker trees, slide down against a large trunk and close my eyes.

I run into the dark wood of my mind and crouch below the branches of great pine trees, heavy with the first snows, crisp and sparkling, which falls in dry flakes that scatter over our clothes like icing sugar. I lean against the great depth of their trunks, crouch lower and lower into their roots for the earth to swallow me up as I hear my mother calling. 'Sigrid . . . Sigrid . . . Come on. Time to go home. We'll miss the plane if you don't come now . . .'

I cover my face and I ache for a past I cannot undo. I listen to the wind blow the tall tops of the firs and bend them and one voice joins another and another until all voices shout and drown each other out.

I make no sound. I am deaf and dumb to all, to everything except this searing, primitive pain. The loss that lives on in me does not diminish, only ages as I do.

Mom, Mother, Mumps, Mama. Why did you never come?

You are gone. And I can never ask you . . . Why?

I bring death with me like a sting. The velvet voice is right . . .

I open my eyes and Jake is standing just off the path by the ditch leading into the wood. He is looking the other way and listening. He half turns as if he senses me, and I freeze. But he doesn't see me crouched down amongst the broken branches and fir cones, in the shadows.

Suddenly, in the distance, there is the sound of voices from the path further up. Jake dives into the wood and moves into the shadow of the trees. He is near enough for me to see his face. My heart jerks about. When they get nearer, I can call out. I can run. Except that Jake is between me and the path.

Two people come into view, talking, carrying walking sticks and maps. They are walking quickly and do not look around them. I try to gauge whether in my crouched position I can get to my feet and run, reach them before Jake reaches me. I look up. Jake's face is in profile, his body still and frozen, staring towards the walkers. Suddenly, he turns and sees me. Stares at me. Something in his face, in the way he stands makes me think of a hunted animal.

I open my mouth to shout out. To yell. And no sound comes. I try and try and no sound comes. Jake's eyes never leave my face and no sound will come. He starts to walk towards me. The moment is gone. I have missed my chance. The walkers are now too far away.

Jake moves quickly towards me. In his face a small tic starts under his right eye, and his face is driven and drawn. This is probably where I am going to die, amongst the trees, with the smell of firs in my nostrils. I am too tired and cold to try to fight back.

Jake bends and lifts me roughly to my feet without a word, and pulls me deeper and deeper into the wood where the saplings are closer and thicker. He swings his rucksack off his back and still without speaking makes me crawl in front of him into a deep hollow of trees like a cave. Then he opens the rucksack, gets out a flask and pours me a black coffee and holds my shaking hands around it. He whispers, very softly, his voice a caressing shiver of wind in the shadows, 'Try to sleep. We are going to stay here until dark.'

I roll away from him on to my side and burrow into the dry fir prickles. I bring my knees up to my chin and I fly away from the wood with my eyes tight shut.

I dream. I dream about days when my mother still laughed. I try to remember the time, when I was very young, when her hair was loose, not in that tight little bun thing which I grew to hate, which drew her face tight too.

I try to remember when she stopped wearing any make-up and the movements of her loose-limbed body changed, lost that little lilt as she walked. As I get older, I realize how young she was when I was small, but she did not seem young to me then.

After she died, I tried to remember conversations I had with her. I

217

tried to hear again the tone of her voice and the way she smiled, and it was difficult. The more I panicked, the more shadowy and insubstantial she became. I could not hold on to anything that gave me a clue to her pain or her happiness. Her hopes or her feelings for me or my father.

I remember her clear joy on only two occasions. One was on a skiing holiday, in France, not in Norway. The three of us. She was in her element, literally. I caught a wonderful glimpse of how she could be.

On skis, she flew, grew wings of delight and lightness. She skimmed over crystal snow like a princess. She shot past us laughing, encouraging me and my father, who were only average skiers.

She was slim and beautiful in her bright ski suits, her blonde hair streamed behind her, she outperformed everyone. I could see that my father was proud; I could see that she bathed in his pride and attention, revelled in her own expertise and the allure of a beautiful woman doing something superbly.

She was exhilarated by the snow, the sun making it sparkle in a hard crust and casting shadows on the mountains. It is the only time I can remember her as sexual, using her body to attract. She was on a high. Ex-Norwegian skiing champion showing the world how it was done.

It is the only time I can remember her like that. Her body was slim and boyish, almost asexual. Deliberately, I thought later. This, this was the life she loved and missed to a degree my father and I could never guess at.

I was much too young to know these things about her. It was only when I was adult and looked at the many photos of that holiday that I could imagine these things.

I was jealous of her on that holiday. Jealous of the attention my father was suddenly giving her. One evening I heard them drinking and laughing in the next room of the chalet we were in. I loved the sound of the laughter between them. I wanted to join in, it made me feel secure and happy.

My father laughed at me in my new pyjamas and pulled me on his knee. 'Look at her,' he said to my mother. 'She is going to be a little beauty.' My heart swelled with pride, for my father rarely appeared to notice me at home.

'She already is.' My mother blew me a kiss and put a thimble of wine into a grown-up glass and gave it to me, and I wiggled with pleasure and flirted with my father and they both laughed.

My father carried me back to bed and tucked me in, kissed me good night. It was the first time I can remember him ever doing it. Usually he was working still when I went to bed.

I think it was the first time he noticed me. I had made him notice me by competing with my mother. So the things that happened later were my fault.

The door was still ajar and I heard my father say, 'We ought to have another child, Kristian.'

'No!' Her vehemence made me jump. 'Never!'

The laughter and the noise of their happiness stopped suddenly like a light going out. I thought she didn't want more children because having me must have been so painful. It was only when she died I learnt that from the day I was born, she never slept willingly with my father again.

Looking back, it seems to me that she stifled her sexuality and her emotions, snuffed out all feeling until she was almost invisible. Whether this was caused by her depression, or whether her depression stifled her life, I will never know. Her paleness, which I have inherited, was accentuated by her white eyelashes. She stopped wearing mascara or colour on her cheeks. Her eyes seemed to disappear into the paleness. I could not read her thoughts or watch any shadows of feeling play across her face.

I cannot sleep. I am too cold, even though a silvery slither, a finger of sun, shines downwards through the branches and just touches my hand. I sit up.

Jake turns and sees me shivering and pulls me to him. 'We need to keep warm, to keep our body temperature up. As soon as it is dark, we'll move.' He too must be regretting this watery sun, too high to warm anything but strong enough to burn the mist away.

Another time of happiness came later. My grandmother had flown in to see us from Oslo. She had been staying with a friend near Salisbury and then moved into a small hotel there.

219

The hotel was a little manor house set in the countryside, covered in Virginia creeper, with sloping lawns that rolled down to a river, like a Constable painting. The gardens were full of colourful shrubs, things my mother could not grow in Scotland.

I was excited. We had come down on the train, my mother and I, and it was an adventure because my mother rarely went anywhere. All that long train journey I anticipated the joy of seeing my grandmother waiting for us on Salisbury station. I missed her so much, I could not believe she would be there, and the reality was as searingly wonderful as the anticipation.

I watched my mother's face light up as the train drew in and we caught a glimpse of my tall, imposing grandmother. A small, passing, wistful flame lit my mother's rather flat and pale features, making her look earnest and very young.

I quickly gathered up all her things, suffused with love for her and excitement, and the pleasure of the two of us doing something together. She couldn't have been much older than I am now.

It was only when we were all back at the hotel, having tea in the garden, that I wondered why my grandmother had not come up to Scotland to see us.

'Too far, darling,' she said. 'I only have ten days, and so much to do, so many friends to see.'

But it was really because she disliked my father.

By the table in that garden of the hotel there was a philadelphus bush, flowering. The scent was pungent, the dry branches heavy with the pure white blooms. Petals strewed the ground and my mother got up repeatedly from the table and bent her face to the flowers, making herself giddy with their scent. Exclaiming in wonder at their beauty, wishing she could eat or paint them. Almost in tears with delight.

It felt so good to see her animated, alive and happy; it was so rare. But I noticed my grandmother looking sad and anxious as she watched her. I was too young to know then that the degree of my mother's reactions to things was not always appropriate or balanced.

Later, after my grandmother showed us our room next to hers, my mother and grandmother went downstairs, back to the garden for an early evening drink, leaving me to unpack my toys and half watch television.

I could look out of the window, where the creeper made fluttery green outside curtains, and see both their heads bent deep in conversation, earnest, serious, grown-up conversation. Bodies tense.

I felt immediately anxious, because sometimes my mother and my grandmother argued. I turned the television off, picked up my book and went down to them. Neither of them saw or heard me behind them.

My grandmother was saying, 'Kristian, please come home for a while. Come for a long holiday. Bring the child. Your father is so worried about you. You know that is why I am here.'

My mother shook her head.

'But why? Tell me why. You are so obviously unhappy. What is the point of making yourself ill?'

'I married a Scot, Mother. My home is there.'

'Even if you do not love him? Even if you are obviously not happy there?'

'You want me to come home so you and Dad can say "I told you so"?'

'We would never say that, Kristian. Your father and I did not want you to marry David, it is true, because we did not think you were over Erik's death and because we did not think David was right for you.'

'But I did marry him, Mother. I've made my bed and I've got to lie on it.'

'And that is the problem, isn't it?' my grandmother said very quietly.

'What?' My mother seemed startled, then embarrassed.

'I am your mother, Kristian, of course I notice these things. You hate David touching you. I've watched you flinch even if he brushes past you. I presume you do not enjoy that side of life . . .'

'I hate it. I loathe it,' my mother hissed at my grandmother, startling her. 'It's gross . . . it's an invasion . . . it . . . it's messy and revolting and painful . . . and I can't bear it . . . I do not want to bear it ever, ever again.'

My grandmother lit up a cigarette. 'Did you feel the same way with Erik?'

My mother grabbed the packet and lit a cigarette with shaking fingers.

'Erik wasn't like David. We were so young, Muma. We had to work so hard to keep fit. Our whole life was skiing. We were ambitious and competitive, and sex was . . . was not important.'

My grandmother stared at my mother, then said in a surprised voice, 'You and Erik did not sleep together? I . . . well, you were so close, I just assumed . . .'

My mother said bitterly, 'David says I'm frigid. I don't know if I am or not. Erik is the only boyfriend I ever had before David. We grew up together, went to school together, always knew we would get married or live together, so I don't know'

My grandmother was silent for a moment, then she said, 'I take it . . . the first time . . . your honeymoon was not a success, Kristian?'

'Awful. Oh, so awful. He was drunk . . . didn't believe I was a virgin . . . He was so rough and loathsome . . . all that sweating and pawing and touching. Where's the love in it, Muma? Where? I can never say "No". He forces me to, however I feel . . . Oh God . . . sex makes me sick with revulsion.'

I thought my grandmother was going to cry. She said, 'Why, why did you not tell me this before? Kristian, you do not have a marriage. Come home. You are wasting your life here and you know it. There are so many things back home that you enjoy. You can teach, you can ski . . . Your father and I will help you. Every time I see you, you are more sad and depressed. What keeps you here? You are not making any sense.'

'If I had not had Sigrid, I expect I would come home. But I had her straight away and David adores the child, and she adores him. She has started school here. I have no right to deny him his child.'

'I am not asking you to. She will always be his child. You coming back to Norway doesn't mean he cannot see her. Am I missing something here, Kristian? What do you feel for David?'

'We have come to an understanding. I will not leave him, take the child from him. He will mostly . . . leave me alone.'

'That's it, is it? That is the sum total of your reason for staying?

222

And, despite not having a sex life, Kristian, do you love him? Is he good and kind to you in other ways? Make me understand.' I can hear the anger in my grandmother's voice.

'I have a beautiful home, Mother. I have lovely things. I have plenty of money. David has to entertain; I help him. I'm not unhappy all the time. I'm not . . . I just get depressed sometimes.' She pauses. 'I don't want to have to live with you and Dad again. I like my own place. I don't want to have to share. With five of us I have had to share all my life. I don't want to struggle for money, and whatever you think of him, he is the father of my child and I am fond of him. I am trying to make the marriage work, have a life of my own . . .'

I make an involuntary movement and my grandmother sees me. She leans quickly forward and says firmly, and I can hear her anger, 'Then for God's sake, try to be happy and cheerful for the child, Kristian. You have made your choice. I am tired of your misery, which I am beginning to think is an indulgence . . .'

My mother scrapes back her chair. I can see her trying not to cry and I am for a moment cross with my grandmother. My mother leaves the garden and I sit in her chair and drink a Coke with my grandmother as dusk comes and bats flit low over our heads and lights come on in the hotel.

I stayed up and had supper with them both in the dining room and I ached for them to be friends again. Later, my mother and grandmother stood in the bathroom while I was in the bath and hugged and hugged each other.

'I'm sorry, my darling. I love you so, so much,' my grandmother said. 'You are my beautiful, talented daughter, and all I want is for you to be happy.'

'I know. I know,' my mother said, and they rocked and rocked, holding each other in the room where the green creeper came in the window.

This was only the beginning, the first of so many circular quarrels that punctured my childhood. My grandmother, protective of me, eventually relinquished my mother for ever.

Chapter 31

When I wake it is almost dark. I am thirsty and the trees are crouched around me, waiting. Jake's body generates heat as the temperature drops and night swoops in. He is very still. I cannot tell whether he sleeps or not. I think about dying. I think of Beth and John in Huer's Cottage . . . Beth getting supper for the twins. I think of Talland House and the photograph I love so much of Virginia Woolf. I see the little gap in her hair where she has pulled it back. The beautifully shaped ear and long flawless neck. The perfect profile. Sensuous lips, large straight nose, heavy eyebrows and serious sad eyes, focused where no one can follow.

The collar of her dress is white and lacy, pure and romantic. Ageless. As if she is caught in this photograph dying young and beautiful. Except the truth is in later photographs. Virginia hanging on to her friend Violet Dickinson in her garden, looking anorexic and haunted.

My mother died young and beautiful. Words never spoken hovered between us, never to be acknowledged. They hung in the air through my childhood and in our eyes, which never met.

When she died, when I was left alone with my father, I thought about running away to Norway, to my grandparents. But my father was so broken. He shrivelled before my eyes, became suddenly old. He employed a housekeeper, travelled more with his job. He never touched me again, after my mother died.

I close my eyes once more. My mother's ghost haunted that terraced house of my childhood. Resentment gathered inside me like the dust on her things. Grew like my father's guilt, until he too could no longer bear to meet the eyes of a daughter no longer a child.

He came home less and less, met his future wife. Left me with a fat and lazy housekeeper. I spent my time working for A levels and riding my friend's horse. Those two years between my mother dying and my going to university seemed the longest of my life.

I never went back. I met Dan on the train to Bristol and wherever he went in the holidays, I went too.

Jake sits up and fumbles around for his rucksack, gets out the flask and hands me the remains of the tepid coffee. 'Ready?' he asks.

We crawl out of the trees and I find I am so cold I am numb. Jake jerks me upright and makes me wave my arms and jump up and down, then we move back towards the path and the river, which has narrowed into a thin stream round the wood. Jake does not speak, just leads me out of the trees, downhill again, following the stream, towards the road. In the distance, some way across the moor, I suddenly see a host of small lights bobbing about. My heart leaps. The police?

Jake stops and watches the lights fanning out like fireflies. 'It might just be army manoeuvres, but I don't think we'll take the chance, darling.'

'We are not going back into the wood?'

Jake laughs shortly. 'As you well know, I am much safer out here where I know every rock and cranny than I am waiting like a sitting duck.'

He listens, then pulls me cautiously across the stream and over the fields. My feet are soaking. Every so often we stop and listen, and I catch the feeling of what it must be like to be hunted.

We make a detour round a farm and I see the lights are getting further away and Jake's strange detachment begins to scare me. We reach the road and Jake hurries me across it. I can see the lights of a hotel to my left and in the distance, a long way away, the tiny squares of a billion lighted windows of the prison loom out of the night like a ship.

Back into the dark, and Jake leads me stumbling over the rocks. Our breath is coming hard and fast, rasping into the dark air as I try to stay upright. We are covering the ground at great speed towards what I most fear.

The quarry looms up in front of us, sinister and overbearing in its desolate, mysterious and sad beauty. It holds all the despair of prisoners in chains with hardly any hope of escape, and it holds the violence of man and nature in its smooth deceptive depths.

Jake pulls me round towards the jagged black rocks that rise dizzily upwards from the edge of the water. It is the terror of my endless dream. It gives reason and validity to the nightmare I have had since childhood. The child in the red dress will rise from the corpse of the adult me in an inevitable and apt ending.

I fight hysteria. There is a difference in Jake. A calmness, almost a happiness, a relief. He is unhurried. As if he has accepted his end. But his end will be mine and I am terrified by his icy impassiveness.

Jake drops his knapsack on the ground and takes out an abseiling rope, puts it round my waist and clips me to him. His face is very near mine.

'I can't climb in the dark,' I say. 'I can't . . . What are—'

'We don't need to climb.' He helps me over the low shiny black rocks to the edge of the water. 'We have to walk around to the other side of the quarry. Step where I step, Sigrid. I don't want to lose you in the dark.'

Jake begins to clamber over the rocks, carefully, almost on all fours, and I follow behind, terrified of losing my footing as we climb round into the deep looming shadow of rock face. I look away across the bleak moor disappearing from sight. There are still lights out there, moving. I could scream out into the night. But I would only frighten myself. Jake is nearer than anyone else to me.

After a while we turn to our right and the rock face falls away as we begin to climb upwards on to marshy ground. 'Stay here a minute.' Jake moves off into the dark and the rope round my waist tightens.

The sky is lightening fractionally and I can see little islands of grass and a small elder tree lying on the surface of the water. All, all around me is the echo and sigh of the wind. The lap of water, like the ripple of a small wave, sounds like voices underwater swirling round the mounds and chambers of the quarry like dark seagulls' wings.

Jake is climbing back down to me. 'Right. Follow me exactly.

Where I shine the torch, place your feet. It's not far. We are climbing up where we can view the world together, darling.'

His voice is gentle, solicitous, honey-coated and mad. I place my feet where he shines the torch and slowly heave myself up after him on the boggy ground. I see we are nearly at the top. I can see the grass overhang of the top of the cliff and tiny flowers like stars are caught in the glow of his torch. Behind him, spanning out over the hillside there are still pinpricks of moving lights.

Jake turns suddenly and bends under the overhang of the cliff, moves carefully over the grassy slippery wet rocks and the lights disappear. If I slip I will gash myself badly. I reach him and he pulls me up on to the shelf of rock, shines the torch in my face. 'There! Well done.'

I crouch next to him, shivering, shuddering with cold and fear. 'Don't be afraid,' he says gently, taking my hand. 'Death is nothing to be afraid of.'

'I don't want to die!' My cry echoes across the rocks and bounces up into the night sky. 'Jake, I don't want to die.'

'Shush. Shush, darling. We are together, that's all that matters. We are together. We will jump side by side and this rope will hold us together for eternity. Isn't that wonderful? Isn't that how it should be? You will never leave me again. And I will never leave you.'

He gets to his feet, holding on to the overhanging rock, and pulls me to him so that I face him and the water below, and he faces me and the rock face, balancing precariously. We are suspended, both of us, like kestrels, high, high up on the edge of the quarry.

The moon comes from behind the clouds for a second and is reflected in the black water below me. It lights up Jake's pale face so close to mine.

'I am afraid, Jake, so, so afraid of that water . . .'

'You have always been haunted by this quarry. And it is so beautiful. You and I will just be two more ghosts joining a myriad others, darling, that's all we'll be.'

'Please, Jake . . .' Desperate, I place my cheek to his. It is so cold. Behind him the moon reflected in the water is already forming features. Clouds blow across the face of the moon and darkness is back, but Jake keeps his face to mine, stays still as if my cheek warms him.

He body suddenly gives a quiver of pain or fear. I don't know which. He presses me close to him. 'The first time you kill is very hard,' he whispers. 'Terrible . . . After that it gets easier and easier. I killed my stepmother because she was cruel and made my childhood a living hell – was vicious to my father in his old age . . . It was not hard to kill her at all. I did not intend to kill the Cornish boy, but I watched you together. It was like Dan all over again . . . He was going to take you away from me.'

I am very still. I listen to his words and I am very still against his body. 'I know you understand. We are alike, you and I.' He pauses. 'Except you are only twenty-four years old and you have never hurt anyone in your life . . .'

His voice wavers as if something is breaking inside him. 'I loved you, I loved you. I would so have loved to have had children with you, but I am damaged, I am flawed and knowing this I wilfully damaged you. I wanted to keep you with me for ever, to love me despite everything, but it won't do . . .'

His hand holds my head to him for a second, his mouth is in my hair. Then he holds me away and shakes me. I look into the depths of his eyes and his pain is exposed, bleak and irredeemable. As sad and endless as infinity. But not mad.

'Yell!' he whispers urgently. 'Yell, Sigrid! Scream! Scream out all that you really feel about your parents, from the depths of your being. Come on, Sigrid, do it! End your terrible silence. Scream out what you have never dared even *think* . . .'

I open and shut my mouth, startled. His voice is rough and angry. 'Scream, damn you! Scream it out now or we'll jump.' He shakes me again, hard.

The moon sails out from the clouds once more and I look down into the water and I see the faces of dead men looking up at me like a hundred moons.

Above me, the blue-black sky is spread with stars like daisies and I feel this huge surge within me as if some monstrous thing were tearing out of my body. A great, overpowering, frightening sound rises up and up and up and bursts out of my heart into the blackness in a strange voice I do not recognize.

'You bastard . . . bastard . . . bastard . . .! How dare you? How dare you think I was yours like a doll? You made me ashamed. You damaged me for ever . . . I loved you, you were my father . . . You were my father . . . I wanted you to love me as your child. But your guilt made you ignore me by day . . . And you took me at night . . . You made me know my body before I should . . . enjoy what was wrong . . . Bastard . . . I hate you . . . hate you . . . bastard . . .'

Jake holds me, tight, tight against the cliff face of the quarry. I breathe. My body quivers and jerks in a terrible paroxysm of rage and bitter grief. 'And you . . .' I try to scream at my mother, but no sound will come.

I hurt. I hurt. A sickness rises in me, more agonizing than any death. A merciless betrayal.

'Yell,' Jake insists in his soft, beautiful voice. Holding me, steadying me, bracing himself against the cliff face. 'Yell loud.'

'You, Kristian,' I whisper. 'You . . . you were worse . . . much worse . . . I was a child and you sacrificed me. In the end you knew . . . You sat and did not lift a finger . . . You watched my life blighted and damned to everlasting nightmares and you pretended it wasn't happening . . .'

My voice begins to rise with this harsh and unbearable anger until I am screaming again. 'How could you? How could you watch? How could you *know*, and pretend it was nothing to do with you? Did you love him so much you would sacrifice anything to keep him? I'll never understand . . . because that love never showed . . . Never. Then you just had enough of life and left me. Bloody hell, Kristian . . .'

On and on and on I yell until I am hoarse while Jake still holds me steady by my shoulders, still braces himself into the shelf of the cliff.

'For both of us,' he whispers with his lovely voice in my ear. 'That's it, yell for both of us. Now, my darling, it's done with . . . Over.'

I hold on to him, tight, tight, sobbing. 'No, it can't be over. It won't ever be over. I hurt. I hurt too much, Jake . . . Oh God, help me, help me. Let's go. Now, Jake, let's jump. Let's do it. Hold me, we'll jump together. You are right, it's the only way . . .'

For a second I see his beautiful face as it was. As it was when I first loved him. Love for me shows in his eyes for a second like a sad glitter of frost. 'No, Si. You are not your mother. You have a whole life in front of you. You can move on now, darling. It's over. It's done with. Move on. Let it all go. I have nowhere to go, but you have everywhere.'

Before I can move, before I can speak, he unclips the rope holding us together and he jumps back, kicking away from the rock face with his feet and he falls, silently he falls, down, down into the black water and disappears.

He does not come up.

'No! Jake! No!' I scream, clutching the rock face. But he does not come up.

The moon lights the thick ripples forming on the water, highlights the small child in the red dress rising up, up from the depths, face upturned this time, not dead, pale as death, but alive and floating.

The bobbing lights have reached me. People are shouting in the dark. I cannot move or stop screaming and the sound rises up from the quarry and echoes again and again, reverberates off the black rocks as if I am being answered by ghosts.

A young soldier in camouflage shines a torch on my face and reaches down over the ledge to grab my arm. 'Ssh . . . Ssh, it's all right . . . It's all right. Come on, love, give me your hand. That's it, good girl . . . Good girl.'

I am surrounded by uniforms. They are soldiers. They are not police. They are just army cadets on exercise. I start to laugh and I can't seem to stop, even when I see the police helicopter hovering above me.

I am wrapped in a rug. A radio crackles. 'Female hostage alive and safe. Repeat, female hostage alive and safe . . . Require frogman and diving equipment. One fatality. Repeat, one fatality.'

Chapter 32

St Michael's Mount is surrounded by a deep violet sea. Yachts are racing, white sails fluttering as the small boats dip and plunge in a steady breeze. I cannot see the white lighthouse from here, but it too will be encircled by this purple sea.

The London train is standing stationary with its doors open at Penzance station while the buffet car is loaded on. The twins, Mutton and Alice pour out of the car noisily and head towards the train. Mutton is quite recovered, thank goodness, and is as greedy and loving as ever, and John and Beth have adopted timid little Alice. John picks up my rucksack and Beth and I gather up my bits and pieces.

Beth is trying not to cry.

'Promise me, Si, promise you will write. Please don't just disappear. I am going to miss you so much.'

I take her arm. 'Beth, of course I'll write. I can telephone you too. It's not for ever. I am not going away for ever.'

'It feels like it.' She puts down my bag of books and holds out her arms.

'You know I'm going to worry about you.'

Beth has been protective as a mother to me. She has fought hard to help me get to this point, confident enough to move forward. I go to hug her. Her baby is due in two months, so it's not possible to squeeze her to me. But I hold her sweet face to my cheek as she whispers fiercely, 'It's going to feel so odd without you in the house. Awful, Si. You are the bravest person I know.'

'Rubbish! You are the most incredible friend I'll ever have, Beth. I owe you and John more than I can ever tell you.'

'Balls!' John says, turning and putting his arm round Beth and then me, drawing us in to him. 'I'm not good at this, Siggi. I hate goodbyes. Will you try to think of Huer's Cottage as home, and Beth and me as aged parents you must visit at very regular intervals or we will be devastated and pine?'

'Especially,' Beth adds, 'as you are now one of my most obsessive Woolfies.'

I laugh and we hug one more time. Then I bend to hold the twins for a second, touch the soft heads of the dogs. Train doors bang. The whistle is about to go. My heart lurches painfully. I will not cry.

John leaps on and puts my things into the luggage rack and jumps off. I get in the train, close the door and lean out. I've done it. The guard blows the whistle, one sharp piercing warning of departure.

A signal. The end of something. An ending.

'You will let me know about the baby?' I cry. 'You will take care, won't you? You will . . .' The train jerks twice and pulls slowly out of Penzance. I lean further and further out, waving and waving as the train draws slowly away.

They are all standing quite still, solemn as I leave. Even Mutton and Alice. I raise my hand in a last farewell until the train turns the curve of the line and I can suddenly no longer see them. I stand for a second, staring at the sea, frozen with terror, the tears rising in my chest like a wave.

The Mount slips by, perched high on the dark rocks like a fairy castle in a Gothic film. The sun lightens the sombre stone, flag flying high. I think of Beth and John driving home, the incandescent sea, which changes as quickly as a mood, on their right. As constant and endemic to their lives as breathing. I think about the lighthouse, always there in the distance wherever I walked.

I think of Huer's Cottage, higgledy-piggledy, facing the harbour and catching the winds, full of children and dogs and laughter and warmth. I think, with a pang, of Talland House, full of haunting memories, of past lives hovering everywhere. Full of old photographs and books. A haven these last few months. This is how I will always remember Cornwall.

I move from the window and find a seat. I check my connecting flight number and times and then put the ticket safely away.

I am so glad Beth and John are helping to preserve the past in that house. Preserving the future. Contributing to the memory of a brilliant and troubled writer who goes on and on touching and reaching the core of people coming after her.

No one can replace staircase and fireplaces. It will never be possible to replace the Victorian greenhouse that was left to rot, or undo the brutal sixties division of rooms into flats. But they can, on windy nights, sit and tell the twins and the baby not yet born about the acres of garden that surrounded that house, full of escallonia and camellia. They can describe the pineapple orchard and the peach trees that grew luscious against a white wall in the sun.

They can try to invoke the echo of children playing tennis and croquet, hide-and-seek and sardines, their long white dresses swishing over lawns full of the shadows of evening.

Already, a Cornish childhood is being invoked and lived in the heart of the twins. A lifeboat being launched in high seas, fishing off the pier. Long wet or hot summers. Wet sand like sandpaper on bare legs. Fresh sardines or mackerel, just caught, at the beach café, where the coast on a hot day glitters and curves away like the Amalfi coast, in a rash of little whitewashed houses.

Hanna . . . Amy . . . at university, soporific on a hot day in a dusty city . . . 'Yes . . . well . . . I *practically grew up* in Virginia Woolf's childhood home, so by the time we were twelve, Mum had made us read *everything* by her . . .'

Sometimes, I have this daydream that John and Beth are able to buy Talland House and the car park and all the surrounding land back, and turn the whole place once again into an oasis, a magic past where life seemed slow and safe. Childhood too.

By drowning in that river Virginia Woolf ensured her own rebirth again and again with each generation.

Next year I am going back to school, to Durham, to read English. I will always paint, it is a part of me. But I have a burning need to read, maybe one day, to write. Not because I have become fascinated by Woolf and her contemporaries – it is more than that.

I know now. Our lives are so fleeting, so small. We are moulded by our background, our parents, the context of our time and place in the world.

Virginia Woolf's views and imagination would have been no less acute if she had been from another class and background, but they would have been different. She might have been freer, less dominated by doubts and madness away from the claustrophobic, incestuous, class-ridden society in which she was born. She might have been a more balanced, happier person and a much less brilliant writer.

This is what I do now, all the time – explore concepts in my head. It is hard to stop. I can't always tell whether I am making great sense or none at all. I have been helped and loved and cared for. I have been cherished and protected for weeks. Now I am my own responsibility.

I was so lucky. I had Beth and John. At first it was very bad. I woke up screaming at night. I couldn't talk about what happened, to Beth or John, or the police. I could not eat.

John sat with me for hours. Just sat and talked until his words reached out and touched me. 'You are going to be perfectly all right, Siggi. You are going to be fine. You have suffered a horrific trauma, you have a right to scream, darling . . . But you are safe and you are going to be well and happy again. Yes, you are . . . You are home with Beth and me and the twins and we love you to death . . .'

I cried and I crawled into Beth's arms and she rocked me like a child. Seeing fear in the eyes of people you love when you believe you are talking great sense and obviously are not is something I won't ever forget.

It must have been hard for Beth and John. There were times when I thought I was going mad. 'There is nothing wrong with your mind, Siggi. You just need to talk it all out with someone who knows how to listen.'

Beth moved my things into Virginia's nursery at Talland House. Where I could watch the sun rise and set. Where I could hide and heal. Where I had space to be, but not alone. This was where John sat with me and Beth held me in the long nights. This was where Virginia sat quite still by my bed and I sat and watched each new day begin and end, until the world became still and full of colours again.

Sometimes the twins took turns sleeping with me, up close,

comforting, smelling sweet and newly bathed. Mutton or timid Alice would rest their silky heads on my arm and sigh deeply.

Without Beth and John, without Talland House full of Virginia Woolf, I believe the memories might have drowned me. I escaped into her world, more real than my own. I read without surfacing. She walked my dreams and inhabited my days. She drove my demons to a distance and her beautiful words filled my mind until there was room for nothing else.

She was beside me when I spoke for the first time about my childhood. My father. I found out later that Beth was so shocked and upset she nearly lost the baby. The ripple effect of abuse, neglect or unhappiness seems endless. Need colours everything. We cling. Damaged people cling so hard one to another, they drown.

I drowned Jake with my vulnerability and when he looked into my eyes he saw only a reflection of himself. I looked into his eyes and was fascinated by my father, excited by the forbidden.

I close my eyes. I must shut off thought. Enough. Writing is what helps most now. No one has to see what I write. I can burn the words on the paper. They are only hieroglyphics on shaved wood, after all.

I open the small pocket of my rucksack again, just to finger the thin cardboard ticket, to make sure it is real. This evening I fly to Oslo. I am returning to Norway to stay with my grandparents, who are still very much alive, thank God.

I go because we are flesh and blood and we have missed so much of each other. We have so much catching up to do. Years and years we can never have back.

I have dreamt about my grandparents and Norway for so long without realizing how I mourned the loss of them. I long to lie under the huge sweet-smelling, rustling pine trees, quite alone in the forest and weep for so many things, for Dan and Matt, who were as much a part of me as a brief, joyous echo.

Jake I can never leave behind me. I have to incorporate him into my bloodstream and renewing blood cells, into my waking and sleeping. Into the pain and knowledge of the past and my hope for the future.

I am bound, like the old man of the sea, to carry him with me always, his legs tightening every so often around my neck. It will never be possible to throw him off entirely.

I talked to the police. I told them about Dan and Matt – that I suspected that Jake had killed them both. They told me what I already knew. That Dan jumped off the suspension bridge full of a cocktail of drugs. They told me it would be impossible to prove after all this time that Jake either injected or forced Dan to take an illegal drug. Or that he encouraged or suggested that Dan jump. He was not on the bridge when Dan jumped.

Matt's death was filed as murder, by person or persons unknown. The police did believe that Jake had injected Matt with a massive dose of heroin, but they could not prove it beyond all reasonable doubt.

Matt had a conviction with Lindsey Anderson, his former girl-friend, for possession. They could not prove beyond reasonable doubt that the drugs did not belong to Matt. Or that Jake went to the flat with the express purpose of killing Matt. Robbie kept telling them it was Lindsey, not Matt, who had kept drugs in Matt's flat and that Matt did not take hard drugs as far as he knew, but Jake was not named as the murderer.

It is hard to realize that my evidence of what Jake had told me, that he went to warn Matt off, not to kill him, counted. As did the evidence of the Judge and his brother, Jake's uncle. They maintained that even if he had been violent to me, it did not make him a murderer. They told the inquest Jake had fantasized about death since he was a little boy. They said Camilla died simply by slipping on the wet floor by the pool and that Jake was nowhere near her, but outside smoking a cigarette.

That is what they said.

You never knew with Jake; you never knew what the truth was.

I went to Jake's funeral. I had to. I was still quite ill then and John and Beth came with me. That day there was a mist on Dartmoor too. He was not buried with Camilla.

His father looked old and defeated and shrunk as he shuffled slowly behind Jake's coffin, but not so senile it seemed to me. His suit hung off him as if there was hardly anyone left inside. Perhaps there wasn't.

I never pray, but I prayed then that somehow Jake had found some peace. His coffin disappeared out of the church gate to be enfolded entirely and eerily in mist as it made for the crematorium. It was like some slow-motion black-and-white film, and Beth and John and I shivered as it finally became invisible.

The judge took both my hands in his own for a minute but could say nothing. As I turned away to go home, Jake's uncle touched my arm. 'If you can, condemn the deeds, not the man.' I looked at him and noticed his dog collar for the first time. He had very blue eyes, like Jake. 'Believe me, Jake had the most horrendous childhood. That much is truth.' He turned away before I could answer, and Beth and John took me home.

I was sad. I was so sad.

Cornwall . . . Huer's Cottage . . . Talland House are slipping away behind me. For the last three months they have been my whole world. Now I'm going home to Norway and I'm excited. I open my book: *The Sayings of Virginia Woolf*, and I smile.

When I am home, I will let myself remember Matt. I will paint as we painted together. I shall walk in the snow and unravel in my mind the tiny fragments I have of his life. So much love and hope in so short a time.

I will invoke our laughter and I will see him flying in on the white froth of waves. I will remember the packed church, bursting, bursting with the young of St Ives at his funeral. People filled the choir stalls, the aisles, they leant on the font, crouched on the floor, overflowed out into the street.

I did not know it was possible for one human being to engender so much love. John stood up and said, to all the people crying silently, that with all this love there had to be hope.

My grandparents still have the log cabin near Voss. I am going to live with them for a while. Perhaps I will discover there, something of the child who was my mother. And the adult I will become.

I will see my first spring there.

This summer I am going to backpack north through Norway. I am going to paint in places my grandfather told me about when I was small. I shall take the ferry across the blue waters of Vestfjorden, to Moskenes in the Lofoten Islands. I shall travel north to Narvik, on and on to Nordkapp, the most northerly tip, where I shall stand and look out over the Arctic Ocean.

From the end of May until the middle of July the sun never sets behind the horizon, but shines all night, filling the houses with dusky light, colouring the land gold and reflecting in the dark water like dull sparks.

This . . . this . . . is how I imagine it.

I am leaving a childhood like never-ending night behind me. Muffled as a footfall. Silenced. I longed for perpetual daylight where there were no shadows. No darkness. No soft, secret and muted footsteps placed carefully upon a stair. I longed for days where all was safe and seen.

I am going home to my grandparents.

My name is Sigrid Olemass and I go to reinvent myself one more time. To be reborn in the land of midnight sun.

Chapter 33

My great-grandmother is watching me ski. I recognize her bright scarf out of the corner of my eye as I negotiate the slalom. This is going to be my last competition for a long time.

She has always worn something bright so that my eyes will find her, since the time I was a little girl at school sports days. As I take off my skis I smile at the memory of her always being there.

She is eighty now, and still beautiful despite the wrinkles that crisscross her face like a beloved map. She is the person I love most in the world. This is the first time in my life I will be spending any length of time away from her.

'Well done, darling!' she cries, kissing me. 'That was very good.'

'I'm going to miss being on skis,' I say.

'Yes, you are, but there are plenty of holidays. What time is your flight?'

I laugh at her, she knows perfectly well, she has asked me a hundred times. She is going to miss me. 'Like your mother, you are my joy . . . my joy,' she will whisper whenever she says good night.

'My flight isn't until ten tonight, Ginna. We've got loads of time.' I tie my skis to the roof of the car and we drive slowly home down the mountain to the village.

I look at her while she drives. She is still so young-looking, despite her age and all the sadness in her life. 'Strong as a horse, darling,' she says, but I see signs of frailty and forgetfulness now. All her life she has had to be strong.

She had her first daughter at eighteen, and went on to have four more, all competing with each other. She never did have the son she longed for, but at least she has five grandsons.

241

Kristian, my grandmother, was one of Ginna's great sadnesses.

My grandmother had been a champion skier but apparently had had a strange need to punish herself. She had been a cool, self-contained child, difficult to get near, unlike Ginna's other daughters.

Her first boyfriend had died tragically in a skiing accident and my grandmother wondered if Kristian blamed herself. She grew up preferring her own company and loathed competing for her parents' attention.

She met my grandfather, David, on the rebound. He had just finished agricultural college and was on a skiing holiday, and he and Kristian were totally ill-suited, Ginna said. She disliked him intensely. She said he was dour but charming on the outside and shady on the inside.

My mother, Sigrid, was born in Scotland. Ginna hates remembering or talking about it, but there was a terrible rift between Kristian and my grandmother when my mother was small. Ginna wanted Kristian to bring Sigrid home to Norway. It is the one thing my great-grandmother can hardly bear to talk about. It is too painful. Unspeakable.

Ginna suspected that my mother was being abused by her father, but they were too far away to know for sure and they were afraid of setting something in motion that was either incorrect or might damage my mother, who would say nothing to them. They were advised that without proof they were on very difficult legal ground.

My great-grandparents tried hard to keep in touch with Sigrid, but their letters were returned. They lost their daughter and their granddaughter in one fell swoop.

After years of depression and breakdowns Kristian committed suicide when my mother was sixteen. 'Your great-grandfather and I were quite unable to understand Kristian's insistence on martyrdom, of suffering an obviously rotten marriage. But my guilt, my darling, is that I did nothing. I left a vital decision to a daughter incapable of making one. I should have interfered and damned the consequences. Maybe I didn't want my suspicions to be true. I should have gone to England and scooped them both up and brought them home where they belonged, but I didn't.

'In those days we did not understand about clinical depression. We were such a strong, healthy, physical family. We were intolerant of what your great-grandfather and I saw as self-indulgence or feeling sorry for yourself.' She had looked at me and said wisely, 'It is possible, I'm afraid, Birgitta, to love one of your children without liking what she has grown into.'

My great-grandparents adored my mother, though. She came back to Norway when she was in her twenties. Ginna had not seen her for fourteen years. My mother was only going to stay for a summer – she had it all worked out. She was going back to England, to university, to read English. She had fallen in love with Virginia Woolf.

Within weeks, she discovered she was pregnant with me, so she stayed in Norway with my grandparents, and she painted. She never went back to England to live, although she visited my godparents in England sometimes.

She was so talented, my mother. I have her paintings everywhere. I was born in Austvåøy, where she was painting in a little artist settlement, much to Ginna's disapproval. In Austvåøy there are days between June and July when there is no night.

Sigrid fell totally and utterly in love with Norway. She did many paintings of Lofotveggen, the vast and startling mountain range that seems to loom forbiddingly above the sea, totally blocking the horizon as you approach the Lofoten Islands. Ginna says she became fascinated by them, a little obsessed.

She painted huge canvases of white-capped mountains reflected in deep black fjords. Snowfields stretching forever to skies the colour of cornflowers. Huge glaciers with arms of cold ice. Gold midnight sun on a clutch of houses. Waterfalls caught in the act of freezing into a strange suspended blue-green.

She travelled to Finland and painted the complicated patterns of lakes. To Lapland, to Russia, and the uninhabited lonely, open spaces. But she never drew people. She became a well-known and sought-after painter in such a short space of time. My heart swells with pride when I look at her work.

My mother died when I was six.

If I try very hard I think I can still hear her bubble of laughter and the way her pale face suddenly lit up. I can remember her small hands always covered in flecks of paint, and her holding me tight. I can remember her long wonderful hair and the way she would throw it back out of her face to smile at me.

To me, she seemed to be always happy and serene. She had an amazing stillness and ability to listen and empathize that drew people like a magnet, and it was this stillness that made her paintings so powerful and personal. People have told me all my childhood, 'Sigrid always seemed so serene, that sudden smile could light up a day . . .'

I check my bags and put them by the door. I am flying to England. I am going to university. But first I am going to see Beth, my godmother, and stay with her family in Cornwall in their cottage by the sea.

Beth and John only spend weekends and summers in Cornwall now. They moved back up to Bristol to be near their parents. I am going to see Talland House for myself, the house my mother was so haunted by. Virginia Woolf stayed there as a child. I am totally fascinated by her. She is part of my literature course and I can't wait to see the house my mother wrote about so impressively in her diaries. A family bought the house and live there now, but Beth is still deeply involved with the Virginia Woolf Society.

Hanna and Amy are going to show me London. Siggi, Beth's youngest, who is only a bit older than me, is home for the summer, so it is going to be fun. I've never been to Cornwall and I've only been to England as a baby. Beth used to fly out here when Muma was alive. She was my mother's best friend so I know there are many things she can tell me about my mother that Ginna cannot know.

As I've grown up, Ginna has told me, bit by bit, the story of my mother's life. She has always been totally honest with me. She says she has told me all she knows of Sigrid's life before she came back to Norway, all that my mother told her. Ginna believes there has been too much silence, secrecy and heartbreak in this family.

Ginna thinks she failed both Kristian and Sigrid, and she is determined to protect me. She says *not* to have told me about my mother's life would have been much worse than my knowing the truth. To find it all out as an adult would have been a betrayal.

She's wise, my great-grandmother. All my life she has intermingled the tragic bits of my mother's short life with the wonderful letters Sigrid wrote to her and Gramps, and to me, while she

244

travelled all over Norway and painted. They are full of her awe and wonder and joy of discovering Norway. Discovering she was having me.

I also have her diaries and her descriptions of Dan and Jake and Matt. All the good, bad, sad and frightening things in her life. I have waited to read the later ones, as I have waited to read the last letter she wrote to me before she died. Ginna has it, safe, for when I finally leave home.

I have in her childish hand memories of a happy skiing holiday with her parents, and a weekend in a small hotel with Ginna and her mother.

There is a little passage about walking down a street with Kristian and noticing all the men looking at her mother and realizing with a surge of pride how beautiful Kristian was. There is one wistful sentence about her father. He took her to her first ballet. It makes me cry when I see that despite everything, the small child who was my mother went on being loyal and loving her parents.

There is the excitement of meeting Dan, her first love, on the train to university. There are photos of Jake Watson and Matt Tregonning. I looked up Dartmoor on an English map. It's a huge expanse of wild and lonely moor in Devon.

The photo of Jake is old, black-and-white and curling at the edges. He was very beautiful. I often look at it. I hold it to the mirror and peer at it and then at my own face to see if I can see any likeness.

There is just one small photo of Matt surfing. I have peered and peered at his face too, so many times, but I cannot really make out his features. I fantasize continually about which man was my father. I have got to that age. Sigrid told Ginna she honestly was not sure. Well, that is what Ginna has told me. She has always stressed she has told me all she knows.

Ginna says I don't need to know who my father is and it would be impossible to find out. This is not true, parentage is easy to establish. Of course she is trying to protect me. But I think she is right; it is probably better if I never know for sure.

There is no name on my birth certificate, and all my mother's documents were conveniently destroyed in a fire so maybe my mother did not want me to be sure, either. I often wonder if she knew.

I gather the last of my belongings. The things I always carry with me. The things my mother always carried with her.

There is a little wooden horse that was carved by a friend of my great-grandfather's. There are two paintings, so very different in style. One is by Matt Tregonning of a wild place called Zennor, which is in Cornwall.

And one by Jake, of my mother. It was painted in Venice. It has the date on the back, which is soon after my mother married him. This painting haunts me. It is a possessed, mysterious, invocatory painting. As if the artist knew something about my mother I will never know.

Whenever I look at it, I see her extraordinary, strange, frail beauty which I have not inherited. I see her passion. In the curl of her lip and the intensity of her gaze. And I *know* the man who painted her touched and ignited something very powerful in my mother. And I shake instinctively as I catch a faint exciting echo of that power.

It is time to leave; the taxi is here. I hug Ginna again and again. She is smiling and crying at the same time. She presses into my hands the last letter my mother wrote to me. I hug my aunts and my uncles and cousins. I hug everyone.

The car slips down the mountain, away from them all and I have my first terrible pang of leaving and the sick wrench of the homesickness to come. I am leaving all I have ever known, for the first time.

I wish my mother hadn't died.

I have a photograph of Virginia Woolf, which belonged to my mother. I have looked at it so often, it is as familiar as my own features. I will touch that face as if it is my mother's face. As if I might, through my fingertips, accept and understand why *my* mother had to die. Why she was taken from me, after all she had been through.

But of course, I cannot. Ginna has taught me that life is not fair.

When I was little, my mother would leave me with Ginna and travel long distances on her own to paint. Sometimes, on the nights before she left me again, she would hold me to her tight, tight, and I felt her stillness like a great sadness that was a secret part of her.

As I've grown up I've learnt to understand her great need to be gone to those vast wastes, to capture in her work some strong element of herself.

None of the family even suspected she was ill. We knew she got severe headaches. She was a bad sleeper, and she had fevers and nightmares all her life.

On her last trip my mother travelled to Honningsvåg where she drove across the wide spaces and hills full of frozen craters, to the great emptiness of the ocean between Nordkapp and the North Pole. She went to paint the northern lights.

All that day she struggled with a bad headache and nausea. She slept in the afternoon and then got up again. When she had finished her painting, she screwed the caps back on her paints and placed them neatly in the mahogany box I still have. She drove a snow-scooter a long, long way across a plateau of sparkling snow where there was not even a trace of birds' feet. She made a bed in the roots of fir trees that protruded up through the snow like bones, and she tucked herself into the snow like an icy blanket, for that last long sleep.

'Why, Ginna? Why?' I would ask as I grew up. 'Why didn't she come home? Why didn't she go to hospital? Why, why didn't she tell us she was ill? I don't understand. Did she want to die? She had me, Ginna . . . she had me . . .'

'Darling, of course she didn't want to die. Of course she didn't want to leave you. You were the most important thing in her life. But she *was* dying, and she did have a choice about how she died. She didn't want long and painful treatment which could not cure her. She did not want you to remember her ill and in pain, but alive and happy. She chose to die in a place she loved and felt part of, a world she had spent so much of her short life painting. You must try to accept and honour that.

'Look at her paintings. Why do you think people stand and cry when they look at them? She has imbued her landscapes with all the ache and shiver and wonder and magic of her mind and heart. With what *might* have been. She has captured the awesome beauty and the acute loneliness of a land just discovered within and outside herself. What a legacy, darling, she has left you. Such an achieve-ment in so short a life. Something to be so proud of. Something of herself which lives on and on.'

They *are* my legacy, these amazing paintings of hers. She does

247

live on in them for me. They are full of the power and wonder of life. Of nature renewing itself again and again. The sheer beauty of virgin snow. Nothing glimpsed on the surface, but within it, under it, near it, secret life and growth, an everlasting pulse like a heartbeat, a small haunting refrain.

As the taxi moves down the mountain, crunching through a heavy snowfall, I read my mother's last letter, crouched in the back of the taxi, leaning towards the light, the dying rays of the sun lighting the pages.

My darling, beloved Birgitta,

Can you ever know the perfect joy you have brought to me unless I tell you? With your birth my true, real and happy life began.

How you loved me to tell you the story of the surprise of you, over and over again at night when I put you to bed! My small miracle!

I had not had periods for so long you were totally unexpected. Oh! I never get tired of thinking about the joy of that discovery.

Without your birth I might never have discovered in quite the same way the wonder of places I could only imagine.

These last six years since you were born have been the happiest and most fulfilling of my life. Forgive me, darling, for leaving you so much with my beloved Ginna (to whom I owe everything). It was not because I did not love you. I carried you with me every minute of every day. It was because I discovered, quite by chance, on a fleeting visit to John and Beth, that I had a malignant brain tumour. I told no one but John and only John, because I needed to know exactly what my life held and I wanted honesty.

Birgitta, forgive my selfishness. There was so much I wanted to do, so many places I wanted to see and experience. And . . . am I vain? I wanted to leave you something of myself in my work, because faces, voices, the memory of people fade, but feelings, secrets and love are captured for ever in paintings. You see, up until your birth, I had limited myself, through fear, to such a small landscape, mostly seen through the eyes of men I loved. With your birth I grew up. I tried my wings and found I could fly. I spread them out . . . and to my great surprise, they were undamaged and I found I could soar, up, up and away to places I had only visited in my head before.

Oh, Birgitta, the wonder, the awe, the magic, the settling of the spirit in the knowledge, the sure and wondrous knowledge, that we will live on and on in the landscape we are part of. The length of a life is unimportant, darling. We live on in the power to express the feeling, the tone, the isolation and beauty, the sheer magic of hidden and unsuspected places.

We live on in words, in painting, in music, in photography. If I am only one brush stroke, one note of music, one letter of absolute and utter love for a small human being created out of passion and chaos, then how lucky I have been!

You gave me another chance of life, darling. And I went for it. Thank you. I wish I could change the circumstances of my past. I wish I could change the discoveries you will make when you are adult. But I can't. I have entrusted your care to the only person with the ability to give you, despite all those discoveries, confidence and a sense of your own self. Never, ever lose it. Always feel cherished, respected and admired. Love yourself, always love yourself as you should. And never keep silent.

I wish I could leave you a different legacy. I wish I did not have to leave you so soon. Leaving those you love is hard. But I want to die with dignity. And I so, so want you to remember me young and happy.

When you feel sad, remember, I am free, little Birgitta. Free. Soaring somewhere, up above the snows in a clear blue sky, hovering with wings *you* gave me. My sweet, happy, laughing little daughter . . .

I fold the letter. I will not cry.

I must hold this vision of my mother's life clear inside me. My understanding, my aching sadness and loss will change and deepen as I have children of my own.

I know. I know the isolated, glittering beauty of the landscape that

249

she chose to paint accentuated powerfully the confusing passion, joy and pain that lay inside her.

Often in the night I think about how it could have been for my mother if Kristian had brought her back to Norway as a child. I would like Ginna to feel the soaring resonance of release before she dies. Whatever she feels she did not do for her own daughter, for my mother, she has done a hundredfold for me. My childhood has been filled with love, security and laughter. She has protected me well, but not from who I am.

After university, I shall come home to Norway to write, and like my mother I will travel and discover the raw places, the open spaces. The lonely maps of the mind.

I know there is a land in each of us where the silence sings because we can make no sound. I know there is terror so vast it swoops like a shadow. I know, I know, that there are desolate icy wastes where the heart aches for someone lost, and is inconsolable.

I grew up with the memory and videos of long, blowing, fair hair, and laughter I can never quite catch, and dreams of a face for ever young. Clear, near enough to touch.

In one of my mother's diaries I found this, by Virginia Woolf. 'We do not know our own souls, let alone the souls of others. Human beings do not go hand in hand the whole stretch of the way. There is a virgin forest in each; a snowfield where even the print of birds' feet is unknown.'

Muma, despite all, despite everything, you never hesitated to bring me into the world. I, Birgitta Olemass, have had the most amazing childhood to cherish all my life. You and Ginna taught me the importance of trying to capture happiness each and every day of my life.

Today, I begin my life away from home. I promise, I promise, I will always search and search for snowfields marked with the delicate, filigree patterns of birds' feet, which confirm and celebrate Life.

And bring hope to the cold places of the mind.